**Also available from Caitlin McKenna
and Carina Press**

Colorado Christmas Magic

Also available from Caitlin McKenna

No Such Luck
Super Natalie
Manifesting Mr. Right
My Big Fake Irish Life
Logging Off

A MOVIE MAGIC CHRISTMAS

CAITLIN MCKENNA

carina
press

carina press®

Recycling programs
for this product may
not exist in your area.

ISBN-13: 978-1-335-45263-4

A Movie Magic Christmas

For questions and comments about the quality of this book, please contact us at CustomerService@Harlequin.com.

Carina Press
22 Adelaide St. West, 41st Floor
Toronto, Ontario M5H 4E3, Canada
www.CarinaPress.com

Printed in U.S.A.

For My Family

A MOVIE MAGIC CHRISTMAS

Chapter One

Catalina sat in the back of an executive helicopter with her squeaky-new assistant, who was already driving her crazy. His nervous chatter, his fidgeting, his spring-loaded moves whenever she opened her mouth were telltale signs that the guy was too green to handle the complexities of the job. Why hadn't her manager, who insisted she hire him, seen it? Now she was stuck with a nervous assistant on a movie whose shooting schedule had been pushed up to accommodate its difficult, high-in-demand director.

Attempting to book accommodations for the cast and crew only weeks before Christmas had proven problematic for the production office. St. Nicholas, Colorado, was a small mountain town with only one decent hotel. They assumed the star wouldn't mind staying in the same location as the crew. She did mind.

Neil's first challenge had been to find her a beautiful, serene place away from prying paparazzi eyes, crazed local fans, and a gossipy crew. Only an hour into his employment and Neil had looked as if he was going to have a meltdown. Everything was booked.

Fortunately for him, she'd received a hand-delivered invitation from the very town they were shooting in, offering her a complimentary one-week stay at a five-star bed-and-breakfast. The impressive invitation was set on shimmery silver card stock embossed with gold cursive handwriting. Worth exploring, especially since the Carroll Inn could be her only alternative to staying in a crowded hotel. She'd handed it over to Neil, who'd secured two rooms for however long the filming lasted. She only hoped the Carroll Inn lived up to its own hype.

Neil couldn't believe their luck, but luck had nothing to do with it. She was always being bombarded with products and businesses who hoped she'd post something nice about whatever they had to offer. Having a celebrity's endorsement, no matter how small, was far better than spending thousands on advertising.

Neil was fidgeting again and stealing glances in her direction. "So…uh…have you been to Colorado before?"

"No."

"Me, neither." He waited for a response, and when he didn't get one, he averted his gaze out the helicopter's window. "Look at all that beautiful snow."

She lived in LA but had grown up in Maine and didn't find snow so charming, especially working in it. "There's nothing beautiful or enjoyable about filming in freezing-cold temperatures."

Neil's agreeable expression turned anxious, and she could only assume he thought she might fire him for saying the wrong thing. She wanted to tell her nervous newbie that she wasn't a horrible, entitled movie star like all the tabloids had portrayed her to be—that she was actually very nice, so he could relax. But she wasn't going to say any of that because she no longer trusted assistants; they often had ulterior motives. A hard lesson she'd learned firsthand.

The pilot made a turn, slowed, and started to descend.

"Looks like we're here, Ms. Jones." Neil gathered his electronics and set them inside his workbag.

Catalina checked her phone, hoping her manager had sent a text informing her that the movie had been postponed until next spring. Disappointed to find no such news, she threw her cell in her winter-white Gucci handbag, put on a faux-fur hat, which matched her faux-fur boots, slipped on a pair of Prada sunglasses, then waited for the helicopter to land.

"Thank you for flying with us, Ms. Jones." The pilot smiled as she made her way toward the exit. "Please let us know if we can accommodate you any further."

She offered a quick nod, then stepped out of the black helicopter and approached the thoroughly decorated bed-and-breakfast property. Over a dozen pine trees were trimmed with shiny ornaments, ribbons, and lights. Several Christmas yard displays dotted the snowy landscape—the largest among them were Santa sitting in a sleigh piled high with bags of Christmas gifts, and a life-size, five-piece set of animated carolers singing "Jingle Bells" along the walkway.

A heavyset handyman hurried past her carrying a tool set and did a double take, which often happened—even from those who didn't really know who she was. If people couldn't place her or recognize her iconic ruby-red lips, high cheekbones, or giraffe-like neck, they often mistook her for a high-fashion model. She stood five-nine in flats and was extremely thin.

She made her way toward the front steps bordered

by evergreen plants and red bows. Fresh swags of garland accented with red berries, pine cones, and red velvet bows were draped over the entrance with two large nutcrackers standing at attention on each side. She was admiring the colorful Christmas wreath adorning the front door when it opened.

A pleasant-looking older couple came out to greet her—and Neil, who lagged behind, weighted down by her ice-blue three-piece designer luggage set.

"Welcome to the Carroll Inn, Ms. Jones," the older woman said warmly. "I'm Mary and this is my husband, Joe."

Mary's bright eyes and cute dimples had Catalina thinking that if Mary were an actress, she'd be typecast as a sweet grandmother who made apple pies all day, while offering sage advice to anyone who came for a visit. The man next to her seemed equally good-natured and clearly looked like he sampled too many of his wife's sweet treats.

Catalina's focus drifted to the picturesque bed-and-breakfast with its rich mustard color and ivory-framed windows outlined in multicolored Christmas lights. In every windowsill sat an old-fashioned incandescent candle. Three inches of pristine-white snow blanketed the roof, and a thin swirl of smoke rose from its chimney.

A tiny, fleeting smile touched the corners of her mouth. "Make sure our location scout is aware of this place."

Neil dropped the luggage and had to catch his breath before he could respond. "Of course, Ms. Jones." He quickly made a note in his phone, then addressed their hosts. "I'm Neil Segal, Ms. Jones's assistant."

"Yes, of course. We spoke on the phone," Mary said.

"Why don't you two go on inside and get warm by the fire while we take care of the bags?"

Catalina wasn't going to argue. She'd only been outside for a few minutes, and she was already freezing.

"So that's Catalina Jones," Joe said quietly as they waited for the pilot to bring over the rest of their guests' luggage. "She's taller in real life."

"Very," Mary said on a laugh. "Did you see how she towered above me? It was intimidating. For a second I thought she might really be that Russian double agent she played in her last movie and was here to commandeer our home."

Joe chuckled. "She sure does know how to make an entrance. I don't think we've ever had a guest arrive in a helicopter before."

"Not what I'd recommend for a movie star who wishes to keep a low profile. The whole town will be talking."

"It's hard to believe that someone who *has it all* is our next Scrooge assignment."

"Not all." Mary raised a brow. "She doesn't have love, and without that, what does she have really?"

Catalina had risen to movie-star status quickly. Her third film became a box office hit, which made her a Hollywood success story overnight. Everyone who met her said she was one of the most genuine, down-to-earth celebrities out there. Mary recalled seeing Catalina and her then-boyfriend Grayson Edwards on a talk show. The hosts rightly pointed out how strikingly beautiful they were as a couple. Catalina seemed so sweet in the interview while Grayson appeared very confident, bordering arrogant, and she had suspected their relationship wouldn't last, which it didn't. Shortly after their engagement, their very public breakup had been splashed all over the front covers of every tabloid in the supermarket. Apparently, Grayson had moved on to his next leading lady, leaving Catalina emotionally shattered. *Such a shame.* Catalina Jones had been a beautiful, kindhearted, talented actress, and now she was known as the Ice Queen.

"This is it, folks." The pilot set four more bags at their feet.

"Fly safe," Mary said, and waved.

Joe lifted the two heaviest bags and groaned. "Nobody knows how to travel light anymore."

Mary opened the door. "Let's get this Scrooge show on the road."

Joe carried everything up to the second floor while Mary went to check on their new guests, who were sitting by the fire at the far end of their living room. Neil was standing in front of Catalina, going over her schedule, as the star sat staring at her phone.

"How about a delicious cup of hot cocoa?" Mary beamed at the two.

"Yes!" Neil's face lit with excitement until he glanced at his boss, who scowled back. "I mean, no. Ms. Jones doesn't do sugar," he said, deflated.

Catalina refused to make eye contact and kept her face buried in her phone. Even though the actress was still wearing her winter jacket, Mary could see she was toothpick skinny and could certainly stand to put on a few pounds.

"How about a nice glass of—"

A knock at the door had Mary going to answer it

when she was cut off by Neil. "I believe that's a delivery for Ms. Jones," he said. "Let me take care of it."

Joe descended the stairs and stood next to Mary as Neil signed for a package at their own front door. "Hot off the press." He handed his boss an express-mail envelope.

Catalina inspected it, turned it over, and was ready to pull the tab to open it when she noticed an eager audience hovering over her.

"Oh, sorry." Mary fixed the back of her hair, hiding her disappointment that she and Joe wouldn't get to see what was inside. "Joe dear, why don't you show Ms. Jones and Mr. Segal to their rooms so they can get unpacked?"

"We'd appreciate that. Thank you, Mrs. Carroll," Neil said politely.

Catalina rose slowly, typing on her phone, and brushed by Mary without saying a word.

As Catalina followed Joe up to the second floor, she inhaled a rich scent of pine and took note of the fresh Douglas fir garland wrapped around the banister. It had been years since she'd smelled real garland. Even the most luxurious hotels in Europe rarely decorated with it anymore. Through her very expensive designer glasses, she judged everything by what was real and what wasn't. How could she not? So much of what she had thought real in her life wasn't.

Joe stopped in front of the last door on the right and the most secluded suite of them all. "The Winter Wonderland Suite," he announced, pushing open the door.

Catalina walked into the room and gawked, frozen

in place, and for a moment she thought she'd actually stepped onto a movie set.

A slim Christmas tree was tucked away in the far corner adorned with silver and gold balls, glass icicles, sparkle-covered pine cones, and a silver angel resting on top. At the base of the tree sat a small white teddy bear in a tiny red train. Snow-white swans cuddled together on a window seat along with a happy Christmas polar bear and a dancing seal.

Sheer curtains were drawn up at each post of a four-poster bed and white fairy lights outlined the canopy above. On the opposite wall from the bed was a sleek quartz fireplace the color of a glacier. Cotton-leaf garland outlined the mantel with an illuminated miniature Christmas village spread across it.

The room's wintry theme made her inwardly smile. Her parents had taken her to an ice castle festival where ice sculptors from all over the country made some of the most gorgeous castles she'd ever seen. Her favorite had been decorated for Christmas, similar to the room she was standing in. That had been one of the best Christmases she'd spent with her dad growing up. He was a military man and had come home for the holidays—something that became more difficult to do in the years that followed.

"Your room matches your outfit." Neil nodded to her white ski attire as he helped Joe bring in her luggage. His mouth turned down when he met her icy glare. He broke eye contact and cleared his throat. "I'll check in with production," he said, and quickly left.

"Here's your key." Joe placed it on a small table by the window. "Holler if you need anything."

After Joe closed her door, she picked up the polar

bear, remembering how she'd received one just like it on Christmas years ago. She used to love Christmas, not so much for the presents, but for the festive season itself. Her mom was always baking something delicious while she and her brother would be outside building snowmen. At night they'd watch Christmas movies and string popcorn. The best part was the feeling of love that permeated the house—along with the smell of hot apple pies and sugar cookies. When her dad wasn't deployed, he'd bring home a freshly cut Christmas tree, and the scent of pine filled their home for days.

Catalina put the bear back. No time to get sentimental. She couldn't afford to relax or feel comfortable. On second look, the decorations were no different than the studio dressing that surrounded her on every movie she ever made. She assumed the staging invoked good memories for other guests, but for her it reminded her of work—a place where she pretended to be someone she wasn't, surrounded by people who barely knew her.

With a deep exhale, she took off her hat and coat, laid them on the bed, then opened the express-mail envelope. She pulled out the contents—her own image graced the cover of *Vogue*. She sat and studied the photo, wondering how the critics would react to her dramatic haircut. Her once wavy, long dark locks were now stick-straight and fell right at her square jawline. She touched the back of her bare neck, missing her most favorite attribute. Her long hair had made it easier to hide from the world when she needed to.

The magazine had selected a shimmery silver dress for her to wear, which electrified her blue eyes. As she stared into the endless black pools of her pupils, she wondered if the real woman behind her new nickname

of the Ice Queen was still in there. She'd been a working actor for nearly a decade, found her way into movies
early on, and had been a household name for the past
five years. She'd been blessed to have such a successful career, and she was only twenty-eight.

Catalina heard her cell ring deep inside her handbag and ignored it. When it started up again, she had
no choice but to fish it out. "Hey, Erin," she said to her
manager, who also happened to be her best friend. "I
just opened it."

"Wasn't I right? You look gorgeous."

"Insisting I cut my hair was a good call, but pushing me to star in *The Scrooge Legend* isn't going to
change my image."

"You don't know that," Erin said. "Besides, you can
stop being the Ice Queen anytime by being less curt
with your new assistant and production crew. They
weren't the ones who broke your heart."

"This isn't about Grayson," she said, even though
that was only a half-truth. "I'm tired of being used to advance other people's careers or raise their social media
status. If I keep everyone at a distance, I don't have to
worry about it."

"You need friends again, and allies."

"I've got you."

"I appreciate that, but you need more than me to be
looking out for you."

Catalina didn't want to have a constant entourage
around her like so many of her fellow actors did. She
missed the days when she wasn't famous. "I can handle the media."

"Not when they blow things out of proportion. And
we haven't even talked about social media. One nega-

tive post from someone in St. Nicholas and your die-hard fans will turn on you, believing the Ice Queen rumor is true."

"But it's my only protection."

"It's beginning to change you, and you're not seeing it," Erin said. "You're acting like a guard dog, biting everyone's hand before knowing who's a friend and who's a foe."

"More foes are being bitten, I promise you that."

Her best friend released a long, exhausted sigh. "Cat, you've recently lost two movies. Do you want to lose your career?"

"Now you're being an alarmist."

There was a long pause on the end of the phone. "As your best friend and manager, I'm going to share something with you that you're not going to like. You didn't land this role because the director thinks you're a good actor. Victor actually thinks you're a Scrooge, and frankly I'm beginning to agree."

Catalina felt the sting in her words. Erin was the only person outside her family she could trust, so her opinion mattered. "How can you say that?" she asked, attempting to mask her wounded pride.

"Because it's the truth. You're so negative and unhappy these days, and I don't know how to get you back." Erin sounded concerned. "You know you're one of my dearest friends. I got into this business because you asked me to, but I won't stay and watch you destroy everything you've worked so hard to achieve."

Catalina had wanted to tell Erin just how miserable she'd been over the past year, but how could she complain when she was living a life many people could only dream of? Instead of being straight with her best friend, she'd created a persona to cope. Her sharp tongue and difficult demeanor kept her safe from men, who'd only break her heart, and assistants, who'd try to end her career. She thought it had been working well until she learned that she'd lost the starring role in a sci-fi fantasy because its well-respected director declined to work with her.

Was it true? Had Victor hired her only because he thought she was a Scrooge? Could her Ice Queen persona be damaging her career more than protecting it?

"I'll work on it," Catalina finally said.

"Thank you." Erin let out a relieved breath. "I really hope you allow yourself to enjoy being part of *The Scrooge Legend*. I know how you love movies based on true stories."

"How true remains to be seen. Christmas magic obviously doesn't exist, which means the screenwriter took some serious liberties when writing Piper's story."

"Hopefully, Piper will be able to sort out what's what when you meet with her," Erin said. "How are things going with Neil?"

"It's too soon to tell."

"Neil's a good guy. He's solid. I checked him out myself."

"I hope you're right."

"I am, so stop worrying." Erin's landline rang in the background. "I've got to jump on another call. Keep me posted."

Catalina hung up feeling a little better about Neil, but trusting those she needed to rely on was hard to do. Every time she let her guard down and allowed someone to get close to her, she'd regretted it soon after. From actors befriending her in hopes of advancing their own careers, to fans seeking autographs they could sell on eBay, everyone wanted a piece of her.

When Grayson came along, she thought she'd met someone who understood what she'd been going through. After all, he'd quickly risen to fame almost as fast as she had. She assumed they'd protect and support each other, so she completely trusted him when their relationship pushed past friendship. Grayson told her how much he loved her, and she believed him. She hadn't realized that he only loved her because she ranked higher in Hollywood than he did. He had used her to further his career, and she'd been in love with him too much to see it.

Splitting with Grayson had devastated her, and having a camera shoved in her face every time she stepped out into the public eye had only made it worse. She and Grayson quickly fell off the covers of magazines, replaced with photos of Grayson and his new girlfriend. The whole experience had made her swear off love forever.

She gazed out the window at a peaceful, snowy scene below her. A single blue jay hovered over a bird feeder while a few finches jockeyed for a better position in its circular seed tray, spraying seeds across the snow-covered ground that had squirrels happily cleaning up the mess.

As much as Catalina wished she'd been offered the lead in the sci-fi fantasy, she would have been working in front of a green screen on an LA soundstage for fourteen hours a day. When she'd finally get off work, she'd be accosted by reporters and paparazzi. At least now she was able to look out a window without seeing aggressive photographers staring back. Maybe taking

The Scrooge Legend had been the right decision after all. She'd forgotten what it was like to take a moment and step out of the chaos. She'd forgotten about the power of being calm, remaining still. She used to draw strength from it, like she had learned to do on her very first film.

Sage Under Fire had been an independent film about a group of high school friends who rescued a girl's horse from a fast-moving wildfire. She'd learned so much about her craft and made many fond memories with the cast and crew. The story itself was a huge undertaking for an independent film, and the end product was impressive. The film took home three awards, including best actress for her performance from one of the biggest film festivals. Her work in *Sage Under Fire* had helped to land her a supporting role in a miniseries, which gave her name recognition.

What she cherished most about that film was how she had become fast friends with the director. Jay Townsend had gone to school for photography and had a true talent for setting up shots—sometimes better than his own cinematographer. He also knew how to get the best performances out of his actors because he had an incredibly calming energy. Jay was the one who had taught her how to shut out all the noise around her, focus energy, and grow strength from being still. He said that everything good comes from being still—the creative inspiration, the true connection, the honest answers to difficult questions.

For three months, she and Jay had hung out together, sharing everything from stories about growing up to cringeworthy accounts about their first missteps in the industry. He never judged her like so many in her life did now, and she regretted how their beautiful friend-ship ended. She had developed romantic feelings for Jay and had wanted to tell him during filming, but she didn't want to jeopardize the outcome of his movie should he not feel the same way.

At an after-party following the film festival's awards ceremony, she summed up her feelings in one kiss. It was a soft, tender kiss, and as she opened her eyes to judge his reaction, his DP and camera crew came bar-reling into the room, dragging Jay away, insisting he meet one of their buddies.

"I'll be right back," he'd said.

Only he never came back. She kept looking for him throughout the night but never caught sight of him. When she was ready to leave the party, she asked if anyone had seen him, and was told that he had already left. He clearly had not been interested.

Over the next few days, they played telephone tag and finally spoke to each other on the phone, but it had been distant and brief. Shortly after, she set off for England to film the miniseries. Jay had been hired to shoot another movie in Florida. For the next two years, she went from one movie set to another, never seeing or speaking to Jay. Later, she learned that he had left the industry. She often wondered if he was happy and content with whatever he was doing.

Catalina unzipped one of her bags, pulled out *The Scrooge Legend* shooting script, and began marking it up at the table. She had no desire to play Ms. Scrooge, especially now that she knew what the director really thought of her. But if she quit, her critics would call her an Ice Queen *and* a Scrooge, and her career would then go into free fall.

At least the shooting schedule was short—three weeks in St. Nicholas, a week off between Christmas and New Year's, and then back to LA for another six weeks. She could handle it. St. Nicholas appeared to be a normal, small mountain town—away from LA, away from the paparazzi, away from chaos. What could possibly go wrong?

Chapter Two

Lying in the prone position, propped up on his elbows, Jay remained motionless on a bed of pristine white— camouflaged from head to toe in stark-white winter wear, silently watching for any movement around a grove of bright-red winterberry trees in the snow-covered landscape. A twig snapped, and then he saw her—a beautiful doe, followed by her fawn, foraging for food.

He began snapping photos. Mama deer must have heard the barrage of clicking sounds coming from the camera, for she glanced up and looked directly into Jay's telephoto lens. He took three more, then paused, not wanting to scare her. The fawn came closer to his mother. They were in perfect alignment with one another and framed so beautifully by the red berries. He snapped one photo, waited, snapped another. The fawn took no notice of him, so he continued to shoot, hoping they would look in his direction at the same time.

A rustling sound came from behind Jay, and for a split second, the deer froze, both staring in his direction. He snapped quickly.

"Achoo!"

The deer swiftly scampered off into the woods.

"I'm so sorry." Hailey blew her nose, then moved

her camping chair away from a cluster of pine trees and into the direct sun.

He got to his knees, dusting off the snow before he took his camera off the tripod, and walked over to where his little sister was surrounded by his gear.

"Please tell me you got the shot." She looked at him anxiously, wiping her red nose with her glove. "Jay, you can't blame me. I told you I wasn't going to be a very good assistant."

"You did warn me." Suppressing a smile, he put the cap back on his telephoto lens and set his camera back in its bag. "And thanks to you, I got exactly what I needed."

Her eyes twinkled with excitement. "You did?"

He nodded as she sneezed again. "And now, I better get you inside before Mom kills me." He reached for two more camera bags and threw them over his shoulder.

Hailey folded up her chair before picking up the remaining bag. "I'm really glad you're staying for Christmas. I don't think I could have taken another holiday with Mom and Dad moping around."

"They're only moping because you'll be leaving for college next year."

"Dad actually thinks I could have a great career as a marine biologist right here in St. Nicholas."

He laughed as his cell buzzed inside his jacket. He took a look at who was calling and answered. "Hey, Tyler. Never thought I'd be hearing from you again."

"You might have quit Hollywood, but we didn't quit you," his old friend and former agent said. "Remember that producer who had been extremely interested in your psychological thriller, *Silencing Sarah*?"

"You mean Peter Wells?"

"Yeah. He's back from Canada and is working right now on the very movie filming in your own hometown."

"I think you've got your intel wrong." Jay walked out of the woods with Hailey. "There isn't a movie shooting here."

"Want to bet on that? Luisa Avalos, a client of mine, is one of the producers. Their still photographer had to bail last night, and she's having difficulties finding a replacement on such short notice."

"Are you asking me to fill in?"

"It would be a great opportunity for you to network."

Jay's departure from the film industry had been messy, and though he'd had a choice to leave the door open with a few vital relationships, he'd slammed those doors in their faces. At the time, he didn't think it mattered. He'd had it with the industry and decided to be a wildlife photographer—something he felt he could be good at, and he wouldn't have a multitude of novice photographers behind him, telling him how to take the shot.

Only he hadn't realized how difficult it would be to sell his photos, and not for very much money. He loved being out in the wild, waiting for that perfect shot, and though it'd helped to clear his head the first year he left behind the chaos of Hollywood, lately that solitude had him missing his friends and the good times they'd shared together. Jay began to question his decision to leave. Was he now getting a do-over? Maybe. But he'd have to swallow his pride and do an apology tour. "I'm a wildlife photographer now. Coming back hasn't really crossed my mind."

"That's not what I hear," Tyler said. "Hudson tells me you're second-guessing your career move."

"Hudson talks too much."

"So he's right."

"Doesn't mean others want to work with me again. I didn't exactly leave on good terms."

"Is that what you're worried about?" Tyler laughed. "We've got actors in and out of rehab, divas making impossible demands, megalomaniac directors, abusive producers. You think fighting for your creative vision and having the stones to walk away when you didn't get it is going to keep you out of the industry?"

"My last film tanked."

"Because they didn't listen to you, which the studio now realizes but will never admit. I wouldn't be calling you if you were washed up, now would I?"

All this time he'd been beating himself up when he should have just picked up the phone and talked to Tyler. "No, I don't suppose you would," he said. "Tell me more about the gig."

"Production will only be shooting the exterior scenes—those needed on location. It will be for three short weeks, and I'll wager the pay is much better than what you're making now."

"How much?"

"Thirty-five hundred a week on a ten-hour day, six days a week, plus equipment rental."

Not even close to what he'd made as a director, but far better than not having a paycheck at all. "That sounds great, Ty, and I appreciate your reaching out, but I can't take it. You know the days will be twelve to fourteen hours minimum, and I came home to visit my folks."

"I hear you. I've made an I'll-be-home-for-Christmas promise myself. But what if the schedule was a sure thing? Luisa said one of the actors wouldn't sign onto the project unless they were guaranteed a ten-hour day max."

"That's a first." Jay glanced at his little sister, who was busy texting someone on her phone. "All right. I'll do it."

"Great. I'll shoot you the production office's address and let them know you'll be over to sign your deal memo. Welcome back, buddy."

Hailey put her phone away. "What was that all about?"

"I just accepted a job." He opened the gate to the back acre of his parents' property, and they walked inside.

"When does it start?"

"Tomorrow."

Hailey frowned. "Jay, you promised you'd stay home for Christmas."

"I am. A movie's shooting right here in town, and you're looking at their still photographer."

She seemed satisfied. "Cool."

He and Hailey went inside his parents' house, dropped off his equipment in the mudroom, then joined their mom in the kitchen, where she was unloading groceries.

"It's a madhouse in town." She set a large carton of eggs in the refrigerator. "A production company has descended on our tiny St. Nicholas."

"We just heard." Hailey helped her unpack the groceries. "Jay's accepted a job as their still photographer."

His mom stopped what she was doing and stared at him.

"I know. I'm sorry, but I promise I'll be—"

"I love it!" She broke into a big smile. "I can come visit you on set."

"Don't know if that's allowed." Jay caught a loaf of bread Hailey tossed over and set it on a shelf in the pantry.

"Why wouldn't it be? I'm your mother for goodness' sake." She folded up the empty grocery bags, then started on the others. "Who's in the movie?"

"Don't know."

"Why would you accept a job you don't know anything about?"

"I'm doing it as a favor to a buddy of mine in LA."

She handed over a bag of pretzels and a jar of nuts to Jay. "I do like their choice of location."

Jay's father came into the kitchen, rubbing his hands to get them warm. "The lights are up." He went over to the coffeepot and poured himself a cup.

"Do you need any help?" Jay asked his dad. "I've got a little time before I meet my new boss."

"What's this?" He turned around, excited. "Are you moving back to town?"

"No. I accepted a three-week job starting tomorrow."

"A movie's shooting in town," his mom explained.

"I told you they'd come looking for you." His dad arched a brow.

Jay chuckled. "The movie has nothing to do with me. I'm filling in for their still photographer."

"Which means Jay will definitely be here for Christmas," his mom added.

"That's a plus," his dad said. "It's hard to be a family when everyone is scattered to the four corners of the earth."

Jay eyed his sister, and she gave him a here-we-go look.

"Hailey, maybe we can turn the room above the garage into your office."

"Dad, I appreciate the offer, but my work is in the ocean."

"Is that a requirement? Everyone works remotely these days."

"Not everyone," Hailey said, "but don't worry. There are things called airplanes that we can use to visit one another."

"Humph." His dad squelched a smile. "Since your brother needs to go into town, why don't you help me haul down the Christmas boxes."

"You mean the boxes stored in the room above the garage?"

"Why do you ask? Are you eyeing that space for your future office?"

She shook her head. "You don't ever quit, do you?"

"How do you think I got your mother to marry me?"

Hailey laughed as they walked out.

"I'm really glad to have you home, even if it's only for a few weeks." His mom emptied the last bag of groceries, then poured them each a cup of coffee before they sat down at the kitchen table.

"It feels good to be home," he said, doctoring his coffee with two sugars. "I love what I do, but I wish I didn't have to live out of a suitcase all the time."

"Maybe you could move your home base back to St. Nicholas? Your father and I could keep an eye on your place when you have to travel—that is if you want to have a place of your own. You could always save money and move into your old room upstairs."

"I appreciate the offer, but I'd never want to be one of those thirty-year-olds still living at home."

"I suppose it wouldn't look good for any woman you might want to date." She eyed him. "*Is* there any woman you might want to date? Maria's daughter just got her graduate degree from the Colorado School of Mines, and she's home for the holidays, like you."

"Thanks, Matchmaker Mom, but I've got my dating life covered, so don't even think about trying to set me up with someone."

"I'm not," she said, truly offended. "I don't meddle, you know that. But I do worry. It's been too long since someone has grabbed your attention."

"No need to worry. I'm fine. And happy." He couldn't blame his mom for worrying about him. He hadn't dated anyone seriously in years, and he wasn't going to tell her the real reason he'd given up on love.

Catalina Jones had been his leading lady in his film *Sage Under Fire*. He'd cast her not because she was beautiful but because she was extremely talented. It shocked him to learn how insecure she was about her own acting. He'd helped her with that, and in doing so, they'd become fast friends. He'd never experienced anything like it—to be thoroughly in tune with another person, to enjoy her company so completely. He found himself always thinking about her, always wanting to be with her. They complemented each other, inspired each other, and created an exceptionally good film together.

As the weeks flew by, his feelings for her moved past friendship. He had planned on telling her how he felt when a miracle happened. She kissed him, and his heart burst open, ecstatic that she might feel the same way. Only they never had a chance to talk about it. They'd been interrupted and separated at a film festival party. He kept trying to look for her, but producers and studio execs kept stopping him from doing so. When he was finally able to break free, he'd learned she had already left the party.

They had attempted to talk over the next few days but something always got in the way. Things were moving fast for both of them, and he suddenly found himself needing to make a tough decision. That decision had affected them both, and even though he still felt like he'd made the right decision, it had cost him the best friendship he'd ever had.

After Catalina, Jay had never shared such a close bond with another woman, and he suspected he never would. Even though she was no longer in his life, he'd always kept up on any news about her. When her breakup with Grayson Edwards became so public, Jay could see by the photos that her ex had done a number on her emotionally. Every picture of her told the same story. Catalina was going through the motions of life in the public eye, horribly unhappy.

Like Catalina, his career as an up-and-coming director had taken off. He'd been hailed as "an exciting new filmmaker who illuminated the real essence of someone in an imagined moment of time." After his third film, he'd been given a big-budget movie backed by one of the major studios. What he assumed would be his best film yet had turned out to be a true disappointment. Every one of his creative decisions had been questioned by the studio. In the end, he walked because the movie had been stripped of bold storytelling and had been watered down beyond recognition.

After Jay left the film industry, he discovered his

love for wildlife photography. Nature was bold and unapologetic. It was pure, strong, and unafraid. One article about his work described him as a photographer "who captured soft moments from beautiful wildlife against an equally mesmerizing background." He'd shot everything from a pair of scarlet macaws perched together in a Brazilian rain forest to baby elephants, their trunks intertwined, with an orange sun setting behind them in Africa.

As much as he loved capturing such stunning beauty of nature, he often had to travel to remote places. It made for a lonely existence—one he no longer wished to maintain.

A text came in on his phone. "I better go find out about this job."

"See who's in it," his mom said. "We could have major movie stars among us. You might even know them."

Jay laughed. "I highly doubt that."

Catalina finished making notes in her script and gazed out the window. A deer and her fawn were walking through the woods behind the back property of the B&B. The little one wasn't watching where he was going and ran into his mom's back legs, making Catalina laugh. The doe looked back as he got to his feet and shook off the snow, his tiny tail wagging.

There was a knock at the door, and Catalina instantly stiffened.

"Ms. Jones?" Neil called.

She hoped Erin was right, that Neil would turn out to be a trustworthy assistant, but she wasn't going to let go of her Ice Queen persona until she knew for sure. She grabbed her phone and stared at the screen.

"Enter," she said in a monotone, slightly curt voice.

Neil poked his head in. "The director has requested a meeting with you in town." She rose without saying a word, so he hesitated, most likely not sure what her lack of a reply meant. "I'll…uh…just wait for you downstairs."

He closed the door and Catalina relaxed. He was still so anxious around her. Maybe she should tone it down. Neil knew her last assistant had been terminated less than forty-eight hours after being hired. He'd seen the whole thing on social media like the rest of the world.

Catalina had been on the phone with a producer when her former assistant began recording her without her permission. Furious that her private phone call was being filmed, Catalina grabbed the assistant's phone out of her hands, deleted the recording, and fired her on the spot.

Later, her then-assistant dragged the deleted file out of the trash, did a little creative editing, and posted a new version—an outrageous lie about what really happened. The doctored video instantly went viral. Catalina could be heard off-screen mercilessly berating her ex-assistant. After the supposed tirade, somehow another phone appeared out of nowhere to record the assistant's phone being smashed into oblivion. Her ex-assistant posted the fabricated ending, fueling the rumors of Catalina being a temperamental celebrity and a true Ice Queen.

Catalina had gone on social media to tell the truth about what happened. Only it was followed up by a deepfake video posted by her disgruntled employee.

Her ex-assistant had cost Catalina consideration for the lead in a historical drama. She was furious that someone she knew for less forty-eight hours had damaged her reputation and greatly affected her career.

Because of her ex-fiancé and her ex-assistant, Catalina had wound up here—stuck in a town that was all about Christmas, playing an unhappy character caught up in some stupid Scrooge Legend. To top it off, it was a romantic comedy. She wasn't funny, and she didn't want to pretend to be in love. This was going to be the most miserable shoot of her entire career.

Chapter Three

Joe watched their only guests pull out of the drive before he went to check on his wife, who'd been clearly stressed all morning. He found her in the kitchen making a Dutch apple pie. "Ms. Jones and her assistant just left for town. I was going to ask if they needed anything, but Neil was talking about a production change, which made his boss look grumpy, so I thought it best not to interrupt."

"I don't blame you." His calm, cool wife looked a little frazzled. She blew a stray hair out of her eyes and kept rolling out her pie pastry with strong, determined strokes. "Catalina might be worse than that doozy of a Scrooge we had after Charley. She doesn't talk, refuses interaction, and she doesn't eat. Who doesn't eat, Joe?" She gently wrapped the pastry around the rolling pin, then opened it up again over her baking dish. "Thank goodness the McCorts are coming. They'll help to balance out all this negative energy."

"About that." Joe leaned against the archway. "Our boss has just diverted them to Hawaii."

"What?" Disappointment flooded Mary's eyes. "Why?"

"He said having a film crew in town is like hosting

a Scrooge convention. There are more people needing his help than we can handle, which is why he's calling this assignment a Scrooge emergency. Apparently, half the crew are pre-Scrooges."

"Pre-Scrooges? What makes them different from Scrooges?"

"No one has dropped their names in his mailbox suggesting them as a Scrooge, so he can't give them the kind of attention they need until someone does."

"Well, we're not allowed to suggest them." Mary threw her pastry into the refrigerator to chill, then began coring the apples. "What's our boss hoping for?"

"That they'll change their ways in order to work together." He watched his wife carefully before he imparted the last bit of news. "Our boss would like a few of them to stay with us."

Her shoulders fell. "Of course he would. Who are they?"

"The director, writer, and director's assistant— though the assistant is not a pre-Scrooge."

Mary peeled the skin off the apples. "I can see why they need to be under one roof. If our Scrooge is having to work with a dysfunctional family, then it's best we help get the dysfunction straightened out."

Joe came over, put his arms around her, and gave her a kiss. "You are an amazing woman, Mrs. Carroll."

A smile finally appeared on her face. "That's because I'm married to an amazing man."

He gave her another kiss, then eyed the cooling rack loaded with English toffee bars.

She chuckled. "You may have *one*."

"Can I negotiate for two? You know Catalina won't eat hers."

"All right, two, but that's it. Catalina might not be interested today, but I'll have her hooked on them before the week is out." She just hoped the pre-Scrooges didn't muck that up somehow.

Jay didn't have any difficulty finding the production office since it had more people coming and going than anywhere else in town. Sitting at the reception desk was a young production assistant with dark hair and purple-framed glasses. She looked up from her computer when Jay approached.

"Hi, I'm Jay Townsend, just hired to be your still photographer."

"Iris," she said. "I'm one of many production assistants you'll meet while we're shooting."

Jay glanced around the busy office setting up shop. He assumed all those above the line—the director and producers—were situated down the hallway in private offices while all those below the line were staking out territory for their workstations. Several crew members were talking to the production manager and coordinator while relaying messages to their various departments through headsets.

"So, what's the movie called?" Jay asked.

"*The Scrooge Legend.*"

His mouth fell open. "You're making a movie about our town's legend?"

"Why not? It's got intrigue, laughs, drama, romance." Her eyes lit up. "Maybe even a little magic."

He couldn't argue with her there. Those were solid makings for a good movie. "Who wrote it?"

"Stan Larkin."

"I don't know that name. I was thinking he might have lived here."

"I'm not sure, but is it true? About the legend? That any Scrooge who enters the town will end up loving Christmas as much as Santa?"

"It's been that way as long as I've lived here."

"Cool. Then I think you'll like the story. We just received script revisions, so after we incorporate those pages, I can get you your copy." She put together a new employee start-up packet from several loose payroll and tax forms arranged on her desk. "This must be exciting for you—to have a movie shooting in your hometown."

"Not really. I used to work in the industry."

"Oh, yeah?" She glanced at him. "What did you work on?"

"I directed *Sage Under Fire, Lost in the Glades, Mr. Templeton, Raised by*—"

"Oh my gosh." She put a hand to her cheek. "You directed *Sage Under Fire*?"

He nodded.

"I love that film. Will you be directing something again soon?"

The million-dollar question. He'd been out of the business for three years. Tyler assured him that Peter Wells was a straightforward producer who despised chaos as much as he did, but Jay didn't know if the man would remember him—especially now. Back then, Jay had been a director going up the ladder of success, not a fill-in still photographer just hired.

"I'm working on it," he finally answered.

Iris gasped. "I just realized something. You're going to be reunited with your *Sage Under Fire* leading lady!"

He cocked his head. "What?"

"Catalina Jones," Iris said, excitedly. "She's playing Ms. Scrooge. How awesome is that?"

Jay was left speechless as his mind raced, wondering how this could work.

Iris handed him a clipboard with a stack of forms. "Here's the call sheet for tomorrow, your deal memo, the start-up paperwork, and our company's safety protocols. Go ahead and fill them out, and then I'll take you over to meet the unit publicist."

He froze. If Catalina was starring in the movie, how could he possibly take the job now? They hadn't spoken in years. It would be so awkward—not only personally but professionally. There'd been a handful of famous directors who began their careers as photographers. Whoever heard of a director hanging it up for photography? Catalina would think him a failure. When she'd seen him last, his film had just won awards at the film festival. He was attracting studio attention and making a name for himself. Now she'd only see him as an inconspicuous still photographer—if she even noticed him at all.

He stepped outside and dialed Tyler.

"Hey, Jay. Did you find the production office okay?"

"Why didn't you tell me Catalina Jones is starring in this movie?"

"Because you would have let your emotions do the talking and not taken the job."

"I haven't taken it yet, and I'm not going to."

"Why not?" Tyler sounded as if Jay had said something inconceivable. "Don't make this about her, Jay. This is about you getting back to what you were meant to do."

"What exactly am I supposed to say to her? She's only known me as a director."

"Which you will be again very soon." Tyler sounded more confident than he felt. "You wrote the lead in your thriller for her. Seems like this is a golden opportunity for you to get both Peter and Catalina on board."

"As a still photographer, I'm going to be a nonentity on set. I bet they don't give me a second thought."

"If that happens, then you will be no worse off than where you are right now."

"Except my pride will resemble scorched earth."

"Do you remember your first interview at the film festival? Your quote became famous and is still repeated by film school professors. 'If you allow yourself to be still, the magic will happen.'"

His laugh was laced with irritation. "That was to my actors."

"It's good advice for anyone—including you."

Jay ran a hand over his face and released a loud sigh. "I don't know, Ty. Out of all the actresses that could be starring in the movie, why does it have to be her?"

"Because life wants to torture you? I don't know. But answer me this. Do you want to get back to directing, or do you want to make pennies freezing your butt off in order to take a few photos of wild animals?"

"One of those *photos* is on the cover of *Nature's Treasure*," Jay said, feeling slighted.

"A decent magazine with a sadly small readership." Tyler softened his tone. "Buddy, I'm not knocking your wildlife photography. You're a good photographer, but a brilliant director. You can always go back to your photography between films. So what's it going to be? Are you in or out?"

A couple of grips came out the door laughing, already entrenched in their on-set comradery. As much as Jay wanted to grouse about the industry, with its demanding deadlines and too many executives who knew nothing about the creative side of filmmaking, he missed having a crew around him who felt like a second family. If he managed to get back in and hated it, he could always get back out again. Besides, he could put up with anything for three short weeks. "I'm in," he finally said.

"You won't regret it." Tyler hung up before Jay could change his mind.

He blew out a breath and heard yelling near a black SUV parked on the street. A stocky forty-something man with curly dark hair was dressing down a young guy who looked no older than Hailey.

Jay rarely heard yelling in his quiet hometown, but when he did, it usually centered around a Scrooge. He stopped to watch it play out, in case the altercation got any worse. He had no qualms about getting in the middle of it, should he need to protect the kid.

"If I wanted it that way, I would have asked for it!" The man threw something in the young guy's face, then stormed off toward the town square. The young guy looked shocked as he adjusted something in his ear and talked into a small microphone.

Only then did Jay realize he'd been staring at the director of *The Scrooge Legend*. It was definitely time to get back to directing—if not for himself, but for this kid, and for all the film crews out there who had to deal with megalomaniacs like Victor Caviano. If Jay could take one directing job away from someone like that, the stress of pulling off a comeback would be well worth it.

Chapter Four

Neil parked near the entrance to the town square and opened the backseat door for Catalina. She put away her phone and braced herself before stepping out, ready to be bombarded with fans wanting autographs and paparazzi taking pictures. But there wasn't a crowd at all. Everyone looked normal, going about their day, as if she wasn't famous. The first woman who passed by her smiled and said hello, but kept walking. The same thing happened with a couple, and then a man.

"Looks like your winter wear conceals your identity quite well," Neil said.

Catalina smiled and dropped her shoulders as she and Neil walked along the meandering path lined with luminary bags. Christmas lights outlined the branches of every bare tree, and she could only imagine how beautiful it was going to look when the town was lit up at night.

Spotted among the decorated pines were elaborate wooden-carved Christmas scenes—a snowman family, Rudolph with his reindeer, and a trumpeting angel over the Nativity. Past a park bench adorned with red-and-green ribbon, a crew was trimming a sixty-foot Christmas tree in the center of the square.

"The set builders have been working overtime," she said.

"These are actually the town's decorations," Neil replied. "But I'm sure our guys will be adding to it."

"Where?" Catalina couldn't find any place that didn't scream Christmas. They walked another fifty feet and saw a set of life-size, animated carolers singing, "We Wish You a Merry Christmas."

She suddenly remembered the trip her family took to Catalina Island when she was a kid. It was the first week of December. She'd been excited to finally see the place she had been named after. Catalina had been eleven at the time and her brother, Cameron, was nine. On their first night there, the town had a beautiful tree-lighting ceremony. Strolling carolers filled the streets of Avalon with their angelic voices as she and her brother met Santa and his happy elves. It had been such a magical experience for her that she decided she wanted to live in a magical land when she grew up. A passerby had heard her comment and said, "Looks like you'll be going to Hollywood, little girl."

"Get rid of those irritating, cheesy carolers!" Victor scowled at a young man by his side. "And fire whoever thought they were a good idea."

"Sir, they belong to St. Nicholas," a skittish-looking assistant said to Victor.

"I don't care who they belong to, Theo. I said to get rid of them!"

Theo scampered off like a scared bunny. Catalina had heard of Victor's short fuse with assistants; it was legendary. Seeing Neil pale before her eyes, she thought it best to take over before her only assistant became the next victim for Victor's target practice.

"Victor," she said with a smile, holding out her

gloved hands. "It's so good to finally be working with you."

"Catalina, my dear." He took her hands and gave her a kiss on the cheek. "What do you think of St. Nicholas?"

"It's no Telluride," she said, ratcheting up her diva attitude, "but I suppose it will have to do."

"My sentiments exactly." His grin broadened. "Let me show you where we'll be shooting the meet-cute at Santa's Mailbox."

Catalina, Victor, and Neil went around a cluster of pine trees to a bright-red mailbox standing alone with a candy cane flag on its right side, and an address stamped on the front which read 1 KRINGLE LANE.

Catalina felt an unexpected sense of security mixed with relief, and she didn't know why. It wasn't as if she were staring at a beautiful blue ocean, or getting never-ending knots massaged out of her shoulders. She was walking toward a red mailbox decorated for Christmas.

"Is this the mailbox that accepts Scrooge suggestions?" Catalina asked, shaking off the odd sensation.

Victor nodded. "According to Stan."

"And the legend," Neil said, but immediately regretted speaking up when Victor shot him a nasty look. Neil lowered his gaze to the ground and took another step back.

"Interesting design." Catalina pulled on the handle, but it didn't open. "Someone will need to fix this."

"You." Victor snapped his fingers at Neil. "Make a note."

Neil nodded and added it into his phone as Theo returned.

Victor studied the mailbox, then snapped his fingers

for Theo. "What's with the candy cane flag?" Victor glared at his assistant as if he had personally put the flag there himself.

"I don't know, sir, but I can find out."

"That was a rhetorical question. I hate it. Get rid of it."

"Yes, sir." Theo immediately got on his phone, which seemed to bother Victor, so he hung up and ran off again.

A young couple approached the mailbox. They stared at a letter in the woman's hand, as if it held their hearts' desires. Then as the woman was about to drop it into the mailbox, Neil said, "That's not a real mailbox. It's a film prop."

The young woman gave him a curious look, opened the door with ease, tossed in the letter, raised the candy cane flag, and walked away with her companion.

"Idiots," Victor said to Catalina. "Let's go to my office and talk about your character. There are some elements I'd like you to incorporate in your portrayal of Ms. Scrooge."

No doubt. Victor was more of a Scrooge than she could ever be, and she wondered how she was going to make it through filming. *Just breathe.* Jay's words suddenly popped into her head. Whenever she'd gotten too stressed out, he'd reminded her to take three deep breaths. It had always worked, so she took those breaths and suddenly became fixated on the town around her.

St. Nicholas had received three inches of snow the night before, covering every exposed surface. The gorgeous swath of pure white glistened in the sun, giving the small town an ethereal feeling, like fairy dust from Tinkerbell's wand.

The early afternoon streets were filling up with Christmas shoppers, smiling, laughing, carrying Christmas-themed shopping bags, and sipping warm drinks. Main Street itself was camera-worthy. Sizable silver bells were draped over the street every thirty feet or so. Boughs of garland and twinkle lights wrapped the trees planted along the sidewalk. Big red bows were attached to every lamppost with little happy elves holding on to each one. Every storefront was decorated with Christmas lights, bows, bells, and garland. Actual snow was piled in the corners of each window instead of the fake stuff they used on sets.

She stopped and stood still, just to take it all in, when a horse-drawn carriage passed by carrying a young couple laughing, smiling, appearing to be deeply in love. For a moment, Catalina wanted to switch lives with that woman—to be so in love that nothing else mattered. Another time, another life. She shook the wish away.

Victor turned toward her. "What's wrong?"

"Nothing." She cleared her throat. "I was just noticing how the town is so picture-perfect."

Victor briefly scanned Main Street. "We can do better." He continued to the production office, and she had no choice but to follow.

Inside, the place was teeming with production assistants, department heads, arriving crew, and producers. Victor headed straight for his office with Catalina close behind. An assistant was taping up storyboards on one of his walls while two others placed large silk olive plants in the corners, bookending the couch. The faux plants made her think of the ocean and summer, which seemed like an odd choice for their location.

"Come back later," he told the PAs. "Theo, bring

us some fresh coffee, and find out when my room will be ready."

"Yes, sir." Theo ducked out.

Catalina studied the storyboards. "When do I get to meet Piper?"

"Didn't you already speak to her by phone?"

"I was supposed to, but with our accelerated schedule, it never happened."

"I'll make sure you connect with her today," he said. "But I'm not worried about your portrayal of her. The movie isn't her biography, so don't sacrifice your acting choices if they don't happen to align with who she is in real life."

"I won't," she said, wondering why he needed to explain that. She could only assume that Stan's script had veered off into the land of ridiculously implausible, instead of aligning with Piper's real Scrooge story.

"Your instincts for playing a Scrooge are right on target—though not a stretch since you'll be playing yourself."

She ignored the backhanded comment as he walked around his desk and sat.

"What I am concerned about is you and Landon." He rocked back, but kept his black, deep-set eyes locked on her. "The chemistry between you two was lacking during the table read."

As much as she wanted to disagree, Victor was right. The original shooting schedule had principal photography beginning at the end of January, not weeks before Christmas. Catalina had planned on going home for the holidays. Her parents lived in Maine and she hadn't seen them in over four years. When she had called her mom to give her the bad news about not being able to make it home for Christmas, her mom had insisted she and her father understood, but Catalina could tell she'd broken her mom's heart. That phone call had happened five minutes before the table read, and Catalina had been miles away when she read her lines.

"I was preoccupied with something else," she told Victor. "But you don't need to worry. You'll get sizzling chemistry between us once the cameras are rolling."

He leaned forward, studying her. "I'm glad to hear that, Catalina. I've seen that intensity in your eyes, and I want it in my movie. I want that incredible vulnerability and that undeniable chemistry you shared with Grayson Edwards in the movie you did together. Tell me, were those scenes filmed before or after you two were an item?"

Catalina stiffened. She knew exactly what he was talking about. She and Grayson had fallen in love during filming. The chemistry was real, as was her vulnerability. Raw emotion and honest moments between two people were always magical, and though actors faked it all the time, it didn't get any better than capturing the real thing on camera.

"It was before," she said, not willing to share the truth. "We dated after we'd shot those scenes."

"Interesting." He held her gaze, as if he were waiting for her to flinch because of the lie she'd just told him.

But she didn't flinch and wouldn't. She had finally learned to embrace the Ice Queen in order to hide what she was truly feeling, and she certainly wasn't willing to give that up for Victor.

"Then you shouldn't have a problem tapping into whatever helped you to deliver that solid performance," he challenged.

"It won't be a problem at all," she said confidently, even though she wasn't so sure. She was not going to revisit those incredibly deep emotions she'd had for Grayson—not for the movie, and not ever.

"Jay?"

He turned around to see the director of photography from *Sage Under Fire* approaching. "Clayton. Hey!" They greeted each other with a handshake and clap on the back.

"Are you working on this?" Clayton asked, motioning to the production office Jay had just exited.

"Yeah. They lost their still photographer last night, and Tyler found out I was here visiting my folks, so he roped me into it."

"You're the still photographer?" Clayton gave him a surprised look. "Not what I expected to hear, but they'll be getting awesome publicity photos with you on board. I've been following your work. You have such a great eye."

"Thanks. That means a lot."

Clayton glanced around to see who was within earshot, then lowered his voice. "I wish you were the director on this thing. VC isn't who I would have chosen to direct a feel-good Christmas movie."

"I've heard the rumors. Yells first, then figures out what he's yelling about later."

Clayton chuckled. "Sadly true, but what are we going to do? His movies end up being huge hits so he'll never be out of a job."

"Not much fun for any film crew who has to put up with him."

"That's an understatement. His last cinematographer

quit after the first week." Clayton eyed Jay. "When are you going to get back to directing?"

"Soon, I hope."

"Glad to hear it. I'd love to be your DP any day."

"Thanks, man. I appreciate it."

"You know who's in this, right?"

Jay rubbed the back of his neck, feeling anxious all over again. "Just heard."

"You can tell me to butt out, but whatever happened between you two?"

Jay shrugged. "Nothing more than what happens to a lot of friends. We got busy, work took us in different directions, and then we lost contact with one another. Have you worked with her since *Sage Under Fire*?"

"No, but a buddy of mine was on her last film, and he says her new nickname holds true."

"Ice Queen?" Jay looked at him skeptically. "So I've heard, but I can't see that. I remember her being a genuinely sincere person."

Clayton blew out a breath. "This industry changes people, and from what I hear, she's not the same person. You're not going to recognize her."

"More like she won't recognize me."

The doors blew open, and a woman dressed in white came barreling out of the production office so fast that Jay barely had time to get out of the way before she ran him over.

"Guess you're right about that," Clayton said with a laugh. "She definitely didn't recognize you."

Jay whipped around and stared after her. "That was Catalina?"

"Afraid so."

They watched her march toward a black town car

with tinted windows. A young man leaped out of the driver's seat, came around to the other side, and opened the door so she could quickly disappear inside.

"We've got a Scrooge for a director and an Ice Queen playing Ms. Scrooge," Clayton said. "This is going to be a blast."

Jay shoved his hands in his pocket, feeling a sudden drop in temperature. What had he gotten himself into?

Chapter Five

Catalina sat in the back of the town car, irritated that she'd let Victor get under her skin. It was bad enough how every time she went to a Hollywood function someone would inevitably mention Grayson's name, but now her director had actually suggested she draw upon her time with her ex to feed her performance. How could he have been so insensitive?

"I spoke with Piper while you were meeting with Victor," Neil said. "She's available to speak with you now or at three, whatever works for you."

Catalina blew out a breath, letting it go. "Thank you, Neil. Now would be great."

Neil took her to Piper's coffeehouse, where she sat with the woman her character was based on, sipping the best cup of coffee she'd ever tasted. Catalina assumed Stan had taken a few liberties with Piper's story, but she had no idea he had practically rewritten her entire life.

Piper frowned, staring at the latest round of script changes. "I don't understand this. The writer asked for my permission to use some of my story, but had I known he was going to do this, I would have never agreed to it."

"So, you never stole cars for a living?"

"No, I *drove* cars for a living as in delivering cars

from point A to point B. That was my job before I moved up here to be with my mom."

"I'm sorry, Piper. Writers tend to punch things up—to make something more dramatic. I'll talk to him about changing it."

"I'd really appreciate that," she said. "What other questions can I answer for you?"

Catalina skimmed her notes. "You said that you and your husband were considered Scrooges. Is that usual with the Scrooge Legend—to have two Scrooges fall in love?"

"It happens as often as it doesn't. The Scrooge Legend brings people together, and how that is accomplished is unique to every Scrooge story."

"The angst you must have gone through when you thought Adam was going to tear down your mother's house, but instead he fixed it up and sold it back to you for a dollar."

"All true," she said, smiling. "Adam was a Scrooge because he had only cared about making a profit before he met me. I thought he was going to be my worst nightmare, but I soon discovered he was my happy ending."

"And you two fell in love with each other during the renovations?"

"We did. At first I didn't care for him. At all." Piper let out a little embarrassed laugh. "But when I made it my mission to watch his every move, I discovered that *his* mission was restoring old homes, not tearing them down. As I continued to stop by the house and question what he was doing, he'd pull up research of old homes from the 1930s, determined to get every detail right, and I couldn't help but admire him. His love for old houses brought us together. When I pushed aside my fear and judgment, I saw what a good, kind man he was, and well, how could I not fall in love with someone like that?"

"It's all about the details, isn't it?" Catalina knew this to be true when it came to acting, but she had never thought about it in terms of a relationship. It was the details that mattered, not some grand, sweeping, one-time gesture. "You've got a great guy. Adam understood that the details mattered from the beginning. Even how he proposed to you was fantastic." Catalina flipped to the last page of the script. "Did he actually tie your engagement ring around the key to your mom's house?"

"That was your writer's idea, and admittedly, it fits better with the story than how he actually proposed."

"How so?"

"Adam took me to an expensive restaurant in downtown Denver where he had our waiter put my engagement ring in the dessert I'd ordered. There was a mix-up with the desserts and mine went to another table with an older couple. A sixty-year-old man got my ring."

"Oh, no," Catalina said with a small laugh. "What happened?"

"It got straightened out quickly. After Adam proposed to me, the older gentleman came over to congratulate us, and said that we had inspired him to ask his wife of thirty years to marry him again."

"How sweet." Catalina was beginning to see a pattern with the Scrooge Legend. Love not only surrounded Scrooges, but it radiated out, and touched the lives around them. It almost made her want to be a Scrooge—and not just in a movie. She glanced at her list of questions. "When did you start believing in the Scrooge Legend?"

"When I saw the synchronicity of how we met, and

how far back the timing of our paths crossing had actually gone."

"What do you mean?"

"Right after my dad passed away, my mom suddenly sold their house and moved up here. I thought she was crazy. My dad had grown up here, but she hadn't, and when my grandparents retired to Florida, we no longer had a connection to this place. I was constantly worrying about her being too isolated, so I came up here to convince her to return to Denver, but I moved in with her instead. I was only given one month with her before she died, but it was the best month of my life. We repaired our relationship, and I learned just how many dear friends she had in town. St. Nicholas has always been a good town with caring people. I thought their Scrooge Legend was a little out there until I lived it. So many horrible things kept happening to me—the worst losing my mom, but through her, I met Adam. My mom had always wanted me to find the kind of love she'd had with my father, and I can truly say that I did. Of course, I would have never met Adam had my mom not moved up here in the first place."

"Forgive me, but your mom also had to die in order for you to meet him."

"No. Turns out she had contacted him as a restoration contractor. She was actually in a meeting with him the day I had arrived. They had even decided on the date he'd begin work. He was already on the way to St. Nicholas when she had a heart attack."

Catalina sat back, blown away. It was quite a coincidence for Piper's mom to literally pick out the guy her daughter would marry. She now understood how a legend became one when coincidences like that happened. "I'm sorry to hear about your mother."

"Thank you. She is very well remembered. The people here are lovely and had taken good care of her, and then me when I lost her."

"It sounds like this is a wonderful place to live. Maybe it's not the Scrooge Legend that makes this place special, but the people."

"I think it's a little bit of both."

Catalina gathered her things. "Thank you for your time, Piper. I truly appreciate it. Will I see you on set tomorrow for our first day of shooting?"

"They've invited me, but I don't know." Piper shrugged. "It sounds like Stan has changed so much of my life that I might freak out watching it."

"The movie is about your Scrooge story. You have every right to speak up and be there during filming, especially since you now know that the character based on you steals cars."

Piper let out a big sigh. "Maybe if we both talk to Stan, he'll change it."

"Can't hurt." She stood. "You might want to mention one other area. The bit about your kids feeding Santa's reindeer in your backyard."

"Oh, that part is true."

"Uh, what?"

"Reindeer need real food, not milk and cookies, in order to deliver on Christmas Eve. It's a lot to do in one night."

Catalina exploded with a laugh, but Piper just stared at her with a straight face, and she didn't know what to make of it. Christmas magic didn't exist, even in a special town like St. Nicholas. Obviously, she was joking. Wasn't she?

* * *

Mary and Joe scanned the diner for their friends, Felicity and Nolan, a young couple who also hosted Scrooges at their own B&B.

"There they are," Mary said, and led the way to a corner booth.

"My fault we're late." Joe took off his coat while Mary slid in next to the window.

Angel, the diner's best waitress who had recently been promoted to manager, still took care of her good friends. She set down four coffees and a coffee cake on the table. "Go ahead and get started without me. I'll be back over as soon as I can."

"Thanks, Angel." Joe sat next to his wife.

"Is everything okay?" Felicity asked, shifting her gaze between the two.

"Define okay." Mary shrugged out of her coat but kept it around her shoulders.

"Is it raining Scrooges like it is at our place?" Felicity asked.

"Got one in the barn and more on the way." Joe grunted. "Just what the heck is going on?"

"We've been wondering the same thing," Nolan said.

Mary shook her head, confused about the change in plans. "We were only supposed to be hosting Catalina and the McCorts, then—"

"Bam!" Joe smacked his fist into the palm of his hand. "A helicopter is landing in our front yard, and our boss diverts the McCorts to Hawaii so that the director, his assistant, and the writer can come in their place. Our house is filling up."

"Ours, too." Nolan's eyes widened. "We're supposed to be welcoming the leading man with his companion late tonight, but we've already got two producers with their assistants, who keep asking us for things we don't have."

"Like what?" Mary asked.

"Cappuccino makers for their rooms, a masseuse on call, a loaner car."

"Movie people," Joe grumbled, slicing off a piece of coffee cake for himself.

"Just how many producers does one movie need?" Felicity asked, irritation coloring her voice.

"Who's your Scrooge?" Mary asked.

"We haven't been assigned one yet," Felicity said. "We think it might be the leading man, but we don't know for sure."

Mary took a sip of coffee, trying to figure it out. "What I don't understand is how our boss allowed this movie to be made in the first place. You know they're not going to portray the Scrooge Legend accurately."

"That's an understatement." Angel pulled up a chair and sat down. "One of the crew members was in here, and I might have peeked at the script. There are talking reindeer."

"Oh, dear." Mary fussed with the back of her hair. "This doesn't sound good at all."

"Wasn't Piper coming to the meeting today?" Felicity glanced out the window.

"She was, but then she got inundated with a ton of orders from the production crew, which is about to happen to me." Angel indicated a growing crowd at the entrance. "Gotta go." She hurried off.

"What should we be doing about all of these pre-Scrooges?" Nolan asked.

"I say we keep our focus on Catalina," Mary said. "She's the Scrooge assignment."

"I'm actually happy to hear it's her," Felicity said, nibbling her piece of coffee cake. "I really like her movies, but her breakup with Grayson changed her, and now she comes off as a diva."

"Grayson Edwards," Nolan grumbled. "That guy could use a serious attitude adjustment."

Mary frowned. "Felicity, please tell me he's not her leading man."

She shook her head. "It's Landon Barnes. He's been in a bunch of stuff. He usually plays the best friend or the sidekick."

"He's a funny guy." Nolan took a drink of his coffee. "I can't see him as a Scrooge."

"Whether he is or isn't, hopefully Mr. Barnes can spread the laughs," Mary said, "because I think we're going to need them."

Chapter Six

"How did it go?" Neil asked as Catalina exited the coffee shop.

"Eye-opening. Piper's real story is far better than the script. I need to speak to Stan. Has he arrived yet?"

"He's stuck in LA until tomorrow, but I can set up a call with him if you prefer not to wait."

She closed up her coat, then slipped on her hat and gloves as they walked to the car. "Text him to see when he's available. Some of the things in the script are too ridiculous."

"Like the Christmas fairies?"

She instantly smiled. "Can you believe he put them in there?"

"Don't forget the talking reindeer."

Catalina shared a laugh with him, then immediately pulled back, realizing she was letting her guard down. They walked in silence, and it was beginning to get uncomfortable.

"Ms. Jones, may I say something?" Neil stopped and turned toward her. "I think what your last assistant did to you was egregious. I completely understand how difficult it must be for you to trust another assistant again, but you can trust me. I respect you, and I respect your work. I would never do anything to jeopardize that."

She wanted to believe him, but that had been her problem all along. She trusted the wrong people at the wrong time. She eyed him for a long moment. He seemed genuine, and the sincerity in his voice was hard to miss. Maybe she could give the guy some slack. It didn't mean she was going to spill all of her secrets to him, but she didn't have to be so closed off.

"Thank you, Neil. I appreciate that."

He nodded with a slight smile and released a breath before they continued to the car. "I almost forgot. I got a little something for your mom, if you want to send it to her." Neil popped the trunk and handed her a small gift bag.

"For my mom?" Catalina looked at him curiously as she reached inside the bag and pulled out a small bakery box.

"This particular bakery is known for the best snickerdoodles in town."

Neil's kind gesture made her eyes misty, and she was glad to be wearing her sunglasses. She blinked, took a breath. "How did you know my mom loved snickerdoodles?"

"An article from 2020. You talked about how you loved making them with her at Christmas every year, and that you were disappointed you'd be missing out on that tradition."

"You do your homework, Mr. Segal."

"I try."

"Thank you for this." She placed her hand on his arm. "It's very kind of you."

He smiled. "It's always good to cheer up moms when

we can't come home for the holidays. Mine wasn't so happy about me missing Hanukkah again."

"I bet she wasn't." She set the cookie box back inside. "If our schedule hadn't pushed up, you would have been with her."

"That's what I told her." He opened the car door. "The production office isn't overnighting anything until tomorrow. Maybe we should try the post office."

A few minutes later, they walked inside. "A fairly large post office for such a small town," Catalina said, looking around.

"And a busy one." Neil gestured to the long customer service counter. "Ten stations and they're all open. I've never seen that in LA, have you?"

"Maybe the magic begins here." She studied the clerks, who appeared quite jolly, and couldn't help but think of Santa's little helpers. "I'm intrigued."

They found the end of the line, which seemed far from the front counter. Already feeling too warm, she unbuttoned her coat and debated whether to shed her hat at the risk of being recognized.

Neil noticed her discomfort and whispered, "I'll be happy to get this out in the mail if you're too hot."

"I'm not boiling yet," she said as the line moved up. "Besides, I'd like to ask some questions. If anyone knows the locals in town, it will be the postal workers."

The line kept moving, and in no time, they heard, "Next."

"That was fast," Catalina said under her breath as she and Neil walked up to the counter.

The post office clerk was a cheery guy wearing a Wyatt name tag and drumming his hands on the counter. "Merry Christmas." Wyatt smiled broadly as he kept beat to "Here Comes Santa Claus" playing over-head. "What can I do you for, movie people?"

Catalina and Neil shot each other a look.

"How do you know we're with the movie?" Neil asked.

"I didn't. But I do now!" He chuckled. "What can I do for you, movie star?" He looked directly at Cata-lina, and she shrank.

"Sir, can you please keep your voice down?" Neil asked. "She doesn't want to be bombarded."

"What do you mean?" He didn't understand, so Cata-lina lowered her sunglasses.

"Oh, my goodness!" Wyatt threw his hands on top of his hand. "I *cannot* believe this." He broke into a big grin, unable to take his eyes off her. "You look exactly like that big-time actress. What's her name? Caroline Jones?"

"Catalina." She put a finger up to her lips in hopes he'd lower the volume.

"Yes, by jolly, Catalina." He struck the counter with his fist, then leaned in. "Are you her stand-in or stunt double?"

"Ms. Jones would—"

"Stand-in," Catalina said. "And assistant to Ms. Jones. In fact, we're here to mail this package for her."

Neil handed over the bakery box to Wyatt.

"Oh, she has good taste. This bakery has the best goodies. And I would know." He patted his belly with a laugh.

"Yes, I hear they're exceptional," Catalina said.

"Okey dokey." Wyatt reached under the counter and gave her a shipping label. "I think you'll want to overnight them." He handed the right size box to Neil, who packaged the cookies before sealing the box.

"Do you by chance know Piper Davis?" Catalina asked as she was filling out her mom's address. "The movie is based on her Scrooge story."

"Mrs. Davis is such a goodhearted woman," Wyatt said. "She lost so much, but she believed in herself and the people of St. Nicholas, and now look at what a beautiful family she has."

"She does." Catalina attached the label to the box. "Do you think the Scrooge Legend had anything to do with her falling in love with Adam?"

"It had everything to do with it. How do you think she met him?"

She squinted at Wyatt in confusion. "Piper's mother had actually contacted Adam to restore her house before she passed away."

"Yes, but that's because it wasn't any old house. It was her husband's childhood home."

"What?" This bit of information was new.

"Came on the market only a week after he passed away."

Catalina felt chills over her body. Piper was living in her mother's house and her father's childhood home. Why hadn't Piper told her about her family's connection to the house? "Quite a coincidence."

"No coincidence. That's the Scrooge Legend at work," Wyatt said.

"So you believe in the Scrooge Legend."

"Oh, gosh golly, yes. Too many Christmas miracles have happened not to."

"And Christmas magic?" she asked. "Do you believe in that, too?"

"Look around. Can you find a more magical place?"

She was beginning to believe that St. Nicholas had a lot more to offer than what met the eye. "Piper said her kids fed Santa's reindeer on Christmas Eve."

"Well, someone has to feed them." He glanced at the sealed-up box. "All done?"

"Yes." Neil handed it over.

Catalina was lost in thought as she paid for her mom's package. She was no longer part of a light romance story. She was playing someone real who'd experienced an unusual chain of events. But to call it a Christmas miracle or Christmas magic? She no longer believed in either. Maybe it was because she knew movie magic was fake. For her, Christmas had become just another day.

"Wyatt, I heard that the Scrooge Legend's magic sometimes continues with those who were once Scrooges. Were Piper's mom or dad ever considered Scrooges?"

"Gosh golly no. However, Barbara, Piper's mom, had wished for Piper's dad."

"What do you mean?"

"Barbara had met him when they were kids, so when Barbara was in college, she came up here to find him by depositing a wish in Santa's mailbox. The very next day she ran into him in the town square."

"Whoa." Neil couldn't hide his surprise.

"A wish?" Catalina cocked her head. "I thought the mailbox was strictly for recommending Scrooges."

"Nope. Christmas wishes are also accepted. In fact—" he leaned in "—the Christmas wish is the original purpose of the mailbox."

Another layer of the Scrooge Legend. Piper's story

had much more history with that odd mailbox than Stan or Piper herself had divulged. "Where's the real mailbox?"

"In the town square."

Neil shook his head. "We were over there earlier and didn't see it."

"It's red with a big candy cane flag on it," Wyatt said. "You can't miss it."

Catalina stared at Neil. "Wasn't that a prop?"

"Here ya go." Wyatt slid two pieces of paper over to Catalina and Neil.

"What's this?" she asked.

"A voucher for a free hot cocoa. You haven't tasted real hot cocoa until you've had one in St. Nicholas."

"Thank you, but I have to watch my weight." She slid it back.

"You're thinner than that flagpole out front." He slid it to her again. "Besides, isn't it the actresses and not the stand-ins who have to do those strict diets?"

"Right." She and Neil took their vouchers.

"Merry Christmas!" Wyatt said with a big grin.

Catalina walked out with Neil. "I've got to see that mailbox again."

"I'm not sure if it's still there." Neil opened the car door for her. "Victor ordered the whole thing to be removed—not just the candy cane flag."

She dropped her shoulders. "He didn't."

"Hopefully someone stopped him."

"I doubt it. The residents seem too sweet to make waves."

Five minutes later, she and Neil were heading up the meandering path to the mailbox.

"Check out the carolers." Neil pointed to a new display that stood in place of the one Victor had removed, and it was gigantic.

Catalina laughed. "I guess the good people of St. Nicholas can hold their own after all."

As the mailbox came into view, Catalina got that strange feeling of relief and a sense of security that she'd felt earlier. She wanted to ask Neil if he was feeling anything similar but knew it would sound too strange.

"I'm glad to see Victor didn't get his way," he said.

"He didn't even get the candy cane flag removed." Catalina pulled on the mailbox handle, and it didn't budge. "This has to be a film prop."

Neil tried it, too, and got the same result. "There's one way to tell." He brushed the snow away from the bottom of the mailbox exposing ornate gilded legs that were bolted to the cement. "I'm not sure if the production designer would have gone to such an extreme."

She studied the thing. "Hard to believe what Wyatt said about Piper's parents."

"It does sound a little far-fetched, but it makes for a nice story."

Catalina walked around to the back side of the mailbox and spied an ornate heart-shaped vintage padlock. She yanked on it, but it didn't open, either. "It's got to be the real one. Check this out."

Neil came around and saw the lock. "That's pretty cool."

"I guess this is where the snowman collects the Scrooge suggestions."

"Do you find that odd?" he asked.

"Which part?"

"The mail collector being a snowman. Wouldn't he melt in the summer?"

She laughed. "A valid note for our screenwriter. Stan needs to keep to the basics. Everyone knows elves help Santa, not snowmen." She started to walk away, but Neil didn't move.

"Do you want to see if it works?"

"What?"

"The magical mailbox."

"Magic, Christmas, unicorns—that's all stuff for kids."

"Hey, I'm Jewish, so it makes no difference to me, but the scientist in me wants to find out." He took out a pen and notepad, then scribbled something on it.

She crossed her arms, refusing to believe that a mailbox could grant wishes. "Good luck trying to get the door open."

"Right." He rubbed his chin, looking at it. "I first wish for the door to open," he said with a chuckle as he looked to the heavens, then grabbed the handle and it opened with ease.

Catalina gasped.

"Yes!" He tore off the paper and dropped his wish inside. "Your turn. Make a wish."

"What could I possibly need?"

"Love."

Catalina frowned and looked away.

"Sorry. I didn't mean to overstep," he said nervously. "I was thinking more in universal terms—that everyone needs love. Heck, I need love. What do you think I wished for?"

"You wished for love?"

"Had to. If I go through one more year without meeting a nice Jewish girl, my mom is going to be moving in with me."

She cracked a smile. She'd never joked around with one of her assistants before. Hopefully this day wouldn't come back to bite her. "In the name of science only." Catalina reached for his pen and paper. "And because I don't believe this thing has any power at all, I'm going to make it really tough on the legend. I'm going to wish for my soul mate to appear to me immediately."

He laughed. "That's genius. If the mailbox holds Christmas magic, he'll pop in like a genie. If no one shows, we'll have proof that it's fake."

Catalina set her hand on the mailbox handle. "To be fair to the legend, asking for an immediate response might actually mean within twenty-four hours. Piper said Scrooge invitations were put in motion within twenty-four hours, so it could be the same for wishes."

"Okay. Then for our experiment, we'll assume the word immediately means that it could take up to twenty-four hours," he said. "We'll need to pay close attention to anyone we meet, see, or briefly run into from now until this time tomorrow."

She nodded. It was silly, she knew that, but what would it hurt to wish for the love of her life? There was no way she'd meet whoever it was in less than twenty-four hours.

"I'm documenting all of this." He glanced at the time, then made some notes in his phone.

She reached for the handle again. "Santa's Mailbox, I wish you would bring me my soul mate, right here, right now, to St. Nicholas, Colorado. Also, don't let it be an actor." She pulled on the door handle, and it opened effortlessly.

"Look at that." Neil's eyes widened. "You didn't even need to say open sesame."

"I've got the magic touch." She shared a laugh with Neil, then she tossed in her wish.

When the mailbox door banged shut, she felt a blast of warm air. She thought it was odd, then wrote it off as warm air coming from inside the mailbox.

"Well, we did that." She brushed off her hands and glanced around. "So, what's next?"

"Late lunch. And then a video call with Stan. Victor and George will be joining."

"Maybe I can get a salad at that diner across the street."

"No pictures!" Neil suddenly yelled at a man directly in front of them. Neil attempted to block the guy, which she found endearing because the man was a good five inches taller and outweighed Neil by fifty pounds.

"Since when am I not allowed to take photos of my own town?" the man said, then did a double take at Catalina as she came closer.

She stared at him, slowly taking off her sunglasses. "Jay?"

"Catalina. Wow…hi." He smiled. "I almost didn't recognize you with your new haircut."

She touched the back of her neck. "I'm still getting used to it myself." She couldn't believe she was standing in front of Jay Townsend. She also couldn't believe how good he looked. When she had starred in his film, he was kind of a geeky but cute guy right out of college. The man standing before her had definitely hit the weight room. He was no longer cute; he was downright gorgeous.

"What's it been? Seven, eight years?" she asked, gazing into his hazel eyes that often appeared to change color. Science dictated that eye color didn't change, that the difference in light only made eyes appear like they did. She happened to disagree. When emotions were high, or when a situation was intense, Jay's eyes had always changed to a deep green—as they were at that very moment.

"Seven and a half years." He brushed his blond hair back with his hand, seeming uncomfortable, but he didn't break eye contact.

She studied his face. It was leaner, stronger, more determined. "I heard you got out of the industry."

He nodded. "I'm a wildlife photographer."

"I had no idea." *We were good friends once. You should have told me.* "Have I seen any of your work?"

"Depends on which magazines you read, but yeah, they're out there."

Was he happy to see her? She couldn't read him anymore. "Are you on assignment here?"

"Oh, uh…" He glanced around, shoving his hands in his pockets. "No, this is my hometown. My family lives here."

So he's married with children. She forced a short-lived smile. "That's right. I remember you saying that you grew up in Colorado." It made sense that he'd come back to a place with good memories to start a family. "I'm…uh…shooting a movie in town."

"I know. I was actually getting a jump on things, taking photos of the town square since we're shooting here tomorrow."

Catalina cocked her head. "Are you *working* on my movie?"

Jay winced, rubbing the back of his neck. "My old agent called, asked me to take over for someone who had to bail, but—"

"Victor is no longer directing?" *Please tell me that's the case.*

"I'm sure he is," he quickly amended. "I was asked to fill in as the still photographer, but you know, maybe I should pass…"

Does he dislike me that much? "Why? Do I make you feel uncomfortable?"

"No, I thought I was making you feel uncomfortable."

You already did that. Just what she needed—an arrogant director and a guy who had no interest in her. "Don't use me as an excuse for not taking a job, Jay. If you want to turn it down, do. If not, I'll see you on set." She turned and walked away with Neil.

What had she ever seen in him? Time warped recollection. She actually thought Jay had the power to calm her nerves when, in fact, he did the complete opposite.

Wow. She had definitely changed, and Jay wasn't so sure if he wanted to be a part of the drama. He headed back to the production office, ready to turn down the job, but then stopped himself. What was he doing? Had he learned nothing from his time off? He couldn't allow one remark to get under his skin.

Of course it was more than that. He didn't want to believe that Catalina had changed so much. He'd always been a great judge of character. He couldn't have been that wrong about her.

But seven and a half years had passed. They were no longer friends; he'd messed that up long ago. He'd had a few chances to connect with her after she finished filming the miniseries in England, but he could never bring himself to call her. It took him years to finally admit to himself that he had been afraid he was no longer enough for her.

And now she was more beautiful and more successful than ever. Even if they could somehow become friends again, what would be the point? He had nothing to offer someone like her who lived in a much different world—a world he voluntarily left.

He'd keep his word, do his job on set, and only if it felt right, he'd approach Peter about his screenplay. But that was it. When they wrapped every day, he'd come home to spend time with his family. He didn't care about Catalina's Ice Queen dramas. He wasn't going to get involved, especially after that last exchange.

He thought he saw disappointment in her eyes when he said he should pass on the job. But why? She didn't know him anymore. He meant nothing to her. *Stop thinking about her. She certainly isn't thinking about you. Is she?*

Catalina marched out of the town square more rattled than she'd expected. She'd hoped St. Nicholas would give her a reprieve from the stress she felt in LA, but seeing Jay changed all that.

"Are you all right, Ms. Jones?" Neil asked, trying to keep up.

"Yes."

"May I ask? Do I need to protect you from that guy?"

She cracked a smile. "I appreciate that, but no." She took a breath, letting her anger go. "Jay was the director of my first movie."

"Oh, yeah? I wouldn't have pegged him for a director."

"That's what made him great." And that's why her

emotions had gone from zero to sixty. Jay had been a great director and a great guy, and she'd obviously ruined the best friendship she ever had. She should have been happy for him—that he had found love and was married—but she couldn't. She only felt the sting that if she hadn't come on strong by kissing him, maybe their relationship could have developed into something more gradually, and maybe he would be with her now.

Neil headed toward the diner, but Catalina stopped at the car. "I'm no longer hungry," she said. "Please take me back to the inn."

"Of course." As he started up the car, a text came in. "Looks like lunch is out anyway. The video call has been pushed up, and Victor is now at the Carroll Inn."

"What?" Catalina stared at Neil through the rearview mirror. "Why?"

"Asking." Neil's fingers flew over his phone. "Victor has moved over there from the hotel. His office is currently unavailable, so he's decided to have the meeting there."

"No." She felt a ball of stress forming in the pit of her stomach. He couldn't be staying in her only haven away from him. Could this day get any worse?

Chapter Seven

Mary and Joe poked their heads out of their kitchen at the growing number of people in their living room. Victor and his assistant, Theo, had commandeered it for their off-site production office, and more people were coming and going than the supermarket in town.

"I threw everything at them, Joe. English toffee, peppermint bark, sugar cookies, my popular charcuterie board, and look. Not one nibble from anybody."

"I don't understand it." He rubbed his chin. "How can anyone turn down English toffee?"

"Not anyone normal," she said before they moved away from the kitchen's entrance.

Joe leaned against the counter. "I thought they had offices in town?"

"They do." Mary shrugged. "But maybe they need to be here for a Scrooge Legend reason. I overheard them talking about adding a scene where the character based on Adam loses the deed to the house in a poker game, but Christmas fairies somehow get it back."

"What kind of harebrained idea is that?" Joe frowned. "Piper stealing cars, Christmas fairies, talking reindeer—this is getting out of hand."

"Piper's very upset about it." Mary quartered a

pumpkin muffin and shared it with Joe. "You know, she accepted the money so the town could finally break ground on the Scrooge Legend Museum. With the increasing number of tourists visiting each year, we really need it. Such a shame that this has happened. Piper now believes they actually paid her off so she wouldn't complain about her drastically altered story."

"Even if she gave them back their money, they're not going to stop filming. Movie people have more lawyers than there are gallons of water in Lake Dillon." Joe popped a bite of muffin in his mouth and brushed the crumbs off his fingers. "Maybe we can knock some sense into them."

Mary led Joe into the living room, but their guests were in the middle of a video conference call with several people. Mary grabbed Joe by the arm, and they scurried back into the kitchen. For the first time in twenty years, she felt like an intruder in her own home.

Catalina and Neil walked into the B&B to find Victor sitting with producers Luisa and George and their assistants in the living room. They were already on the video call with Stan, executive producer Peter Wells, and some of the department heads.

"I'm not liking the cost," George said. "But it's your call, Peter."

"If it will make everyone's lives easier, I'll approve it."

"Catalina, come sit." Victor patted the couch next to him. "Everyone, we have Catalina with us now, so let's switch gears."

She sat as far away from Victor as possible but was still able to see everyone on the call.

"Good to see you, Catalina," Stan said. "How do you like the latest rewrites?"

"Hey, Stan. I spoke with Piper today, and she never stole cars for a living."

"Yes, I'm aware, but it will make your character's Scrooge turnaround more dramatic."

"I told her that, but she wants it changed."

"The movie opens with Blake being chased by the cops into St. Nicholas," Stan said evenly. "They certainly wouldn't be chasing her for a broken taillight."

"Stan is right," George said. "And this is what the studio has already signed off on."

Catalina ignored George and eyed Neil, who read her mind and handed her a script. She turned to the scene. "Stan, you have the police losing sight of Blake's car the second she crosses into the town of St. Nicholas, so what does it matter? For the record, Piper delivered cars to clients. She didn't steal them."

"We need action, excitement, intrigue, Catalina, not just a bunch of talking heads." Stan defended his words.

Catalina's lips tightened. "Piper doesn't want her friends and family to think she used to steal cars, and I happen to agree."

"We don't want to put any local residents in a bad light," Luisa said.

Stan slumped on camera. "Victor, help me out here."

"I like the drama." Victor spoke directly to Catalina and Luisa. "And so does George and the studio execs. Piper got paid, so it makes no difference if she's happy with the end product. Besides, you're going to make her look great. Right, Catalina?"

I'll do more than that. I'll refuse to shoot the scene.

"At least speak with her, Stan. Moving on. Why did you make Santa's helper a snowman?"

"Just trying to think out of the box." He sounded a little snippy.

"But, as you know, Santa's helper has never been caught on camera here in St. Nicholas. A snowman isn't exactly fast moving, and they melt in the summer, which would mean Scrooge suggestions can only be picked up in the winter, which also isn't true." She glanced at Neil, since it was a good catch, and he smiled.

"Santa's helpers don't really exist, so this is a moot point," Stan said.

"Not to the people who live here, and you should know that. How long did you stay here doing research?" she asked.

"I've never been."

"Come again?"

"No reason to, Catalina. I use the internet like everyone else."

"You think so? Let's talk about the confrontation scene. My understanding is that Piper confronted Adam in the diner, but you've placed it at a ski resort."

"Just keeping the action going. Skiing is better than talking in a diner."

"How much did you learn about St. Nicholas's ski resort?"

"Quite a bit."

"St. Nicholas doesn't have a ski resort."

It was difficult to see Stan's reaction since six others were sharing the computer screen, but his silence told everyone that he'd been caught in a lie. "What mountain town in Colorado doesn't have a ski resort?"

"St. Nicholas," Catalina repeated. "Look, if you want

to have the confrontation scene at a ski resort, fine, but put it inside a ski lodge. My character would recognize her nemesis a lot faster at a diner or a ski lodge, instead of catching a glimpse of him when skiing by him."

"If you reread the script, you'll see I have them running into each other after Blake gets off the chairlift," he argued.

She was getting nowhere, and Stan was getting testier. "I'm just trying to look out for you, Stan. You've written a really great speech, very similar to Piper's. When she called Adam on the carpet, in front of everyone at the diner, you could hear a pin drop after she was through. How can Blake's speech have the same effect outside with a bunch of skiers and snowboarders who don't know them personally?"

"I appreciate your concern, Catalina, but this is supposed to be a romantic comedy. Her nemesis takes off down the slope and does a face-plant afterwards. There's the comedy."

"But it takes away from the seriousness of her speech," Catalina reiterated.

"We're already over budget," Peter on video piped in. "The diner or lodge would be a better fit, and we can shoot it in LA."

At last. A voice of reason. "Thank you, Peter."

"Stan, make the changes," Victor said.

Stan rubbed his eyes. "I'll have them for you later tonight."

The video conference continued for another hour, and Catalina felt it was an hour well spent. Luisa sided with her most of the time, and Peter helped her fight for a few more sticking points in the script.

After everyone signed off, Victor clapped his hands

together. "Good meeting. Let's have a drink and get something to eat," he said to Catalina directly.

She'd already been warned to stay clear of any "impromptu" meals with Victor. She'd heard stories about his unconventional way of directing. Victor would manage to get the actors to loosen up, feel safe, and then they'd talk too much. He'd discover their vulnerabilities, so he could use them against the actors on set. His favorite tactic was to spring something on them right before filming, stating he always got the best performances that way. Catalina didn't have much to hide beyond what the media had already reported on, but she certainly wasn't going to put herself under the microscope when the cameras weren't rolling.

"I'm afraid I'll have to pass," she said as she stood. "I've got a lot of prep work to do before tomorrow morning."

"Another time, then." Victor's eyes bored into her like he was a hunter studying his future prey.

Not if I can help it. Catalina walked upstairs with Neil following close behind, wishing she hadn't been so short with Jay. She prayed he didn't turn down the job. Neil wouldn't always be on set with her, and she would feel so much better if Jay were nearby.

Chapter Eight

"Catalina Jones is in it?" Jay's mom was agog as she unwound the fairy lights and garland, then fed them to Jay to attach them to the stair railing. "What a strange coincidence for the two of you to be working on a movie about the Scrooge Legend right here in St. Nicholas. Maybe you can have her over for supper."

It seemed like moms across the world had one thing in common: they never thought anything was impossible. "She's a superstar now."

"Superstars don't eat? If I remember correctly, you two used to be good friends."

"That was a long time ago." Jay moved down a few steps, threading the decorations through the banister, and continued to wrap the lighted garland around the railing.

"Still, it has to make you wonder if the Scrooge Legend has brought you together for a reason."

Though he'd never admit it to his mom, he'd been wondering that very thing. Everyone who lived in St. Nicholas knew the Scrooge Legend was real and that Santa's mailbox worked. Good intentions, wishes, prayers—they were all powerful tools which reunited loved ones, connected soul mates, and changed lives. Had they been brought together by a Christmas wish?

"Have you seen her yet?" His mom dug out big red bows from a plastic container.

"I ran into her briefly." He plugged in the lights.

"She was happy to see you again, wasn't she?" His mom handed him two bows for him to place on the outer side of the banister.

He'd thought that at first—the way her eyes ran over him, taking him in, not believing what she was seeing—as if he was a ghost back from the dead. But then she'd turned on him so quickly, and he wasn't exactly sure what he'd said that set her off.

"I don't know." He tied the bows tight before grabbing a few more out of the decoration box.

His mom watched him carefully. Even though he'd never shared with her how much Catalina meant to him, it had been obvious to anyone because back then he couldn't stop talking about her.

"Looking past her stardom, is she the same Catalina Jones you remember?"

He hated to think for one moment that she might have embraced her Ice Queen nickname. "Not really. She's a little cold."

"Oh, that's too bad." His mom sounded as disappointed as he felt. "I remember how well you two had worked together." She set longer bows around the bottom posts. "I've seen every one of her movies and loved them. I remember you telling your father and me how sweet and kind she was, but that was before she became so famous. Do you think that's what did it? The fame?"

"In part." He assumed the drastic change in her was mostly because she had given her heart to Grayson, who had stomped all over it. Jay had felt guilty about that, too. If he hadn't made that one decision, maybe she would have never dated Grayson in the first place. "People change, and sometimes it's not for the better."

His mother suddenly gasped. "What if Catalina's a Scrooge?"

"She's *the* Scrooge in the movie."

"Yes, but maybe she's a real-life Scrooge who needs an invitation. You could put her name in the mailbox to help her."

Could Catalina be a Scrooge? No, if anyone was a Scrooge it was Victor. "I think I just need to concentrate on my job." *If that's at all possible.*

His mom tossed Jay another bow, then took the last one out of the box. "What exactly will you be doing as a still photographer?"

"Taking production photos that will be used for marketing and publicity, but I'll also be responsible for taking all the set stills for continuity purposes."

"That sounds important," she said, opening another box to find four Christmas stockings.

"It is. I relied heavily on my still photographers when I was a director."

"Do you miss it? Directing?" She hung the stockings on the fireplace mantel.

"Yeah," he said, and he must have sounded more melancholy than he thought because his mom gave him a look of concern.

"Maybe you'll be able to connect with those who can help you direct again."

He hoped Peter would remember him, and he also hoped to get to know Luisa since she was a client of Tyler's. "There might be an opportunity. Clayton, my cinematographer from *Sage Under Fire*, is also on the movie."

"Is that so? Your industry is smaller than I thought it was. How's he doing?"

"Really well, and I'll be catching up with him soon."

"It will be good for you to be among your old friends again."

Jay unwrapped his grandmother's Nativity set. Would he be able to call Catalina a friend ever again? For a moment, he'd thought he saw something in her eyes—that maybe she had missed him as much as he had her. Had she ever thought of him, ever wondered what he was doing? Had she ever wanted to pick up the phone and call him like he had wanted to do thousands of times? Was it possible to change things between them after so much time had passed? He only had three short weeks to find out.

Catalina sat in her room, going over the script, but she couldn't relax. She wondered what Jay was doing at that very moment. Was he having dinner with his family? What did his wife look like? She was probably beautiful, kind—considerate like she remembered him being. She assumed he had children since he said his family lived here. Did he have a little boy, a little girl? Maybe he had one of each. No doubt they were adorable and looked just like him.

She threw her script aside and pinched the bridge of her nose. She was torturing herself, thinking about Jay's perfect private life that didn't involve her. If she hadn't blown their friendship, maybe she would have been his family. Even if he never felt that way about her, she would have wanted to remain friends with him. Then she would have at least been part of his life, and she would have known about his exit from the film industry.

But they weren't friends, which meant she wouldn't be spending any time with him at all. She was stuck in a small town with no friends and a hotheaded director just down the hall from her. The only thing working seemed to be Neil. He'd noticed how upset she was over Victor's move and immediately began searching for a house to rent. So far, his efforts had been unsuccessful due to the busy time of year.

She heard a knock at the door and ignored it knowing that if it was Neil, he would say so. There was another knock, followed by a woman's voice.

"Ms. Jones. It's Mary. I have a delivery for you."

"Just slide it under the door, please."

"I can't."

Irritated, Catalina got up and opened the door.

"I know you don't drink hot cocoa, but I thought you'd like a cup of hot cider and a little snack." Mary was holding a food tray in front of her with a large mug of hot cider and a charcuterie board covered in fruits, cheeses, crackers, and nuts. "I always serve an afternoon snack for my guests, but you were in a meeting."

She loved cheese. It was her weakness—though she hadn't had a craving for it in a while, and she didn't want to trigger it. "This is very thoughtful of you, but I have to pass. I'm on a strict diet."

"Too strict, if you ask me. If a good wind kicks up tomorrow, I'm afraid you'll blow away. Now, please, at least take the apple cider. It has so many health benefits. It's loaded with antioxidants, and it's a great stress reducer."

"I didn't know that." She picked up the mug. "Thank you."

Mary suddenly got a strained look on her face. "Ow, my wrist!" She pushed past Catalina and dropped the tray on the table next to the window. "Oh, my goodness." Exhaustion colored the woman's words as she rubbed her right wrist. "I sprained it last month, and I'm beginning to wonder if I'll ever get my strength back in it."

"I'm sorry to hear that."

"Hazards of my line of work. But enough about me. Since you have dietary restrictions, what would you like for tomorrow's breakfast?"

"I have to be on set at seven, so I won't be eating."

"What?" Mary looked stunned. "You have to eat something. How else will you keep up your strength?"

Catalina fought back a laugh. She wasn't going to be chopping wood. "The production will be providing breakfast. Most likely none of us will be eating here since we'll all be on set."

Mary frowned. "But I've already made blueberry muffins and rum raisin cinnamon bread for everyone."

Catalina felt like she was gaining weight just listening to Mary's menu. "I'm sorry. Neil should have let you know earlier."

"It's all right, dear. I suppose I could use a break from the kitchen. Perhaps I'll do some Christmas shopping, maybe even get it done early." She headed to the door.

"Don't forget your tray."

"Oh, you know, my wrist is so sore." Mary was now rubbing her left wrist. "How about I leave it in case you want to nibble?"

"I won't," she said firmly, now that she knew Mary's injury was all an act.

"You never know, and you can always set it outside if it's in your way. Have a good evening."

Catalina sighed as Mary closed the door behind her.

Wondering if there was any truth to her health claims about apple cider, she decided to taste it. *Wow.* It was really good. She took another sip as she inched her way over to the charcuterie board and realized the foods were arranged as a Christmas wreath. She grabbed her phone and took a picture. Five types of cheese, green olives, red cherry tomatoes, ribbons of prosciutto. Even the crackers were in the shape of stars. It looked gorgeous. And appetizing.

Her stomach grumbled. Now she wished she hadn't missed lunch, and she had just skipped dinner. She would have gone into town for a quick bite, but she feared she'd run into Victor. Perhaps she should eat a little something. She was extremely thin, and people were starting to talk. The gossip media was already speculating about diet pills or an eating disorder, but the truth was she couldn't eat when she was stressed, and she'd been stressed a lot lately.

Maybe just a taste. She reached for a small piece of cheese and took a bite. Manchego. *Heaven.* Why had she stopped eating cheese? She tried another. Camembert. *Delicious.* She let out a long breath, savoring the flavor, and sat down, feeling much better about things.

She eyed the fruit—blackberries, grapes, and a beautifully cut pear splayed out over red foil, looking like a bow on a wreath. She tried a few of each before she took a handful of almonds. It was all so scrumptious, so she ate a little more.

No doubt Mary's blueberry muffins and cinnamon bread would be equally delicious. Maybe she should take one of each before leaving tomorrow morning— just so they wouldn't go to waste. Besides, it wasn't like she'd have to eat all of it. She'd insist Neil take a muffin and a piece of bread as well. Like her, he was skipping too many meals.

She had another slice of cheese, this time Asiago, making the apple cider taste even better. Perhaps she should remain at Mary's B&B after all.

Chapter Nine

Right at seven, Catalina and Neil arrived at their new shooting location—a quiet five-acre residential property on the outskirts of town. The movie was no longer allowed to film in the town square. City officials had not taken kindly to a movie crew dismantling their animated carolers display and attempting to remove their iconic Santa's mailbox, so they revoked their permit. The set builders then had to recreate a portion of the town square.

As Neil walked with Catalina to her trailer, he opened the small paper bag Mary gave him. "These muffins are enormous." Neil twirled one in his hand before he bit into it and moaned. "Wild blueberries are overtaking my tastebuds."

Catalina laughed. "You should have seen the charcuterie board Mary made for me last night."

"She brought me hot cocoa to help me sleep," he said with a mouthful. "Who does that?"

"Better service than any five-star hotel, that's for sure."

"Let me go grab you some protein to have with your muffin," Neil said. "Are you good with your usual hard-boiled egg and strawberry smoothie?"

"Sounds perfect. Thank you, Neil."

As he hurried off in search of the breakfast tent, she spotted Jay arriving with his gear. *He took the job after all.* A sense of relief washed over her.

"Morning, Ms. Jones," the second assistant director said. "Here are the revised pages for the first scene. You're wanted in hair and makeup in fifteen. I'll be back for you shortly."

Catalina walked into her trailer and found her usual asks spelled out in her contract: a small refrigerator fully stocked with Voss artesian still water, a Himalayan salt lamp, several quartz crystals, and a comfortable suede couch with a sixty-inch TV in her lounging area.

She opened a water, grabbed the bag with Mary's goodies inside, and sat on the couch to look over the revised dialogue. Her first scene was with Landon at the fake Santa's mailbox. She hardly knew him, but he was a good actor. And though Victor had issues with their chemistry at the table read, Landon was funny and genuine—something she needed on her first day of filming.

Of course, she'd be working with Jay as well, but she really wouldn't have much interaction with him except between scenes or setups when he needed to document the film. She regretted storming off the way she did, and he probably deserved an apology.

Why was she thinking about him? She needed to be concentrating on her work, not the guy who had disappeared out of her life for seven and a half years.

Jay was saying hello to everyone, as if it were his own crew. He couldn't help it. He couldn't suppress the grin on his face, or the elation he was feeling inside. He loved being on set again—the constant activity, the camaraderie, the way it all came together very quickly to create something out of nothing.

He spent the first hour reviewing a shot list with the unit publicist. He was the only person authorized to take photos on set and would be responsible for detailed documentation of the sets and actors, along with the director, producers, and the different departments. He'd also be shooting additional photos for scene continuity, but hair, makeup, and wardrobe would be responsible for their own continuity shots and would be taken in their respective trailers.

He then met the first and second assistant directors, and Clayton's camera crew. He was hoping to say hello to Peter Wells, but learned that he wouldn't be arriving until later in the week. Jay then met the infamous Victor Caviano.

"I'll try to get as many stills as possible during rehearsal and right after you call cut," Jay said. "Any angles or specific shots you'd like me to capture, just let me know."

Victor gave him a quick once-over. "You can do your job by staying out of my way," he said, then walked away with the first AD.

Clayton had heard the exchange and came over. "He's like that with everyone."

"I figured as much."

"If you need a place to stash your equipment, we've got room on the camera truck."

"Thanks, man. I appreciate it."

Jay took a moment and became still. He watched the easygoing crew get whipped up into a frenzy whenever the director said something. He sensed that Victor had been chosen to direct this particular movie not because the studio wanted him, but because the Scrooge Legend had invited him to town. Victor had to be a Scrooge.

Unfortunately, this meant that Catalina would be a player in his journey, which was unfortunate. It seemed like she'd been through a lot lately. Perhaps it was a good thing after all—that he had taken the photography job. Now, he'd be on set with her. Since he'd grown up with the Scrooge Legend, he might be able to help her avoid getting mixed up in it—unless of course she was meant to, then there would be nothing he could do.

He opened one of his equipment bags, got to work, but kept an eye out for Catalina, hoping their next exchange would be better than the last.

Catalina sat in the makeup chair, not saying a word. Her personal makeup artist, who had been with her for the past five films, was unable to join her on this one. Now, this new young artist was doing everything she could to make Catalina feel like she could trust her.

"I've studied the makeup stills from your past three movies," Alyssa said. "I like your eyes in this photo, and I believe I've matched it fairly well. But you be the judge."

Alyssa stepped away so Catalina could see herself in the mirror. Her eyes were bold with dark eyeliner and false lashes, and her eyeshadow was a combination of gray and copper, which made her blue eyes pop. "Yes. Good."

Alyssa let out a relieved breath. "I really like your new hairstyle. It's modern and chic, and seems like it will be the perfect look for your character."

"Thank you."

There was a knock on the trailer door, and Alyssa excused herself.

Alyssa gasped before saying something in excited tones to whomever she was talking to. A minute later, she came back, flustered.

"Everything okay?"

"Yes, sorry," Alyssa said, avoiding eye contact. Everything was not okay, but Catalina assumed Alyssa didn't want it to affect her work. "Let me get your lipstick on, and then I can get you out of this chair."

Catalina noticed a slight tremor in her hand as she applied her lipstick. Whatever news Alyssa had been given had truly rattled her.

Chapter Ten

Jay had to laugh. The studio had sent an entire production crew here to film in the real location, but instead they were using on a mockup of the town square. Victor was to blame. He was the one who'd ordered the removal of the real Santa's mailbox to replace it with a fake one. He alone had gotten them banned from shooting in the town square or anywhere near it.

Jay stepped onto the set. The talented set builders had changed the back acreage of the Andersons' property into a portion of the town square. With camera in hand, he began taking pictures. He admired the crew's detailed work. They had laid down a meandering path with a bank of snow on each side, giving the impression that the walkway had just been cleared of snow. A few park benches were dotted around the area with an abundance of Christmas decorations sprinkled in. They'd even incorporated perfectly placed faux trees among the real ones to match the town square. It was impressive. The only error was a big one—Santa's mailbox.

Per Victor's instructions, the fake Santa's mailbox didn't look a thing like the real one—no gilded ornate legs, no candy cane flag, no address stamped on the front. The body of the mailbox was an exact replica of an ordinary blue USPS mailbox, which deviated from the flat top found on the real Santa's mailbox. As for the paint color, it was glaringly wrong—a red-orange, not Santa red.

Jay sighed. Maybe it was for the best. If the movie was a success, he imagined busloads of tourists coming to town to take selfies in front of the famous mailbox. Now, they'd walk right by the real one, thinking it was a Christmas decoration.

"Rehearsal in five," Mark, the first AD, called out, and everyone moved into high gear.

Voices quieted as Catalina made her way onto set with her assistant by her side. Neil directed Catalina to her set chair, but she continued on to the fake mailbox.

Jay stepped out of the way as she walked past him, focused on the mailbox. She studied it and frowned, then pulled on the handle, and it opened. As she walked around it, Jay tried to move out of her sightline, but he didn't move fast enough.

She did a double take. "Glad to see you chose to take the job." She gave him a slight smile. "What do you think of our rendition?"

"Not an exact replica."

"Not even close," she said with a laugh. "But at least this one opens."

"Was the real one in town giving you trouble?" he asked, suddenly realizing she must have been coming from the mailbox when they ran into each other at the town square.

"It was, but I got it open. Eventually."

He was surprised to hear that. "You must know a real Scrooge."

"Too many to count." She looked away. "I actually deposited a Christmas wish."

"Someone has done their homework." He took a step closer to her. "Not everyone knows Christmas wishes were the original purpose of the mailbox. I'm glad to hear you believe in the magic of Christmas."

"I don't." Her eyes blazed, making it clear how she felt on the matter. "It was a science experiment I agreed to do with my assistant."

Experiment or not, Jay knew the mailbox wouldn't have opened unless her intention behind the wish was genuine. He eyed her, curious as to what she wished for.

"You've got an interesting hometown here. How come you never told me about it?"

He'd learned long ago that people thought him crazy when he spoke of a magical town where Christmas wishes were granted and lives were turned upside down for the better. "I guess I was too focused on making magic of my own," he said, thinking about directing her in *Sage Under Fire*.

That made her smile again. She studied his face, moving a little closer, right as Victor stepped on set.

Jay disappeared into the background as Victor walked up to Catalina. The way the guy strutted onto the set told Jay everything he needed to know. Victor loved power, and he didn't care who he hurt to get it. Jay realized, right then, that his first priority of connecting with Peter Wells had to be pushed aside. He needed to keep an eye on this guy and protect Catalina if she needed it. Not that she asked him to do so, or would want him to, but something was way off with this director, and he wasn't going to remain a quiet still photographer if something went seriously wrong.

* * *

"Good morning, Catalina." Victor sauntered over. "Ready to get to work?"

"I'm always ready." She smiled. "Where's Landon?" She looked past Victor, expecting to see him.

"A little tied up." Victor scratched his nose and broke eye contact. "But we can start without him." He moved into her personal space. "I want to make sure you get this first part of the scene right. I want to feel Blake Dickens's desperation. Your character lost her job, left her friends, and moved to St. Nicholas in hopes of getting her relationship with her mother back on track. And now she's died. You feel so alone. You have no one, and you want to feel that safety and security you'd felt from your previous boyfriend, who has also died."

Catalina frowned. "Piper never told me about a previous boyfriend dying."

"Who cares about Piper?" Victor swatted the thought away, like an annoying fly buzzing around his head. "This isn't a biopic, Catalina. I'm talking about Blake Dickens. Please stick to the script."

Catalina rifled through her sides. "I understand that, but I don't see any information about Blake's boyfriend dying in the revised pages."

"Must have been in a previous version. It doesn't matter. The point is you're desperate to have someone in your life again, and I want to see all of that pain before you drop in your Christmas wish of finding your true soul mate."

"She does what?" Catalina stared at Victor. "That isn't in this revision, either." She held up her sides, irritated and flustered at the same time. "Blake is at this mailbox, trying to mail an overdue bill, but the door won't open. Oh, and by the way, *this* door opens, so someone needs to nail it shut." She flicked a hand toward the mailbox. "Blake gets so frustrated that she angrily turns on her heel and runs right into Remington Savage."

"Not anymore." Victor snapped his fingers in the air. "I want my new pages!"

A few seconds later, a PA ran over with two copies in hand. "We just received them," the PA said, out of breath. "Here they are, sir."

Victor snatched the pages from the PA's hands, skimmed them quickly, then gave one set to Catalina. "Stan called me an hour ago. This is much better."

Catalina ran through the revised scene. She happened to agree. It was better, but why did the revised scene suddenly mirror her own actions from yesterday? "Give me a minute to look these over." She marched over to Neil. "A word."

Neil followed her off the set, and once they were out of earshot, she turned on him. "Who did you tell?"

"I'm sorry?"

"Do you think I'm stupid? Blake is no longer trying to pay an overdue bill—she's wishing for her soul mate. Sound familiar? You are the only one who knows that I wished for my mine, and I did that for *you*." She poked him in the chest. "For your foolish science experiment."

"I... I haven't told anyone." His eyes were wide, full of fear. "I swear to you. No one."

"Then how did it end up in the script?" She shoved the revised pages on him.

His eyes flew through the new dialogue. "I don't know." He kept shaking his head. "I said nothing. You've got to believe me."

"Are you trying to tell me that this is a coincidence?"

"Finding one's soul mate is a universal theme. Now, if Blake had suddenly decided to conduct a scientific experiment, I would absolutely believe a crew member had overheard us, but no one was around us because I kept checking."

She studied Neil's face. He seemed truly upset by her accusations, which meant he was probably telling the truth. She took a breath and thought back on when they were at the mailbox. She'd felt ridiculous throwing in a wish, so she too had been scanning the area for any curious onlookers. How could she have let her insecurities mess with her head on day one?

She shuffled through the sides. "This revision is actually better. I get a nice moment." She let out a sigh and eyed Neil. "Maybe it is just a coincidence. I'm sorry I accused you. I really am. It's like I have PTSD when it comes to assistants."

"It's okay." He pushed his glasses up on his nose. "After what your last one did, I would, too."

"Thank you for understanding. Okay. Let's do this." Catalina walked back on set, where she was miked up. She then did a run-through on her beginning beats of the scene. Landon still wasn't on set, and she was beginning to feel like she was being kept in the dark about his whereabouts.

Landon's stand-in approached her, saying he'd been sent to run the scene with her, which was totally inappropriate. She was ready to walk off the set when Erin's face popped in her head. Landon's stand-in was nervously shaking, so she relented and ran the scene. Just as they finished, crew members suddenly started scrambling.

"What's going on? Has something happened to Landon?" she asked Mark.

"I sincerely apologize for the rocky start, Ms. Jones, but there is nothing to worry about," Mark said. "We've got it covered. Why don't you go ahead and take a break while we finalize everything for camera?" He called to the crew, "First team stepping off, second team up."

Catalina searched for Jay, but he had already cleared out. Neil hurried over with a cup of warm tea, which she gladly took. "Have you seen Landon?"

"No, but I was told he's in makeup."

"Something's going on," she said. "Something regarding Landon."

"I heard he was really late, which stressed everyone out. I imagine that's the tension we're feeling."

"Victor better get his act together and learn to communicate properly. He shouldn't have me standing around, looking for answers, or rehearsing with a stand-in. If he thinks this is acceptable, he'll be finding someone else to play Ms. Scrooge."

"I'll make sure your concerns are conveyed," Neil said.

As they walked back to her trailer, she spotted Jay talking to Victor, and neither one looked happy.

The production was already behind two hours and had yet to film one frame of the scene. Another round of script revisions had come in and were awaiting approval. In the latest version, when Catalina's character turns from the mailbox, she's very unhappy to run into Remington since she believes he's after her mother's house.

Victor and the producers signed off on the changes.

Catalina made short work of memorizing her lines with Neil's help and was back on set, ready to, at last, rehearse with Landon.

She took her place as Landon's stand-in approached her, which shot her blood pressure through the roof. "Take a break," she told the stand-in before he could say a word. "Victor!"

Victor stepped away from the camera and came over, all smiles. "Is there a problem?"

"You have exactly two seconds to tell me what's going on or I am walking off set permanently."

"Yes, Catalina. Of course." Victor rubbed his forehead. "Landon got scratched in the face by his girlfriend's cat, and now the makeup department is working overtime to conceal it."

She glared at him. "Why didn't you tell me this in the first place?"

"My apologies," Victor said calmly, and looked almost giddy, which didn't make any sense. Why would he be happy when he was hours behind schedule and his leading man had been injured?

"He's ready," Mark called to Victor.

"We're so far behind that I'd like to shoot the rehearsal," Victor said. "Good with you?"

"Fine," Catalina snapped, then took her place.

Victor nodded to Mark.

"Shooting the rehearsal," Mark called. "Last looks."

Catalina inhaled deeply, shook off her anger, and got into character. She became still, releasing a breath as Jay had originally taught her, and for a moment she wondered if Jay would be able to tell that she still used his method when connecting to her characters. She let those thoughts float away as she allowed Blake's sadness and grief of losing her mom come over her. She thought about how scary it was to face her life—one without a job, parents, siblings, or even a boyfriend. The people of St. Nicholas were very kind to her, but at the end of the day, she went home alone, to her mom's empty house, mounting debt, and no way to pay for any of it.

As the camera started rolling, Catalina as Blake stood in front of the mailbox. A single tear ran down her cheek. "What do I wish for? I wish I had my mom back." She looked off in the distance. "But I know that's impossible. Truth be told, I don't want to wish for anything, but I will. To honor my mom. When I moved in with her, she had wanted me to wish for someone to share my life with, but I refused. I don't believe in Christmas magic. She always hoped I'd find true love— like the true love she'd had with my dad. I'm not sure if that's possible, but for her, here goes."

Blake wrote something down on a piece of paper, then placed her hand on the door handle. "It's very difficult for me to believe in Christmas wishes after everything that's happened. But, for my mom, please grant me this one wish. I wish for a soul mate, my soul mate—one who's as honest as my dad and as kindhearted as my mom." She opened the mailbox door and tossed in her wish. She remained still for a moment, lost in thought, then she finally turned and ran right into Remington.

Catalina gasped, shock written all over her face. Her eyes narrowed on her leading man. "You," she seethed with so much hate—it was as if venom was shooting from her tongue. "What are you doing here? You have no right."

"Don't I?" He locked his gaze on her. "Can't I mail a letter?" her leading man asked innocently—only it wasn't Landon Barnes who spoke the lines. It was her ex, Grayson Edwards.

Chapter Eleven

"Our star walked off the set, Victor! What were you thinking?" Luisa screamed, which Jay overheard as he was walking by Victor's trailer.

"I got the shot, didn't I?" Victor yelled back. "That is money."

Luisa found a few more choice words to hurl at Victor before Jay moved out of earshot.

Victor was a real piece of work. Directors were supposed to take care of their actors and create a safe environment for them—not make them feel uncomfortable, humiliate them, or cause them emotional distress.

Jay still couldn't believe what he'd witnessed. His heart almost stopped when he saw Grayson Edwards approaching the unsuspecting Catalina. He had to summon all of his willpower to keep from walking through the shot and ruining the take. He'd thought about refusing to shoot any pictures at all, but changed his mind— realizing it would be better for him to document the gotcha stunt for Catalina should it be helpful to her later.

He had pushed aside what the stunt was about to do to her and taken a series of photos in quick succession. The images on her face went from sadness of her character's mother's passing, to measured hope of her wish coming true, to shock, anger, betrayal, and bitter hatred upon seeing her ex in real life. She was beautifully brilliant in those stills, and now he had mixed feelings about whether to turn them over to publicity. He wanted to discuss it with her before he did anything, but Catalina wasn't coming out of her trailer. It had been over an hour since she walked off set, and she refused to speak to anyone—even Neil.

Jay knocked on her door and waited. Chances were good he'd be out of a job in a matter of minutes. At least he'd go out on an honorable note. He knocked again and called out, "It's Jay."

A few seconds later, the door whipped open so fast that he had to dodge it in order not to get hit.

"Were you in on it, too?" Her eyes blazed with fury as she towered above him, staring him down.

"No. Never," he said emphatically. "Victor pulled me aside and instructed me to keep shooting no matter what happened. I asked what was going on and he threatened to fire me. When I finally found out what was about to go down, I tried to find you, to warn you, but you were already on set, talking to him."

"Did you?" She crossed her arms. "Keep shooting?"

He slowly nodded. "In case you wanted documentation. I'm expected to turn the photos over to publicity, but I won't without your approval." He held up his camera.

The anger in her eyes changed to surprise. "You'd do that for me?"

"Of course."

Catalina drew in a long breath, then stepped aside and let him in.

Her script had been thrown in the trash, and her

pages of notes were torn in half on the floor. Texts were flying in on her phone, followed by it ringing. She marched over to her cell, looked as if she was about to chuck it out the window, then hesitated and turned off the sound instead.

"What Victor did was unconscionable." He shook his head. "And I'm not the only one who thinks that. I overheard Luisa chewing Victor out a few minutes ago."

Catalina seemed happy hearing that, or at least it calmed her down somewhat. She sat at her worktable and ran both hands through her hair. After a long minute, she finally made eye contact with him. "Victor's cruel stunt didn't only affect me. Apparently Landon got canned last night. Do you know he'd turned down another role in order to do this film?"

"I hope his attorney sues," Jay said, leaning against the kitchen counter. "People like Victor are why I left the industry. They shower you with praise, tell you you're talented, but then don't trust you enough to do your job."

"I know exactly what you're talking about—only in my situation, the people surrounding me either expect me to catapult them up to the top or are jealous and want to ruin my career."

"Our industry seems to be lacking in trust and ethics these days."

She expelled a one-note laugh. "The understatement of the year." She took a breath and studied him. "I can see why you came back here. The people of St. Nicholas seem a lot kinder to one another."

"They are, but then most of our residents tend not to have high-pressure careers, which often bring out the worst in some people. This town thrives on tourists who can't get enough of Christmas. It's difficult to make a mistake with one of the most-loved holidays."

"I bet Victor can with his rendition of the Scrooge Legend."

"I stand corrected."

Catalina gave a slight smile, got two bottled waters from the fridge, and tossed one to him. "Let's see those photos." She sat on the couch.

Jay took a swig of water, then sat next to her with his camera. He cued them up. "You still amaze me with your acting. Your expressive face tells it all."

She scrutinized each frame as Jay clicked through them. "They're better than I thought they'd be, but everyone will know I wasn't acting."

"How? You didn't miss a beat. You said your first three lines."

She shook her head. "You're giving me too much credit. Those lines are something I would have said to Grayson anyway. I'm sure Victor and Stan had it planned that way."

"Well, you handled it incredibly well," he said. "And I have the photos to prove it."

"Which Victor will take credit for."

"Only if you let him."

She rubbed her arms and cast her gaze to the floor. "Then I'll shut him down by quitting."

"Is that what you want to do?"

"Yes. No." She sat back with a sigh. "I really do want to quit, but then he'd win. And so would Grayson."

"Have you talked to either of them yet?"

"Why would I?" She took a drink of water. "Victor is a lost cause. He loves power too much to see how he's hurting those around him. As for Grayson, well, I'm sure I'll have to talk to him at some point, but what is there to say? Victor orchestrated this whole thing, and Grayson went along with it. Besides, he'll only pry into my personal life."

She licked her lips, breaking eye contact—one of her mannerisms he remembered her doing when she was uncertain about something.

"You can always do what your character did in *Sage Under Fire*," he said. "If Grayson asks a question you don't like, reply with one of your own."

Her mouth raised into a small half smile. "I already do that with aggressive reporters. I never thought to do it to him."

Her phone lit up with the name Erin, and she ignored it.

"I didn't want to come here to St. Nicholas," she confessed. "I didn't like the script. I'm not one for miracles or magic, and Piper's story sounded too far-fetched for me to believe any of it. But then I met her, and she seemed so genuine, so down-to-earth."

"She is," he said. "She's a good person—a hardworking woman who constantly gives back to the community. She's a great mom, and she and Adam are one of those perfect couples you don't believe exist."

"That's the sense I got from her. I have to admit, I was ready to punch as many holes in her story as I could. But after five minutes of listening to her tell her journey, I realized how wrong I'd been to judge her so quickly. If anything, Stan hasn't done her justice."

"Maybe you can change that."

"I'm trying to—only you can see I'm off to a bad start."

"You're not. They are."

She sighed. "Does anything ever change for the better?"

"Sure. All the time."

"Like what?"

Like me seeing you again. "Like you being here. You're out of LA, which gives you a break from the paparazzi. When was the last time that's happened?"

"Never."

"Small town St. Nicholas does have its advantages."

"I suppose," she said unenthusiastically.

"No, I get it." He sat back. "You're not the first to say that my hometown is an acquired taste."

"It's not that. It's just the whole atmosphere here, the vibe, it feels so foreign to me. Everyone is so happy and so upbeat that it doesn't feel real."

"I can understand that. You're not used to what happens here, but I grew up in it—the small miracles, the crazy coincidences that come from the Scrooge Legend. We have a lot of positive energy here. It's real. I can promise you that."

"Then I envy all of you." Her voice was filled with sadness, or was it loneliness? "Christmas is no longer the warm, fuzzy holiday our industry sells it to be. It's hard to believe that a town like this exists, and that owners of a B&B, who don't really know me, actually care about what happens to me."

"Of course they care. Mary and Joe are good people. They love being in the service industry because they care what happens to every guest who stays with them."

She gave him a small smile. "I swear Mary is casting magical spells on her guests with her snacks and treats. Have you tasted her muffins?"

He chuckled, nodding. "Her family used to own a bakery."

"That explains a lot." Her phone lit up with Erin calling again. "It's my manager waiting for an answer."

"What are you going to tell her?"

"I'm not sure yet." She held her phone in her hand, looking absolutely lost.

"Would you mind if I weigh in?"

Her conflicted gaze met his. "I was hoping you would."

"Stay." He looked deep into her eyes. "I've got your back on set—as much as a still photographer can. And I've got your back off set, if you need a friend."

Her eyes misted over, and she blinked to clear her vision, then met his gaze with a softness to her expression. "Thank you, Jay. I'm really touched. It means a lot to me to hear that, especially with everything that's been happening…" She drifted off with a shake of her head, then focused back on him. "You know, your job as a still photographer is an important position. You're the gatekeeper. You alone will decide what images are passed on for public consumption, and I can't think of anyone more trustworthy than you to hold that position."

The way she looked at him was the Catalina he remembered—the gentle soul who was entrusting him with her feelings, her image, her career.

"I won't let you down," he said as a promise. "The only photos the publicity department will receive are those that will make you shine."

Her whole body seemed to relax upon hearing his declaration. He hadn't thought much about his temporary job, but by viewing it through Catalina's eyes, he realized that he could help dispel the Ice Queen image by what he shot. Together, they might be able to repair her reputation and melt the Ice Queen image for good.

As for Victor and Grayson, he wouldn't do anything to make them look bad intentionally—but he certainly wouldn't stop them from doing it to themselves.

Chapter Twelve

As soon as Catalina passed through the hands of her hairstylist and makeup artist, she was back on set, standing in front of the mailbox, getting into character. She sensed that strange sensation of safety and relaxation which she'd felt standing in front of the real Santa's mailbox, but this time, it came from Jay—his calmness, his innate sense of finding the truth through all the noise, the way he methodically thought things through, looking at every angle, anticipating the various outcomes. She felt so relieved that he wanted to help her.

His desire to protect her against Victor and Grayson was incredibly attractive. She realized that she'd never be more than a friend to him now that he had a family of his own, but she was grateful to be getting back the most valuable friendship she'd ever had. Talking things through with him had helped her make a rational decision instead of making one from anger. No matter how she looked at it, if she had quit, it would have felt like she was being forced out instead of leaving on her own terms. Staying had been the stronger move, and she already felt more secure and more grounded for it.

Unfortunately, none of that helped push back clueless Grayson, who never understood personal space. Every disc in her spine stiffened, every muscle in her body tensed as he leaned over and whispered, "I was shocked but flattered when Victor reached out to me personally." He smirked. "After Victor explained that the chemistry between you and Landon didn't come close to what we had, well, I had no choice but to come to your rescue."

Her breaths became shallow as she started shaking, fury building from his sheer arrogance. She turned away and caught Jay's eye.

He mouthed *Are you okay?*

A moment of real connection, and his concern for her was like a shot of B-12. She nodded, amazed how Jay was so in tune with her when they hadn't seen each other for so long. She took a deep breath before squaring her shoulders, then focused on Grayson. "Don't flatter yourself. Landon and I barely knew each other. We hadn't even shot one scene together before he was rudely dismissed."

Grayson gave her a questioning look. "Huh. I guess Victor must have been talking about the table read. But don't worry, Cat. I'm here to make you look good."

"You could never do that. You're nothing more than an annoyance," she said as the Ice Queen emerged, glaring at him. "You're like a fly that I can't quite reach to kill."

"Oh." He chuckled, putting his fist over his mouth. "Game on."

"Games are for children. Stay out of my way, if you know what's good for you."

"Picture's up. Quiet on the set," Mark yelled out. "Places, please."

Catalina stood on her first mark, her heart pounding. How could she perform like this? She'd made a terrible mistake staying on the film. She should have quit when she had a valid reason to do so.

She eyed Jay, who was focused completely on her. He gave her a slight nod and mouthed *You got this*. She closed her eyes, became still, and pushed it all away. She breathed in the moment, steadying herself, picturing Piper, connecting to her character Blake. She heard the sticks hit, marking the scene and take, then she opened her eyes. When Victor called action, she let every emotion of Blake's loss wash over her. She took her time as Blake, wanting to take a chance on a Christmas wish for her mother's sake.

Blake made her wish, turned away from the mailbox, and ran right into Remington Savage. She felt off center but in control.

"You," she seethed, her eyes narrowing on the man who was trying to steal her mother's house. "What are you doing here? You have no right."

"Don't I?" He locked his gaze on her. "Can't I mail a letter?" Remington asked innocently.

"Not at this mailbox." She raised her chin defiantly and stared him down.

"Why not?" Remington gave Blake a baffled look.

"You don't know anything about this town, do you, Mr...?"

"Savage."

She scoffed. "Your name suits you."

Remington was ruffled by her acerbic tone, but he wasn't going to let it get the best of him. "I'm sorry, but have we met?"

"You're so blinded by money that you don't even remember meeting me," Blake said. "But I remember you. You're the shark sent by Harris and Klein to steal my mother's house."

"Oh." He drew out the word, finally recalling their brief encounter. "Yes. You're Blake Dickens. I was planning on stopping by your house to discuss your mother's property."

"Save your breath. I'm not interested in anything you have to say." She hit him on the shoulder as she brushed past him.

"Ms. Dickens, hear me out. I know your mother's house is about to go into foreclosure. Don't you want to hear how I can help you?"

"The only help I need is for you to get in your car, drive out of this town, and never come back." Blake turned and stormed off.

Remington watched her go. "A little firecracker," he said under his breath. "And I thought this place was going to be boring."

He continued to stare after her until Victor called, "Cut! Beautiful. Let's go again."

"That felt fantastic." Grayson grinned at Catalina, but she refused to acknowledge his presence. Because of Grayson, the Ice Queen had been born, and it was time she froze him out.

Jay sat back on his heels, doing a quick check on his latest round of photos before they started filming a second take. Catalina would be pleased when she saw the dailies. She commanded the scene. Not one moment of hers read false, which was impressive for it being the first take after Victor's gotcha stunt.

All eyes had been on Catalina when she arrived back on set. But she'd ignored everyone, remained focused on her job, and taken her position in front of the mailbox, as if nothing out of the ordinary had happened at all.

Jay began clicking away, the second he saw her. She was so incredibly composed—too composed, and he'd worried whether she'd be able to get through the scene.

Then something happened. Grayson, who was already in position, moved closer to her. Jay couldn't tell what was going on because he was too far away, so he zoomed in with his camera, and realized that he was watching the Ice Queen he'd heard so much about. It amazed him how different Catalina looked—her eyes were so cold, her jaw was set slightly forward, her mouth taut, and though he knew it was physically impossible, she looked two inches taller, casting a shadow over her ex.

Grayson, on the other hand, looked like an untrained army going up against an impenetrable fortress, attempting to chip away at Catalina's self-confidence with nothing except for whispered words. But the Ice Queen held her own. She was playing offense, and Grayson was floundering. It was almost comical to watch, and rewarding to see Catalina's strength. Jay could now understand why she hadn't wanted to let go of her alter ego.

Even though the Ice Queen had its advantages, it also had a negative impact on her. When Catalina caught his eye, he could see how draining it was for her to be someone she wasn't. He remembered how strong Catalina used to be in the sense that she wouldn't let criticism affect her in a negative way. Now it did, but only because she'd been knocked off her feet so much lately.

Maybe Catalina didn't have to retire the Ice Queen entirely. Like another tool in an actor's toolbox, she could bring her out only when necessary. Then when Catalina was finally able to view herself the way he did—as a strong independent woman who didn't take crap from anyone—perhaps the reputation and the Ice Queen nickname would slowly fade away. Until then, things could be a little rocky—especially since the Scrooge Legend was very much involved.

Chapter Thirteen

"Cut! Good work," Victor said to Catalina and Grayson as they finished the last take needed for full coverage of their scene.

Surprisingly, with every take, Catalina felt more confident working with her ex. It obviously helped to have a scene where she was in control, but something else was happening. Even though her dialogue was written for Blake, it could have easily been words coming from her own mouth. Like Blake was with Remington, Catalina was no longer interested in anything Grayson had to say.

"And that's lunch," Mark called out.

A beautiful bouncy blonde, who had been hanging out next to the camera operator, ran up to Grayson and gave him a kiss. "You were amazing," she told him in a baby voice.

Neil hurried over to Catalina's side and tried to block her view of them, which Catalina found endearing. A week ago she would have been upset to see Grayson kissing another woman right in front of her, but today she felt nothing.

"You were great in your first scene," Neil said as they headed toward her trailer.

"Thanks."

She glanced around, looking for Jay. He'd been called to Victor's side right after they cut. Hopefully it was only for him to take photos, and not be pressed to keep shooting during another gotcha stunt. She was still furious with Victor. She should have known he was up to something. He'd expressed his concerns over her lack of charisma with Landon yesterday and had probably replaced her costar the second she left his office.

"Is there a way to find out when Grayson's flight was booked?" she asked.

"Sure," Neil said. "I can ask Iris. She's been handling travel arrangements and the deal memos."

"Iris? Did I meet her?"

"I don't think so. I only met her this morning. She's the pretty PA in the production office."

"Listen to you." Catalina nudged Neil. "Does pretty Iris have an admirer?"

"Kind of," he said, seeming embarrassed.

"Maybe your wish is already in the works."

"My wish?" He looked confused. "Oh, right. I forgot about our science experiment."

Catalina hadn't since she spent the entire morning doing take after take, wishing for her soul mate as her character Blake. Every time she said her lines, she couldn't help but be reminded of wishing for her own soul mate.

"Come to think of it, I met Iris within twenty-four hours of making my wish," Neil said. "You shouldn't write off your soul-mate wish just yet."

"I don't believe in soul mates or Christmas wishes," she said.

"Neither did Piper, and look how her life has turned out."

She wouldn't mind believing in something so wonderful if she thought it would make a difference. When Neil had asked her to make a soul-mate wish, she did—pretending she was only going through the motions, when in reality she'd had a moment of weakness. She'd wished that if soul mates actually existed, could she find hers immediately? Afterwards she'd felt ridiculous. None of it was real.

"Let me get you something to eat," Neil said. "I'll text you the lunch choices."

Catalina nodded, and he hurried off. She stepped into her trailer right as she heard a familiar voice behind her.

"That was a good scene," Grayson said, standing below her. "I'd forgotten how well we work together."

She inhaled sharply, not wanting to deal with him. At least he'd ditched his bubbly companion. "What do you want?"

"Thought I'd come in, and we could talk."

"There's nothing to say."

"Cat," he said on a sigh. "Since we're working together again, don't you think we should settle a few things?"

"Like what?"

"Can I come inside?"

"No."

Grayson's mouth tightened and his jaw tensed. He seemed irritated that he wasn't getting his way. "Look, I'm sorry that I didn't want the same things as you, but I realized being tied down in a relationship was going to get in the way of my career."

"That would have been helpful information a year

ago." Catalina leaned against the door frame. "Does your current girlfriend know how you feel?"

"She's not really my girlfriend."

"You might want to tell her that."

"I can't control the media any more than you." He huffed. "A lot of it isn't true, you know that."

She crossed her arms. "What are you talking about?"

He hopped onto the bottom step, getting closer to her. "I heard you really spiraled after our breakup. I know it didn't help for you to see me with Raquel on so many magazine covers, but they painted our relationship more serious than it was."

"That's strange because they painted our relationship exactly as it was—serious."

"I'm not denying that." He took another step up and tried to see inside her trailer. "Why do you think I want to talk?"

She blocked his way. "So talk."

"Not like this." He tried to force himself inside, and she pushed him back.

"I said no."

Grayson backed off and jumped to the ground.

"Does Raquel know about bubblegum girl?"

"Her name is Brandi, and we just started dating. Raquel and I split."

"Good for Raquel."

Grayson sighed. "Can we be civil with one another?"

"Aren't we doing that?"

"Why are you being so cold?"

"Why are you here?"

"I told you. Victor asked me, as a favor, to step in. I had planned on taking the holidays off, but he said you needed my help, that you had asked for me specifically."

She laughed. "Hardly. The part of Remington Savage had already been cast, and even if it hadn't been, why would you ever think I'd want to work with you again?"

"Because we sizzled on and off-screen."

"That was months ago. I barely remember it. But you and Victor can relax. I'll be faking it just fine for the cameras."

The stunned look on Grayson's face almost had her laughing. She quickly turned her back on him, walked into her trailer, and firmly shut the door.

Unbelievable. If what Grayson just told her was true, then Victor was one of the worst human beings she'd ever met. It was bad enough to fire Landon, but then to blame it on her? It went beyond the pale. As soon as they wrapped, she'd speak to Landon directly and let him know exactly what happened.

She took a big breath and let it out. She had to stay focused on her job, and not get wrapped up in any kind of petty game Grayson or Victor was playing. Erin wanted her to drop the Ice Queen persona, but she needed to lean on her now more than ever.

Jay stood in the lunch line listening to the LA crew complain about the menu because it didn't include quinoa kale salads, pho, or green tea matcha lattes. One of the cooks from St. Nicholas's twenty-four-hour diner had been hired as the caterer and knew nothing about trendy foods. His specialty was good, hearty, home-cooked meals, and Jay was willing to bet the crew would change their tune when the temperature started dropping.

He grabbed a good helping of beef stew, some warm molasses bread, and sat down next to Clayton.

"You've got a great hometown," Clayton said, working his way through a grilled chicken sandwich. "Seems like this would be a good place to unplug."

"It is." Jay took a healthy spoonful of his stew. "I didn't appreciate it much when I was a kid, but it sure helped me to decompress after I left Hollywood."

"How does it feel to be back on set?"

"I'm loving it more than I expected, and I'm considering getting back in." He eyed Clayton. "How's the environment out there?"

"Plenty of product, but the budgets aren't what they used to be. We still have the same problems as we've always had—too many talented people vying for the same jobs. If you're serious about coming back, you might need to have a project with financiers already in place in order to attract attention from one of the major studios."

"I figured as much." Jay tore off a piece of his bread. "Have you worked with Peter Wells before?"

"First time." Clayton took a swig of water. "So far, he's easy to work with, but I've only dealt with him over video calls for production meetings. I hear he's very approachable, if that's what you're asking. He should be up here tomorrow or the day after."

Jay nodded. "I met with him before I left the industry, and he seemed very knowledgeable about securing funds and creating realistic budgets."

"You should definitely reconnect with him." Clayton finished off the rest of his homemade potato chips. "Catalina's got to be happy to see a friendly face, now that she's surrounded by VC and GE."

Jay leaned in, lowering his voice. "I still can't believe Victor did that to her, not to mention the actor who lost his job."

"And this is only day one."

"Don't remind me." He sat back. "How long are you shooting in LA?"

"It'll be another six weeks to shoot the interiors, after our one-week winter hiatus," Clayton said. "Aren't you staying with the film?"

"I was a last-minute fill-in. I assume they already have a still photographer in LA to take over, but I'm going to check with Luisa on that."

"Good. I'm sure she'll want you to stay on for continuity purposes, and with the amazing shots I've no doubt you're getting, I imagine publicity will also want to keep you around."

Jay would have never considered it when he accepted the job twenty-four hours earlier, but now that he'd spent time with Catalina, he not only wanted to stay on, he wanted to be the one in charge of the publicity photos. As she pointed out, he was the gatekeeper, and he didn't want to relinquish that job to anyone.

Chapter Fourteen

Catalina was still seething over Victor's stunt. Neil discovered that Grayson's travel plans had been booked through Theo, so there was no way to know exactly when Grayson had been hired. The more she thought about the orchestration required to get Grayson up here on such short notice, the more she realized Victor's choice for the leading man must have happened before the table read, which meant his concern over her lack of chemistry with Landon had also been a lie.

Victor might have filmed the raw reaction he'd been hoping for when she first laid eyes on Grayson, but he wouldn't be getting any vulnerability from her going forward—especially in the next scene. It took place much later in the story, when Blake had fallen in love with Remington, which meant she had to pretend to be in love with Grayson. That was going to take some serious acting. She didn't want to cuddle with her ex on a park bench, or have to kiss him as the script required her to do. She didn't want to feel his lips on hers again, or have him be so loving toward her. What she did want was to never again have to work with someone as incredibly manipulative as Victor.

On set, she braced herself and rallied the Ice Queen in order to get through the scene.

"Picture's up!" Mark called.

The camera and sound crews got ready to roll while Catalina and Grayson took their positions on the park bench.

"This is a much better scene than our first one," Grayson said, sliding his arm around her.

She tensed. "Yeah, because the day is almost over."

"You haven't enjoyed any of it?"

"One part. When Victor calls cut."

Grayson frowned and seemed to be lost in thought when Victor called action, which made him miss his cue. She had thrown him off and had to squelch a laugh. At least it now made it easier for her to have a true smile on her face as she put her head on his shoulder.

"Action," Victor called again.

Grayson cleared his throat, then spoke as Remington. "You want me to believe that the red mailbox over there brought us together?"

"It's our town's history," Blake said. "Santa's mailbox began with Christmas wishes. I've never believed in the magic of Christmas or the granting of wishes, but for my mother's sake, I wished for my soul mate, and then I turned around and ran right into you."

"Actually, you yelled at me and accused me of being a house thief."

She laughed. "I didn't know you then. If I'd been able to see what you were going to do to my mom's house, well, maybe I would have called you a house savior instead of a house stealer."

Remington played with her hair. "I like that. I'm a house savior. I might have to put that on my website."

He studied the mailbox. "Who picks up the wishes, and where do they go?"

"Like the Scrooge suggestions, they go to Santa, and they're collected by one of his helpers."

"Santa and his helpers?" he said sarcastically.

"Right around this time of day."

He shook his head. "If you say so."

She braced herself as Grayson leaned over and kissed her. She feared her true reaction—that she would like the touch of his lips against hers again, but she didn't. She didn't feel anything at all, and was smiling inside.

Off-screen, someone jingled bells, their cue to break apart.

Remington squinted at the mailbox. "Is that…?"

A background performer dressed in a snowman costume was doing all he could to collect pieces of paper from the back of the mailbox.

"Oh, my gosh. It's Santa's helper!" Blake exclaimed, and Catalina broke out laughing.

"Cut." Victor did not sound pleased, but she didn't care.

"This is absurd, Victor." She stood, motioning to the costumed extra. "What happened to Stan revising this scene? You can't tell me that the snowman works."

Victor rubbed his forehead, then snapped his fingers. "Theo!"

Theo instantly appeared at Victor's side. "Get Stan on the phone."

"Take five," Mark called out as Victor walked off the set. "First team hold for stills, please."

Jay quickly stepped in and started shooting Catalina and Grayson on the bench. As he bent down next to her for a closer shot, he said, "The mail isn't collected until late at night."

Grayson stared at Jay. "Did we ask your opinion?"

"He lives here. He would know." She glared at Grayson. "Now, what were you saying, Jay?"

"The mail collector only works at night and has never been caught on camera—though several residents swear they saw an elf collect the mail when a previous Scrooge and her boyfriend had rigged the mailbox with a motion-sensor floodlight."

"A floodlight? That's genius," she said with a laugh. "I automatically assumed Santa's helpers were elves. I even brought it up to Stan. But now I can confirm it. Thank you, Jay."

"No problem." He shared her smile.

"Collecting the mail at night is smart, too," she said. "Easy way to stay hidden."

"Why is this a discussion?" Grayson scowled. "Elves aren't any more real than snowmen. This is a movie, not real life."

"This is based on someone's Scrooge Legend story," she reminded him. "And I'm going to bring it to Victor's attention."

"Whatever." Grayson rolled his eyes, then looked to Jay. "Publicity will want a few photos of Catalina and me kissing."

"I already got that shot." Jay stood.

"Great." Catalina shot up off the bench.

Grayson frowned at Jay, then turned on the charm with Catalina. "Good to know that we still have it."

"Have what?"

"The sizzle. We're still great kissers."

"At least I am, anyway." Catalina walked off, and she could swear she heard Jay snicker behind her.

Catalina went in search of Victor. Though she didn't believe in Santa or elves collecting mail, she loved the idea of the floodlight. It intrigued her to learn that a former Scrooge had gotten the townspeople so involved in attempting to see an elf that they actually did. Talk about the power of suggestion. It irritated her that Stan hadn't done his research. She would have loved to shoot a scene like the one Jay had just described. Instead, Stan's magic in the script had no connection to the Scrooge Legend or to the story he was trying to tell. She really wished Stan would pay more attention. She did not want to be filming her first flop.

She finally found Victor and relayed what Jay had told her, along with her thoughts on the magic aspect of the script.

"I'll talk to Stan about it," Victor said. "I happen to like the snowman over an elf since everyone already expects it to be an elf, but the snowman was too comical in how he moved."

Catalina agreed, and then her mood changed on a dime. "I want to be clear about our relationship going forward."

"Oh?" A tiny smile played on his face.

"You might feel your gotcha tactics are what's needed to get a certain performance out of an actor, but don't mistake me for any actor. You do that again and I'm gone."

His smile immediately vanished. "You should want my help. I know you've been turned down for some very good roles lately. You need a win again, and I'm here to deliver it for you."

"Anything you're doing is for you, Victor. But if you really want this movie to be successful, you need to realize that we're supposed to be on the same team."

"We are." Victor smiled, patting the side of her arm. "Trust your director. He knows what's best for you." He walked away without giving her a chance to respond.

Anger rushed through her. She closed her eyes and took a deep breath to calm down. Victor's arrogance had no bounds, and working with Grayson and Victor simultaneously would truly be testing her limits. How was she ever going to survive the next several weeks?

Chapter Fifteen

The rewrite was going to take longer than anticipated, and they were losing the light, which meant they had to wrap for the day.

Jay was pleased with the shots he'd taken—especially with the ones he captured of Catalina. She had been beautiful when he'd worked with her years ago, and now she was downright gorgeous. She'd be one of those women who became more and more beautiful as she aged. He reached her trailer right as a PA was leaving. "Is this a good time to show you today's photos?" He held up his camera.

"I skipped lunch, and I've got to get something to eat before I faint."

"I can go with you, if you'd like."

"Thanks, but I'm sure your wife is expecting you home for dinner."

Jay cocked his head. "I don't have a wife. Heck, I don't even have a girlfriend."

Her brow furrowed. "But you said you lived here with your family."

"Ah." Jay smiled. "I now understand the confusion. No, I meant my parents and my sister live here. I'm only visiting them for Christmas."

A broad smile spread across Catalina's face. "Well, that's great. I mean about visiting your family. That doesn't include a wife." She laughed. "Or a girlfriend." She shook her head and rolled her eyes. "Now I'm babbling."

His grin widened. "The lack of food will do that."

"Yes, well, that seems to be the case." She turned red, laughing at herself. "So...uh...where we can eat and look at your photos?"

"The twenty-four-hour diner is very popular. It has really good food, and you can get anything from soups and salads to dinner entrees."

She hesitated. "How popular? I'd rather not spend another half hour signing autographs."

"It's a fairly big restaurant with three separate sections—one of which is only used when it's a full house. I know the manager, and she might be able to sneak us in through the back."

"That'll work."

Jay called the diner and ten minutes later, they met Angel at the back door.

"Thank you for doing this," Jay said as Angel led them to a booth in a closed section.

"Anything for you and Ms. Jones." She handed them both menus, then eyed Catalina's hair. "I love your new do."

"Thank you." Catalina looked over the menu as a waiter brought over two waters and set them on the table.

"Tonight's specials are cranberry pot roast, rosemary chicken with acorn squash, and pulled pork grilled cheese sandwiches," Angel said. "Anything to drink?"

"I'm fine with water," Catalina said.

"We're good for now. Thank you, Angel."

After she left, he studied Catalina. It had been years since he'd seen her, yet he still knew how to read her. She was rubbing her arms while reading the menu, which meant she was uncomfortable. "If you're not finding anything you like, we can go somewhere else."

"No. The problem is it all looks too good. I don't want to get myself in trouble here."

"You shouldn't worry about that. You look like you've lost a lot of weight, and in my humble opinion, you're too skinny."

She shut the menu, her mouth turning down. "Why does everyone keep saying that?"

"Because it's true." He kept his eyes focused on her. "Is everything okay?"

"Aside from the usual stress like today's big surprise? Sure." She didn't sound very convincing, but he wasn't going to push it.

He took off his coat and sat back. "Tell me what's happening in your life."

She blew her bangs out of her eyes. "You pretty much know all of it. I've been filming, breaking up with fiancés, firing assistants."

He knew there was a lot more to her life than what *Entertainment Tonight* had reported, but she obviously didn't want to share that with him. "How are your parents? Do they still live in Maine?"

She nodded. "My dad just had knee surgery, but they're good."

"It's great that you've been able to take time off to see them."

"Actually, I haven't been back home in four years. My brother was there for Dad's surgery since I couldn't get away. I'd planned on going home for Christmas this year, but then our shooting schedule was pushed up. The way things are going, we'll be lucky if we get time off for Christmas Day."

"It's only the first day of shooting. We'll make up time somewhere," he said optimistically—though he could tell she was expecting the worst. It was sad to see her so pessimistic.

"What about you?" She took a sip of water. "Why did a talented director give it all up for photography?"

"In three words, not enough control. The bigger the budgets, the more opinions, and too many suits don't understand the basics of filmmaking."

"I know exactly how you feel," she said on a sigh. "I've been flirting with the idea of getting out for the very same reason—not enough control."

"That's surprising to hear. You used to live and breathe acting."

"Simpler times."

The Catalina he'd met had never wanted to do anything but act. Now she seemed beaten down, which he could understand if she continually had to deal with situations like today.

"Have you ever thought about forming your own production company?"

Her eyes shot up to meet his. "It's funny you should ask that. I was seriously considering it when Grayson proposed, then when that fell apart, I tabled the idea."

"It would certainly give you more control," he said, rubbing his chin. "With Hollywood being so fractured these days, it might be worth looking into."

She nodded with a distant look on her face, and he wasn't sure if she was seriously considering it, or if he had sent her back to some past conversation she'd had with Grayson.

"Anyway, I really hope you don't give it all up," he said. "Too many fans would be devastated, and speaking from experience, it's better to take a break than to give it up for good."

"Are you regretting getting out?"

"A little." He took a drink of water. "I can't believe I'm about to say this, but I miss it. Not the budgeting and scheduling chaos or the endless studio notes, but I miss being in it with the actors and the crew—creating something that others might find as meaningful as I do."

"You said earlier that you were visiting your family for Christmas. Where do you normally live?"

"Out of hotels, usually. Once I committed to being a wildlife photographer, I didn't see the sense in paying for a place that I only needed for a few days out of a month."

"You sound like me—traveling all the time. I have a place in LA, but it doesn't feel like home because I'm rarely there. Do you like being on the road?"

"I used to, but it's getting old, living out of a suitcase. My parents want me to come back home permanently, or should I say, take up residence in St. Nicholas again."

"Is that what you want to do?"

"I seriously thought about it. I love the peace and tranquility of St. Nicholas, but I need to be back in LA if I'm to have any hope of directing again."

Angel came back over with order pad in hand. "Are we ready?" She looked to Catalina.

"I'll take a small dinner salad, vinaigrette dressing on the side, and a cup of your butternut squash soup."

"And for your entrée?"

"That is my entrée."

Angel's eyes widened. "You'll lose weight just chewing so few calories. How about a homemade chicken potpie?"

"Sounds tempting, but too many carbs."

Angel gave Catalina a once-over, shaking her head. "Hollywood ought to be ashamed, putting you on such a strict diet." She looked at Jay.

"Upgrade her cup of soup to a bowl, please. I'll take your cranberry pot roast and your rosemary chicken, only can you divide them between two plates, and give her one?"

"Done." Angel smiled, then hurried away before Catalina could protest.

"First Mary, and now you?" Catalina stared at Jay. "Just because it's in front of me doesn't mean I'm going to eat it. I make my living in front of the camera and can't afford to gain weight. You of all people should understand that."

Jay took out his camera and flipped through his photos until he found one of Catalina with her coat off as a sound assistant attached the radio mic to her sweater. "If you were one of my subjects, an animal in the wild, I'd believe you were starving." He handed it over for her to see how her ribs were showing through her thin sweater. "You're getting too skinny." He flipped to another photo—a close-up of her face. "You can see what I'm talking about in only a few photos, but in this one here with the way the angle is, you look gaunt."

A tiny hint of surprise registered on her face. "I don't feel like I'm this thin."

"That's because you can't see it in the mirror every day. Subtle changes over time are harder to detect, but

I'm telling you, as a friend, you are at least twenty pounds underweight."

She sat back. "I haven't been hungry."

A flicker of sadness in her eyes told him that she was an emotional eater, or in her case an emotional non-eater. He wanted to ask her why she ate so little, but he assumed it would shut down whatever appetite she had.

"Been there," he said instead, keeping it light. "The good news is you've come to the right town to love food again. Promise me you'll try one bite of everything I ordered."

"One bite," she said on the verge of sounding angry. "But only if you don't bug me about it again."

"Deal. Now, let me show you the rest of these photos. I got some really good ones of you, and maybe some not so great ones of Grayson."

A smile played on her face. "You didn't."

"They just happened. Here's one with his eyes closed." He passed it over to her, and she laughed. "Here's another good one with his nose running from the cold."

She was clearly amused.

"And here you are, Ms. Photogenic. Not one bad picture of you."

"The gaunt-looking one isn't so flattering."

"One out of dozens. Here, you can scroll through everything I shot by hitting this button." He showed her on his camera.

She took his camera with both hands and studied his pictures. Her expression continually changed with every photo she viewed. She was grinning one moment, and looking slightly embarrassed the next. "I definitely approve of all the photos where I'm letting Grayson, I mean Remington, have it," she said.

He chuckled, then watched her mouth turn down. "Which ones don't you like?"

"They're good. Nothing on your end. But these last three here look like I'm really enjoying Grayson's company. Of course I'm acting and that smile is for the character Remington, but anyone could take it out of context."

He studied the photos and could see how easy it would be to add an inaccurate caption like: *Catalina and Grayson are back together.*

"Understood." He made note of them. "What about the ones where you're talking to Victor before rehearsal?"

"I'm fine with all of those." She continued to click through them. A minute later, she burst out with a laugh. "The snowman looks as absurd on film as he did in person."

"I have to agree," Jay said, taking a look at it again. "It's a perfect example of something not translating from paper to film. Is Stan going to change it?"

"I didn't talk to him directly, but Victor said he'd discuss it with him." She clicked to the next frame. She was looking right into the camera, directly at him. There was warmth in her eyes and a softness to her, as if she were listening to a heartwarming story, and he wished he knew what she had been thinking at that moment. She stared at her image, possibly remembering what was going through her mind, because she pulled away, seeming a little embarrassed.

"A truly beautiful photo of you," he said.

"Oh." She gave off an embarrassed little laugh, then

flicked him a glance. "You're still incredibly talented with a camera."

"You make my job easy."

She smiled at the compliment before she suddenly got a very serious look on her face. Her mouth opened, and she took a deep breath. "Jay, I've wanted to—" She shook her head.

"What?" He set his camera aside. "What were you about to say?"

"Nothing." She tossed her head back and forced a smile. "Just that I'm glad we're working together again."

He knew that wasn't it, and wanted to ask again, but he saw Angel coming with their food, so he let it go. "I am, too, Catalina."

Chapter Sixteen

Joe finished off a gingerbread cookie, then got to loading the dishwasher. Mary wasn't her usual, confident self on this Scrooge assignment. He wasn't worried, and she shouldn't be, either. "The Scrooge Legend will help straighten things out. It's no coincidence that the writer will be staying here with Catalina and Victor."

His wife glanced at the clock on the wall. "He sure is late."

"Not to worry," Joe said. "He probably went straight to the set." When the doorbell rang with a chime playing "Joy to the World," he added, "I bet that's him right now."

Mary dried her hands, and they both went to see who it was.

A disheveled midthirties man, with bags in hand, stood on their front porch.

"Evening," Joe said.

"I'm Stan Larkin." His voice was layered with exhaustion.

"Come in out of the cold, Mr. Larkin." Mary motioned him inside. "I'm Mary and this is my husband, Joe."

"We've been expecting you for hours." Joe relieved Stan of his bags.

"My flight out of LA was delayed, then the airlines lost one of my bags. I've been on the phone the entire time up here with either the director or one of the producers. Then just outside of town, traffic came to a complete stop for a...snowman race."

"Oh, that's right." Mary gasped, looking at Joe. "We forgot all about that."

"We sure did." He shook his head, disappointed. "Not that I would have been a participant in the actual race," he said to Stan, "but I wouldn't have minded the snacks afterward." He chuckled.

"A snowman race?" Stan gave them a skeptical look. "I've never heard of such a thing."

"It's a thing," Mary said. "An annual thing. For charity. Everyone participating runs in a bulky snowman costume."

"I'm all for charities, but my driver and I waited twenty-five minutes for all of the runners to pass."

"Well, snowmen aren't supposed to be fast, now, are they?" Mary raised a brow.

"No, they aren't." Stan stared off in space as if something important had dawned on him.

"You look exhausted, Mr. Larkin. Why don't you come sit down and warm up a bit before unpacking?" Mary showed him into the living room and had him sit next to the fire. "Would you care for something to drink? Coffee, hot apple cider, hot cocoa—"

"You have apple cider?"

"Of course."

A smile emerged on Stan's face. "I'd like that, please."

"Back in a flash."

Mary hurried into the kitchen while Joe set Stan's bags by the stairs, then threw another log on the fire. "So, you're the movie writer."

"Screenwriter." Stan took out his phone and checked his emails.

"How long have you been writing?" Joe asked.

"About ten years." Stan answered an email, then set his phone aside.

"Have I seen anything you've written?"

"I wrote *The Lake*, which was out last summer."

"Sounds familiar." Joe rubbed his chin. "What's it about?"

"It's a teenage slasher movie."

"Ah." Joe looked away, wondering whose bright idea it was to put a horror writer in charge of a Christmas movie. "I didn't catch that one. Any other movies?"

"I've written two other slasher movies and a few action thrillers. I have one about the CIA you might be interested in. It's in preproduction."

Mary came back in with three hot ciders, a tray full of Christmas cookies, nuts, and some cheese and crackers. "Here you are." She handed a mug over to Stan.

"Thank you." He perked up as he took a sip. "It's very good. My grandmother used to make hot cider every Christmas. I haven't had a cup since I moved to LA."

"I'm glad you like it."

He eyed the tray of food.

"Help yourself," Mary said as she and Joe sat down. "Did I hear you say you wrote action films?"

"Yes." Stan took a piece of cheese and gobbled it down. "That's what I enjoy writing the most."

"He's also written a few teenage slasher movies," Joe added.

"Oh." Mary couldn't hide her shocked expression. "What got you interested in a story about the Scrooge Legend?"

Stan grabbed a handful of nuts and tossed them in his mouth. "My girlfriend's favorite blogger stayed up here last year. A woman by the name of Charley Dawson."

"Is that so?" Joe shook his head, delighted. "Charley was one of our favorite guests."

"She stayed here? In this very inn?"

"Why, yes," Mary said proudly. "She and her fiancé, Jack, are coming up right after Christmas. They fell in love here."

"For such a small town, there certainly seems to be a lot of people who fall in love." He crunched on another handful of nuts, and then his face lit up with excitement. "I should change your town's name to St. Valentine." He quickly grabbed a pen and scribbled a note for himself.

Mary shot Joe a horrified look before setting her gaze back on their latest guest. "I'm no writer, Mr. Larkin, but when you mention St. Valentine, I think of Valentine's Day. Do you really want to mix holidays?"

He tapped the pen on his chin. "I hadn't thought of that."

"Perhaps you can save St. Valentine for a future screenplay."

"Maybe another teenage slasher," he said.

"Or maybe a nice romantic comedy." She smiled sweetly.

"Your script isn't about Charley, is it?" Joe asked, though his tone came off more as a warning.

"No, I interviewed a lot of former Scrooges and originally tried to combine about four of the stories, but it wasn't working," Stan said. "So I then decided to make it mostly about Piper's story."

"How did you get to know Piper?" he asked.

"Charley had spoken briefly about Piper in one of her posts. I've wanted to write a more character-driven screenplay for a while now, and it was actually my girlfriend who suggested I write about this place."

Mary set her cider aside. "I have to be honest, Mr. Larkin. I'm surprised you didn't come for a visit before taking on such an important project."

"My girlfriend said the same thing. She wanted to come for a week's stay, but then work got in the way for both of us, and well, I figured it was just as easy to make calls and figure it out long distance."

"How did your girlfriend like your finished version?" Mary asked.

"Scripts are never finished, even after shooting," Stan said. "There's always revisions all the way through post production. But, as far as my screenplay is concerned, I made the stakes higher and punched up the magic. Everyone who's read it absolutely loves it, which is why I hadn't expected the onslaught of major changes I've recently received. Actors are now asking for changes, as well as Piper, on top of the changes requested by the director and producers. I'm starting to lose my vision of the story."

"Perhaps we can help." Mary smiled. "We've lived here for years and can answer just about any question you might have about St. Nicholas and the legend."

"The thing is, not every true story adapts perfectly to the big screen," Stan said. "There are always adjustments, and in my case major adjustments, so I've stopped running things by Piper."

"I see." Mary shot Joe an irritated look. His wife was extremely protective over anything that had to do with the town or the Scrooge Legend itself. There was no way Stan would see his vision hit the big screen if Mary didn't approve of it. "If you're having difficulties with your revisions, you're welcome to run anything by us for an honest opinion," she told Stan. "Anything at all."

"All right." Stan tapped the tips of his fingers together, mulling it over. "Here's one. St. Nicholas is supposed to be magical, right?"

"It's magical in a spiritual sense because we have quite a few miracles happen every year."

"The problem with writing about miracles is some people will think the story is too preachy while others will think it's pure fantasy. In order to avoid that, I've decided to focus on the magic."

"Miracles aren't magic," Mary warned.

"I'm not talking about the storyline," Stan said. "I'm talking about everything that surrounds it. For example, every Christmas we see decorations everywhere, people caroling, trimming trees, and though everyone says Christmas is the most magical time of year, where's the real magic? I felt it was time to address this falsehood, so I've incorporated talking reindeer and Christmas fairies."

"What now?" Mary turned her ear toward him, as if that would help her to hear better.

"Who doesn't love a talking reindeer. Am I right?" He eyed Joe with a laugh. "The kids are going to love it!"

Joe sighed, rubbing his brow. He now understood why so many movies bombed.

"I can see why you haven't run this by Piper." Mary forced a smile.

"To be frank, my movie isn't a biography about Piper's life," Stan said. "It follows her story, but I've incorporated my own magical ideas. I'm thinking of adding talking bunnies, too."

Joe let out a disgusted sound, and Mary quickly put a hand on his leg, reminding him to keep his opinions to himself. It was a good thing she did most of the talking because he sometimes had a hard time being so cordial.

"Sounds like your screenplay would be a fantastic story for kids," Mary said. "However, the Scrooge Legend is for adults. Scrooge invitations are literally addressed to adults who have lost their way. Adults are the ones who have stopped believing in the magic of Christmas miracles, not our children."

"All the more reason to have talking reindeer and Christmas fairies."

"Mind telling me how these nonexistent entities fit into Piper's true-life story?" Joe squinted in confusion.

"I've made it work beautifully," Stan emphasized with a flourish of his hands. "The tiny talking reindeer and Christmas fairies lead her into St. Nicholas."

Mary shook her head like there was water in her ear. "Piper's mother lived here. The entire town knows that. Piper came up here to see her mother."

"But in my story, Blake, my character based on Piper, hasn't spoken to her mom in years. She's busy stealing cars."

"Oh, dear." Mary sat back, playing with the back of her hair, looking very uncomfortable. "Mr. Larkin, I know you're an action and slasher writer, but don't you think Piper might be upset if you defame her character?"

"You just said the Scrooge Legend is about adults who have lost their way. I'm raising the stakes. Why can't I have her stealing cars?"

"One of your fictional characters can steal cars, but not our sweet Piper."

Stan ping-ponged his gaze between him and Mary. "I don't understand what the problem is. Piper's been paid for me to tell her story."

"But this isn't her story," Mary pressed.

Stan took a deep breath, shaking his head. He looked irritated.

"Cookie?" Mary picked up the platter, held it out to him, but he shook his head.

"They're really good," Joe said. "They help me figure things out all the time."

"You mean like magical cookies?" Stan had sudden interest in them, so he took one and bit into it. "These are insanely good."

"Thank you." Mary looked pleased.

He ate the rest of the sugar cookie and took another, sitting back, seeming to think about his script. "Everyone hates my magic spin on Piper's story except for Victor and one producer. I wouldn't be here if it weren't for them. I can't change it just because my girlfriend, Piper, you two, Catalina, and all of the locals don't like it."

"Why not?" Joe asked. "Seems like a no-brainer."

Stan looked offended.

"What my husband is trying to say is, how do the talking reindeer add to the story?"

"They show us that the place is magical."

"But you don't need Hollywood magic to have a

place be magical. Isn't a sunset magical or a summer night walking along the beach with your girlfriend magical?"

"I get what you're driving at," Stan groused. "Okay. I'll see if I can come up with something just as good." He took another cookie off the tray. "I better get to work. I have a feeling tomorrow is going to be a longer day than today—if that's at all possible."

Chapter Seventeen

Jay didn't want his evening with Catalina to end, but she needed to prep for tomorrow. He had so much to say to her. He wanted to clear things up between them, but he also needed to move slowly with her to rebuild her trust. She was no longer an easygoing, carefree twenty-year-old. She was cautious, measured, and even skittish if she wasn't in control of the conversation or the situation. He couldn't blame her. Too much was out of her control, like with Victor and his stupid, insensitive stunt. If anyone had even thought about doing that to an actor on one of his sets, he would have fired them on the spot.

Catalina had relied heavily on the Ice Queen between takes, when she had to deal with Grayson, but the more takes she filmed, the more confident she'd become without her alter ego. It was an incredible transformation to watch—one he hoped would continue.

He pulled in the driveway to find his dad and sister attempting to haul in a seven-foot Christmas tree on their own.

"Hold on!" Jay ran to help. He took the heavier end and had his dad take the other. Hailey opened the front door and steered them into the living room, where they set it down near the big picture window.

His dad wiped his brow and took a breath. "I'm out of shape."

"I can help you with that," Hailey said. "I jog every morning at seven."

"I'm not that out of shape."

His mom was carrying hot plates of food to the dining room table. "We'll trim the tree later. Wash up. Dinner's ready."

"Thanks, Mom, but I already ate." Jay grabbed his knife out of his bag, cut the twine off the tree, and fanned out the branches.

"When?" She looked at him, confused. "It's only six thirty."

"We wrapped early, and I ate while I was in a meeting, reviewing the photos I shot today." He thought it best not to bring up his dinner with Catalina. "I'm sorry. I should have thought to call and let you know."

"At least come sit down and tell us about your day," his mom said.

"You're not going to want to miss dessert," his dad said to him when everyone finally made it to the table. "Your mom made your favorite. Chocolate silk pie."

Jay was absolutely stuffed, having eaten more than he had intended, but he'd felt if he stopped eating, skinny Catalina would, too. "Thanks, Mom. You didn't have to go to all that trouble."

"It wasn't a big deal." His mom passed around the mashed potatoes. "Now, tell us about your first day. I've been dying to know."

"We were filming on the Andersons' property. The

set builders did a fantastic job recreating the town square there."

"Why didn't they just shoot in the real town square?" his dad asked.

"Someone from production removed the animated carolers, then attempted to get rid of Santa's mailbox, so our permit was revoked."

His entire family erupted into laughter, knowing that Santa's mailbox was indestructible.

"Sounds like you had a lot of laughs your first day," his mom said. "How did the scenes go with Catalina?"

"Great, under the circumstances. Grayson Edwards is now the male lead."

"No way!" Hailey's face lit up with excitement. "Can I come visit you tomorrow on set?"

"No, you can't," his father said. "You're not old enough."

"What are you talking about? I'm eighteen, Dad, not twelve."

"That actor has too many women fawning over him, and you're not going to be one of them."

Hailey rolled her eyes. "Mom, would you please tell Dad he's being ridiculous?"

"Not when I agree with him. Grayson Edwards is too rich and too handsome for his own good." She eyed Jay. "Poor Catalina. I'm sure he was the last person she wanted to see."

"Yeah," he said. "Not many laughs for her today."

"Can I see what you shot?" Hailey asked.

"Camera's in my bag."

Hailey ran over, dug it out, and brought it back to the table.

"Did you make any good contacts?" his dad asked.

"I'm working with my old cinematographer, and I hope to be talking to a couple producers over the next few weeks."

"These are really good, Jay," Hailey said as she clicked through the photos. "Catalina looks great."

"Let me see." His mom reached for the camera, and took a look herself. "She's so beautiful. Don't you think so, Jay?"

"All right, give me back my camera." He held out his hand.

"Let me see a few more." Hailey intercepted it, and kept clicking through them. "You have a lot more of Catalina than you do of Grayson."

"She's the star."

"But isn't Grayson as well?"

"No. The movie is about Catalina's character."

Hailey brought the camera closer, staring at one photo. "Wow. These look like the same shoes that Dad caught on camera at the mailbox stakeout last year. You saw that photo, didn't you?"

"Everyone saw it," Jay said. "But I didn't take a picture of elf shoes."

"Are you sure?"

Jay took back his camera and looked for himself. Sure enough, there were small green turned-up shoes with bells at the tips, which could clearly be seen beneath the mailbox. He'd taken the photo right after Victor called cut. He'd been concentrating on the actor in the snowman suit, who was walking out of frame, trampling over tiny slips of paper littering the ground. The pieces of paper were used for the movie's Christmas wishes and Scrooge suggestions, and Jay had wondered how many takes Victor would do before he realized the costume was too bulky for the actor to collect little pieces of paper.

"What the..." Jay zoomed in on the image. The elf shoes weren't under the mailbox but behind it. He had captured a side view of the shoes with the back heel lifting off the ground, as if whoever was wearing the shoes was bending down to pick up the discarded paper. "I never saw the shoes when I was shooting."

"I never saw them, either," his dad said.

"Let me see." His mom held out her hand.

"Hold on. I want to import the photos into my computer first." Jay grabbed his laptop out of his bag and set it up. "Dad, do you still have that photo?"

"Of course we do." His mom pulled out a photo album and handed it to Jay. "I even printed the before- and-after frames, but you can only see the shoes in one shot. It's out of sheer luck we got it. Your father was snapping away, deciding whether or not to have the automatic flash on or off, and happened to be taking a picture at the exact moment the floodlights were triggered."

He studied his parents' photos while his were still uploading to the computer. Small green shoes were turned up with little silver bells on each tip. It was the clearest image the town had of the mail collector—only the photo proved nothing.

As it had been debated by locals, skeptics, and online elf enthusiasts alike, everyone reached the same conclusion. Though the photo was clearly in focus and had captured a pair of shoes that looked like elf shoes, who was wearing them could not be confirmed. And like the continuous video cams monitoring Santa's mailbox that always received interference whenever the mail was collected, his father's before-and-after shots were blurry beyond recognition.

Throughout the years, many locals and tourists had tried to capture the entire image of the mail collector on camera, but to date, no one had been successful. The photos were always out of focus, ruined, or caught such a tiny portion of the collector that what or who it was couldn't be determined.

Jay zoomed in on his photo to compare the shoes in both pictures as his family stood behind him, doing the same. Even though his photo was a side view of the shoes, and his dad's photo was a front view, they looked like the same pair.

"They're identical," Hailey said.

"I don't understand this. No one should have been behind the mailbox. We had just filmed the first take." He blew up the image as far as it would go, looking for anything unusual in the frame. "Did you give your photo to the local paper?" he asked his parents.

"Of course," his mom said proudly. "We were the only ones who caught something. A copy of it is also in the library."

"That would explain how someone on set could have seen it," Jay said. "Whoever it was could have been crouching down, behind the mailbox, ready to play a prank."

"Why would anyone do that?" His mom gave him a bewildered look.

"To lighten the mood. The director is intense and many thought it was ridiculous to have a snowman pick up the mail."

"Yes, that is ridiculous," she said. "That doesn't even make sense."

"I think it's real." Hailey threw in her two cents.

"Steven, what do you think?" his mom asked.

"There's a guy dressed up in a snowman costume walking out of frame. Not a stretch to believe that someone else put on an elf costume. Besides, this isn't even the real mailbox."

"That's right," Jay said. "It can't be real."

"Why not?" Hailey kept scrutinizing the frame. "If a wish is thrown in a similar-looking mailbox, maybe Santa's elves are required to collect it."

"Could be one of the Andersons' grandkids," his dad offered up, "but more likely it's someone with the film."

Jay agreed. It had to be someone with the film. Only he couldn't figure out when the prankster had moved behind the mailbox. The actor playing the snowman would have seen him. The camera operator would have seen him and stopped filming.

Jay inspected his photos of the scene he'd taken before they filmed the first take. The shoes weren't in any of those photos. Like his father, Jay had only captured the shoes in one shot. He spent the next hour going through all of his stills, hoping he'd see which crew member had been behind the mystery prank, but he hadn't caught anyone with the shoes on camera. He also hadn't seen any kids in his stills or on set that day.

Hailey brought up an interesting point. There had never been a fake Santa's mailbox in town before. Catalina, as her character, had wished for her soul mate out loud over and over again. Could it be possible that she'd gotten the attention of the real mail collector? Jay wasn't quite ready to believe that.

Unable to figure it out, he found himself studying Catalina's expressive face in the pictures he'd taken of her. Damn, he had missed her. It had been a mistake to let so much time go by without calling her. She had become such a good friend. If they had remained in each other's lives, maybe he wouldn't be where he was now.

And what about Catalina? If they had remained friends, things would have probably been different with Grayson. Maybe her relationship with him wouldn't have happened at all. So many disappointments had taken a toll on her, and it had diminished that spark in her eye. He felt partly to blame, so he wanted to do whatever he could to help her get it back.

One thing he knew for sure: they were better off when they were together than when they were apart. Whether that meant as coworkers, friends, or even something more, they needed to be involved in each other's lives again, and he needed to make that happen.

Chapter Eighteen

Because Victor was now staying at the B&B, Catalina thought it was best for Neil to pick her up at the diner instead of Jay dropping her off. Who she spent time with after work wasn't any of Victor's business, but he'd make it his, and the last thing she wanted was for her controlling director to fire Jay out of spite.

"How was dinner?" Neil asked as he headed to the bed-and-breakfast.

A smile instantly touched her lips as she sat in the back of the town car. It had surprised her—how strong her attraction was for Jay again. When he'd taken off his coat, she couldn't help but notice his muscular frame. He'd been wearing an army-green long-sleeve Henley, which fit nicely over his well-defined chest and sculpted biceps. They'd started the evening sitting across from one another but by the end of it, they'd moved closer, their arms brushing against each other as he shared pictures with her, making her laugh.

She had really needed that and wished she could have stayed with him longer. "It was good. Any revisions come in?"

"No, but it looks like we have a location and scene change on the call sheet for tomorrow."

"Stan must still be working on the rewrite. I really hope his changes are in alignment with the Scrooge Legend."

"Yeah. You don't need another eventful day like today."

"Amen to that."

She really couldn't believe how much had happened in one day—from Victor's gotcha stunt with her ex, to having two heartfelt conversations with Jay. And if she hadn't been able to talk things through with him right after the stunt, she might have ended her career today. Jay had helped her figure out her next move. They had once been so good like that—working through problems on and off set together. Now she was beginning to care about the movie she never wanted to be a part of, and she was beginning to care about him.

"Where's our new location?"

Neil pulled into the driveway of the B&B and parked. "Right here. We're starting with scene nineteen in the morning."

As soon as Catalina and Neil came through the front door, Mary was there to greet them with a big smile. "Good evening!"

Joe threw another log on the fire for Victor and Theo, who were working in the living room, before he joined Mary. "Ms. Jones, we heard you suggested our inn for the exterior bed-and-breakfast scenes. Much appreciated. Mary and I had no idea how well it paid."

"I was happy to do it. Your place is too picture-perfect for it not to be in the movie."

"Someone from production originally told us our shooting day would be next week," Mary said, "but we were just informed that it's moved up and everyone will be here early tomorrow."

"We just received that change as well." Neil glanced at the call sheet on his phone again. "Looks like we're shooting two scenes and will be here until lunch."

"Won't that be exciting?" Mary clapped her hands. "We'll get to see you in action, Ms. Jones."

"Guess I'd better start learning my lines," she said with a laugh.

"Catalina," Victor called out, and motioned for her to come into the living room. "Stan finally made it here. I let him know what you said about the mail collector, so we'll pick that up tomorrow afternoon."

"That's great, Victor. Thank you." She turned toward the stairs.

"Why don't you stay and have a drink with me?" He patted the couch next to him. "Theo was just leaving."

Theo collected his things and walked away.

Catalina remained firmly planted where she was. "I need to get to work, so I'm prepared for tomorrow."

"I can help you." He smiled at her pleasantly. "I am your director after all."

"I'm sure you have plenty of work to do as well," she said. "Neil is great with running lines."

"But our hosts are talking his ear off. Sit."

Catalina glanced over her shoulder. The three, indeed, were still standing in the foyer chatting away. Victor rose and went behind the Carrolls' minibar, rummaging around in the cabinets. "They must have something stronger to drink than hot cider."

"Do you need something?" Joe asked, suddenly appearing right behind Catalina.

"Looking for a nightcap while I help Catalina with her lines. All I see are bags of hot tea and sodas."

"How about a hot chocolate, apple cider, or a ginger-bread spiced coffee?" Mary asked, joining Joe.

"How about something stronger?" Victor asked again. "I'm sure Catalina would like a glass of wine."

"I can speak for myself, Victor, and no, I don't want a glass of wine. Maybe you should go back to the hotel, where you can get room service."

"It's lousy there like it is here."

"I'm very sorry to hear we're not up to your standards," Mary said to Victor.

"Mary's hot cider is very good," Catalina said. "You should try a cup."

Joe nodded at Catalina's suggestion. "My wife makes the best in town."

"I don't want hot cider, or hot chocolate with little marshmallows, or any other Christmas drink! Theo!" Victor slammed his hand down on the minibar counter, and Theo came running back into the room. "Grab my things," he said to Theo, then marched out the front door, leaving everyone speechless.

Catalina couldn't believe Victor's behavior. Jay would have never done something like that. She hated to admit it, but she'd thrown a few temperamental scenes throughout the years. Even in her foulest of moods, she would have never dreamed of yelling at such a sweet couple as Mary and Joe. Having just witnessed it, she now realized how rude and unbecoming it was, and how it had made Victor look so petty.

"My apologies for our director," Neil said to Mary and Joe, taking the words right out of her mouth.

"You are a dear," Mary said to him. "Poor man ap-

Caitlin McKenna   163

pears to be under a lot of pressure. I do hope he will come around. Now, what I can get you two? Hot cider, hot chocolate, a hot toddy?"

Neil's eyes widened and he looked to Catalina.

"I thought you didn't serve anything stronger than hot chocolate," she said.

"To a hothead, no. But for you two…" She shrugged.

Catalina laughed. "Though very tempting, I'd better pass on a hot toddy, but I'd love a cup of your delicious hot cider."

"Wonderful. And for you, Neil?"

"Hot chocolate for me, please. And uh… I'm fine with the marshmallows."

Mary laughed. "Back in a flash."

"Why don't you relax by the fire, Ms. Jones?" Joe stirred up the embers. "Or would you prefer that Mary bring your drink up to your room?"

"Please, call me Catalina, and here is just fine." She sat in the wing-backed chair by the fire and stared into the flames. "My parents live in Maine and always have a fire going in their living room during the winter. It's so inviting and relaxing there. I miss having one myself on cold days, but LA doesn't get very chilly, and I'm rarely at home anyway."

"No, I don't suppose you'd need a roaring fire much in sunny California," Joe said. "How did your first day go?"

Catalina shared a look with Neil. "Victor is full of surprises."

"And Ms. Jones handled everything like a pro." Neil sat across from her.

"Good for you," Joe said as Mary came back in with

their drinks and handed them off. "At least he's not the only director in town."

"I can certainly drink to that." Catalina lifted her cup of cider in the air, and then took a much-needed sip.

"Why do you think he's so angry?" Mary asked.

A question she had asked herself. "The pressures of the job, perhaps, but I don't know for sure."

"Actually, I did some digging." Neil took a drink of his hot cocoa as he pulled up his notes on his phone. "Turns out Victor lost his parents on Christmas Eve when he was a boy."

"Oh, how horrible." Mary put her hand to her cheek.

"That explains a lot." Catalina thought back on Victor's aversion to the Christmas decorations, the mailbox, his preference for Mediterranean plants over a Christmas tree in his office.

"Who took him in?" Joe asked.

"His Italian grandmother. She raised him and his siblings. She passed away twelve years ago."

"No wonder he's having a hard time," Mary said. "Why on earth would he choose to direct a Christmas movie?"

"Money talks," Catalina said. "Though I'm not sure why he would want to torture himself when he could have easily passed on the project. I have my own hang-ups with Christmas, but Victor seems downright uncomfortable being surrounded by anything Christmassy."

"At least he's come to the right town for an attitude adjustment," Joe said.

"Thank you both for the insight. It's very helpful." Mary picked up a dirty mug and plate off the bar. "Joe and I will get out of your hair. Let us know if you need anything."

"Thank you." Catalina studied Neil as he opened the script to help her with lines. "What made you do research on Victor?"

"I wanted to help you deal with him," he said. "I thought if I found something you two had in common, he might begin to show you more respect."

She had really lucked out on getting such a thoughtful assistant. "Thank you, Neil, for taking the time to do research. I truly appreciate it. Did you find anything else in your search?"

"Nothing else worth noting."

"He seems more human, now that I know what had happened to him." She wrapped her sweater tighter around her body. "I actually feel bad for him."

Neil watched one of the logs break in two as the flames engulfed it. "I'll never again complain about my mom wanting me around for the holidays."

"I hope we're able to get our one week off. I'm feeling a little homesick myself." She sipped her apple cider. "Does Victor have anyone special in his life?"

"Not that I found. I don't see any pictures of him on IMDB with a spouse or a significant other. Most of his family lives in Italy."

"He has no one here?"

"He's got a brother who lives in New York."

"Not exactly close." She mulled his situation over. "He could make the crew his family, like Jay did on *Sage Under Fire*, but he doesn't seem to want that."

Neil shrugged. "Some people seem happy being miserable."

"Maybe he's miserable because he feels so isolated." She thought about that. "You know what he needs?"

"What?"

"You already said it. Love."

Neil nodded. "Why don't we add Victor to my science experiment and deposit a Christmas wish for him?"

"I've got one better." She sat up, excited. "What if we recommend him as a Scrooge?"

"Brilliant, though what if Victor finds out?"

"We'll make sure no one is around when we deposit his name," she said. "If Santa's mailbox truly works, we need to help him shed his Scroogey ways."

"He'll thank us for it later." Neil smiled. "And so will the crew."

She sat back and tilted her head. "I wonder what a happier Victor would even look like?"

It took forever to learn her lines because she couldn't stop thinking about the mailbox. Could it possibly have the power to change lives? Neil had deposited a wish and he'd already met someone he was very interested in. With her wish, she'd made it difficult by not only asking for immediacy, but by the nature of the wish itself. She hadn't wished for love from just anyone because anyone could break her heart. She had wished for her soul mate—the one person who was guaranteed by definition to be perfectly suited to her. The only person she just might take a chance on.

But she didn't believe in soul mates, and she certainly didn't believe that Jay, who she ran into right after she had made that wish, was her soul mate. How could he be? He hadn't even liked her kiss seven and a half years ago. No. Running into Jay was nothing more than a coincidence, especially when human collisions happened all the time. That was what happened when people were more engrossed with whatever was on their phone than the real world around them. It certainly didn't mean they were soul mates.

But there was something different about St. Nicholas that she couldn't quite identify. It was as if everyone in town was in a time warp, where positive energy supercharged the atmosphere, causing so many good things to occur in such a short amount of time. When she considered what had happened in twenty-four hours—having an about-face on Piper's story, Neil meeting Iris, her reconnecting with Jay—could these positive things have happened without the Scrooge Legend and Santa's mailbox?

She'd never know. But if she were to make a Scrooge suggestion for a mean, manipulative megalomaniac like Victor and he actually changed, well, that *would* be a miracle. If he had a dramatic change of heart, she'd know, without a doubt, that the Scrooge Legend was real.

It was late in the evening when Catalina and Neil went to the mailbox.

"It's so quiet out here," she said as they got out of the car and walked along the town square's meandering path.

"Well, it is after ten on a cold winter's night in a small, sleepy town," Neil said. "The only thing open is the diner."

She came around the corner and saw Santa's mailbox with the candy cane flag in the raised position. "Good.

The mail still hasn't been collected. We should hang around and see who picks it up."

Neil raised a brow. "We could be out here all night."

"According to Piper, it has to be collected by midnight, but we don't have to stay if you don't want to."

He zipped up his coat. "I'm good if you are."

"Do you have the paper with his name on it?"

"Right here." He took it out of his pocket and handed it over. "Are you supposed to say something specific when suggesting a Scrooge?"

"I don't know, but I think we can wing it." Catalina put her hand on the mailbox door. "I'm suggesting Victor Caviano as a Scrooge. Please help him find his Christmas spirit, find love, and be happy again." She looked to Neil.

"That should cover it."

Catalina opened the door with ease and dropped in the piece of paper. "The flag's already raised so I guess that's it."

Neil glanced around the area. "I think if we sit on that bench over there and remain quiet, whoever collects the mail won't know we're here."

"Perfect," she said in a hushed tone.

Right before they reached the bench, they heard tiny bells jingle behind them. Catalina whipped around and gasped. "The flag's down."

"Maybe it fell down."

They walked back to the mailbox. Neil tried to raise the flag, but it wouldn't budge. Catalina tried, too, but it didn't move for her, either.

"Okay, that was weird." She looked around. "Where did those bells come from?"

Neil looked up. "Maybe they've placed them high up in the trees."

"Makes sense—adding to the legend illusion." She tried to see the bells hidden in the branches above her, but she couldn't spot any. "We'll have to try catching the mail collector on another night."

"Yeah." Neil pulled out his key fob as they walked back to the car. "If by chance it is real, I wonder how fast we'll see a change in Victor."

"I don't know, but *now* isn't too fast for me." She laughed.

"It would be amazing, wouldn't it, to work with a respectful and considerate Victor?"

She put her hands together in prayer and glanced up to the heavens. "Dear Lord, let it be real."

Neil chuckled. "I second that."

Chapter Nineteen

Catalina awoke to a radio alarm by the bed playing "White Christmas." She'd forgotten she had set it, thinking she'd wake up well before it went off. To her great surprise, she had actually slept through the night. She hadn't done that since before her breakup with Grayson. Mary's warm apple cider might have helped her to sleep, but it was really Jay who had helped her turn off the anxiety channel continually playing in her head.

She'd really enjoyed going to dinner with him. She felt more relaxed than she had in months. He'd even reminded her of what it was like to be her old self. Before she was famous, they'd hung out together and talked about anything that came to mind. She really missed sharing food with him, swapping stories, not being in a hurry, or having to worry about anything but the present moment.

But now, she was incredibly busy. She didn't have time to squeeze a relationship into her life, so why was she entertaining the thought of spending more time with Jay?

Because he hadn't changed.

Unlike so many in her life, he didn't hold back when he had something to say. He was the only person she'd known who would always tell her the truth. Even Erin would sometimes say what Catalina wanted to hear instead of what she needed to hear. That's why she took it to heart when Jay told her she was too skinny. Her first reaction had been anger, a habit she needed to break. She respected him for not backing down. Maybe she was too skinny.

A text came in from Neil, and she confirmed that she was awake by replying with a smiley face emoji, something she wouldn't have even considered a day ago. He was proving to be a great assistant, staying one step ahead of her.

Catalina threw back the covers and got out of bed. She shut off the radio, then reconsidered. She hadn't played Christmas music in years. She turned the radio back on right as the song changed to "Carol of the Bells," her absolute favorite Christmas song of all time. It was her mother's favorite, too. She had to get home for Christmas this year. She missed her mom and dad, and she missed the homey feeling of having loved ones around.

Even her visits with her little brother had become scarce. He'd recently moved his family back home and now lived less than a mile from their parents. Cameron and his wife were expecting their second child in May, and she didn't even have a boyfriend. Would she ever have a family of her own? She wasn't getting any younger. Where would she be when Hollywood told her she was too old, and the job offers stopped coming?

Being in St. Nicholas, she was continually reminded that there was nothing more important than love. She immediately thought, *You can't pay the bills with love.* But was she better off? She had plenty of money to pay the bills. She had a successful career, she could go anywhere, do anything. As much as she wanted to tell herself that she was perfectly fine being single, she wasn't. She was lonely. Maybe that needed to change.

"Good morning, Stan. Coffee?" Mary asked as he sat down at one of the tables in the dining room.

"Always, and as strong as you got it," he said with a yawn.

"I'm delighted to see that at least one of our guests is taking advantage of the included breakfast." She set down a small bread basket.

"That's production people for you." He stirred in a splash of cream. "They clock a lot of hours, so they usually grab something to eat on set."

"Did you get your rewrite done?"

"I struggled with it," he admitted. "I was told that the mail is collected here at night, but the scene needs to be shot in the afternoon. Clearly, the snowman is out, but I couldn't replace him with an elf, either."

"What did you do?" she asked, slightly alarmed.

"I tried everything, and then all of a sudden it popped into my head. They don't need to see a mail collector. They'll look away, only for a moment, and that's when the mail is collected."

"Excellent," Mary said. "That's how it always happens."

Stan gave her a surprised look. "It does?"

"No one ever sees the mail collector. You know, Stan, you really should stay awhile."

"I should." He looked a little lost, as if he realized he could have saved himself a lot of time if he'd just traveled to St. Nicholas in the first place.

"For breakfast, you have a choice of waffles, a spinach and cheese omelet, or steel-cut oatmeal. Sides are bacon, sausage, or mixed fruit." She motioned to the bread basket on the table. "Inside are cinnamon twists along with my special cranberry and eggnog Christmas muffins to get you started."

Stan's eyes widened. "I thought breakfast consisted of a dried-out roll and coffee."

She chuckled. "Perhaps at some of the B&Bs in Los Angeles, but certainly not here."

"Wow. Okay. Uh… I'll take the omelet with fruit, please."

"Very good." She headed back toward the kitchen.

"Mary? Are you and Joe going to watch the filming today?"

"We wouldn't miss it."

"Good because I have a nice surprise for you."

"Oh?"

"You inspired me so much that I changed the character names of my B&B hosts to Mary and Joe, and I've also modeled them after you."

"How lovely." Mary smiled. "Joe and I are honored."

Stan stretched out his arms. "And now, back to the robbery scenes." He opened his laptop and pulled up his script.

"Robberies?"

"Yes, a couple of guys who Blake knew in her previous life follow her up here and start breaking into people's homes to steal their Christmas gifts."

"Oh, dear," Mary said under her breath. She should head back to the kitchen, mind her own business, and let it go. But how could she? Anything that could negatively impact her town *was* her business. "One thing. Do the robberies all happen on Christmas Eve?"

"No." He stopped typing and looked up at her. "Why?"

"Well, in many homes, Christmas gifts aren't under the tree until Christmas Eve, and sometimes not until early Christmas Day."

Stan frowned. "I didn't think of that."

"And won't your thieves be competing with your leading man, who is thought to have *stolen* Piper's home?"

"I didn't think of that, either."

"Maybe you don't need the robberies at all."

Stan slumped back in his chair. "No, I guess I don't."

"Feel free to run anything by me before you spend so much time writing it," Mary said.

He rubbed his face. "Maybe I should."

"Wonderful. Now, I best get your delicious breakfast started for you before it's time for lunch." Mary walked away humming, leaving Stan a bit confused.

Chapter Twenty

Before going to the set, Jay dropped off a flash drive to the film's publicist minus the gaunt-looking picture of Catalina, the other photos she hadn't approved of, and the mysterious elf shoe shot. His logical mind told him that it had to be fake since they were filming at a fake mailbox. But he couldn't get over how he never saw the shoes while he was taking the picture. As a wildlife photographer, his senses had been trained to see any movement wandering into frame. He hadn't seen any movement, other than the snowman, and yet the shoes could clearly be seen.

Catalina must have distracted him for a split second, like she was doing at that moment. He couldn't stop thinking about her and immediately began looking for her when he arrived on set at the Carroll Inn. As he made his rounds, dropping off flash drives to the various departments to help with any continuity issues, he kept an eye out for her. He wanted to wish her a good morning.

What was he thinking? He was getting ahead of himself. Just because he'd envisioned—all night—how their relationship could easily fall back into a comfortable friendship before quickly moving beyond that, he had no idea if she felt the same way. She had been through a roller-coaster ride of emotions yesterday, which had her sharing things with him that perhaps she wouldn't have done on a less stressful day. Did she feel differently about their conversations now that she'd had time to reflect on them? He hoped not.

He headed over to the camera truck and saw Clayton and his crew pulling out their equipment. "Looks like we have a busy day today."

"I'll take busy over drama."

"Then cut the trees down!" Victor yelled at Luisa as the two approached the set. "I don't want them in the shot."

"It's supposed to be scenic," Luisa said. "That's why we're here, Victor. We're not cutting down trees."

"Why not? No one is going to miss them. They're everywhere."

"The owners will miss them, and even if I got their approval to remove them, that will cost us valuable time and money, neither of which we have. Talk to your DP." Luisa motioned to Clayton.

"Is there a change in our first setup?" Clayton asked as Jay took a step back and pretended to be cleaning his camera lens.

Victor motioned to the Carroll Inn with a quick fling of his hand. "Just look at it."

Clayton studied the inn. "Uh…what am I specifically looking at?"

"Those gargantuan pine trees. I don't like them framing the inn."

"What's wrong with them?"

"It's all about them. They dwarf the inn—an inn I don't even like. Who signed off on filming here?"

"I did," Luisa said. "This is the most picturesque B&B in all of St. Nicholas."

Victor got in her face. "One more time, I want the audience to be paying attention to the actors, not the trees, and certainly not the inn."

Jay almost laughed out loud at Clayton and Luisa's stunned expressions.

"The trees will only be seen in the establishing shot," Clayton said. "Blake's exchange with the inn's hosts is at the door, then when she talks to Remington, I can make sure they're not in the scene."

"Fine. Do it," Victor said, and walked away.

"Thanks, Clayton." Luisa already looked worn out. With a sigh, she followed after Victor.

"Am I missing something?" Jay asked. "If I were directing and shooting here, I'd be ecstatic. It's enchanting, warm, inviting. This inn, with its beautiful hundred-year-old pine trees, could be on the cover of a Christmas card."

"I don't get it, either," Clayton said, watching Victor chew out someone at craft service. "It's like he hates any reminders of Christmas. Do you know he didn't want Santa's mailbox to be in the story at all?"

Jay laughed. "That mailbox is the sole reason for my town's very existence. It's why we have the Scrooge Legend."

"Other than reconnecting with you, I'm not sure what the benefit is for the studio to have brought us out here when our director is trying to remove anything that looks like St. Nicholas. We could have shot the whole thing in LA on a sound stage where we wouldn't be freezing our asses off at the same time as getting them chewed out."

"I have to agree." Jay debated whether to tell Clayton about the intricacies of the Scrooge Legend. He knew why this was all happening. Victor hated Christmas, but was directing a Christmas movie and was staying with Mary and Joe because someone had suggested him as a Scrooge. And Victor wouldn't stop being a Scrooge until he found love and the Christmas spirit. It sounded so simple, but it never was to people who hadn't ever been involved in a Scrooge journey.

As soon as there was a break in the action, Jay would find out from Mary and Joe if there was anything he could do to help move Victor in the right direction. He hated seeing Catalina swept up in it, and the sooner Victor was no longer a Scrooge, the happier everyone would be.

"We're ready for rehearsal when you are," Mark said to Catalina as she opened the door to her trailer.

She nodded, then saw Jay and waved him over. "Morning." She was all smiles. "I wanted to thank you again for dinner last night. I really had a nice time."

"So did I," he said. "I'm glad we finally got to catch up."

"Did you see the rewrite on the mailbox scene?" She picked up her revised sides.

"Just got them."

"Thanks to you, the scene is so much better. Stan opted not to show the mail collector at all."

"That's awesome. I'm glad to hear he finally saw the light."

"Yeah," she said, laughing, and she didn't know why. She couldn't seem to stop smiling, but Jay was smiling almost as much as she was. "What did the publicist think of your photos?"

"She seemed pleased."

"She should be. You frame photos so well, as if you're telling a story with each and every one. I'm the worst at taking a good picture."

"I'll be happy to give you a few pointers," he said, his gaze locked on her.

"I'll take you up on that." She pictured him leaning over her shoulder, cheek to cheek, as they set up a shot together.

"We'll have to do dinner again soon," he said.

"I'd like that." She no longer felt a heaviness from trying to predict what would be thrown at her during the day, and it was making her giddy. "Will you be stopping by after we wrap to show me your photos?"

"Of course."

"Good." She just stood there, smiling, not able to break eye contact. His grin widened, and then he finally took a step back. "I guess I better get out there."

She nodded. "See you on set." She watched him go, looking so strong, carrying all of his equipment. He seemed so at ease, back in his element.

"Hey, Jay," Valerie, the wardrobe supervisor, who was in her midfifties, called out. "If you have to take any pictures of me, please get my good side."

"They're all your good side," he replied, which made her smile.

"Yo, Jay. It looks like your Broncos are against my Chargers this weekend," one of the grips said.

"I'm not worried."

"You should be. They're going to wipe the floor with your guys."

Jay chuckled. "We'll see about that."

Catalina laughed. Jay was more popular with the crew than the director, and it was only day two.

Chapter Twenty-One

"Can I get you something warm to drink?" a PA asked Mary.

She and Joe had come out to watch the filming and were given chairs and warm blankets.

"Oh, goodness," she said, taken off guard. "I'm the one who normally asks that. Thank you, but I'm fine for now."

"I could use some coffee," Joe said.

"No problem." The PA talked into his headset mic as he walked away.

"Didn't you just have a cup?" Mary eyed her husband.

"Yep, but I'm beginning to like this film business. We've got chairs, a good view, people waiting on us. It's great to be in the middle of the action."

"Are you going Hollywood on me?"

"Just for the day," he said, relaxing back and putting on his sunglasses.

"Here you are, Mr. Carroll." A different assistant handed over a cup of hot coffee, then hurried away, talking to someone over his headset.

Joe took a sip and made a face. "It tastes like motor oil."

Mary laughed, happy to know she couldn't be so easily replaced by all the glitz and glamour.

"Well, what do you think?" Stan asked, coming over.

"I now understand the phrase 'Don't make a production out of it.'"

Stan laughed. "Good one. Oh! I have someone I'd like you to meet." Stan walked over to another couple sitting in chairs, spoke to them, then brought them over. "Mary, Joe, I'd like you to meet Mary and Joe."

Mary stared at a couple in their early thirties wearing matching Christmas sweaters. The woman was drop-dead gorgeous with strawberry blond hair, and the guy looked like her twin.

"We're your upgrades!" the man said, laughing.

"Come again?" Mary shifted her gaze between the two.

"We're playing you two," the woman clarified. "I'm Isabella, and this is Elliot."

"Oh." Mary finally got it, trying not to look offended. "Nice to meet you."

"Do you have any questions you'd like to ask us about running a B&B?" Joe asked.

"No," Isabella said. "Seems fairly simple."

"We got this." Elliot high-fived Isabella.

"Rehearsal's up!" Mark called out.

"That's our cue," Isabella said.

"Time for the pros to go to work." Elliot offered them a big grin, then headed to the front porch.

"Aren't they just perfect?" Stan said, looking quite pleased with the casting.

"Oh, uh, they seem capable," Mary said.

"They look just like us." Joe stared after them.

Stan laughed hard. "The best part is, in another

scene, I reveal that they are actually in their sixties, but they look so good because they put a wish in the mailbox to be forever young and beautiful."

"Oh, dear." She wrung her hands, not knowing where to start on how his idea was totally inappropriate.

"It doesn't work that way," Joe spoke up. "Only wishes regarding love are answered."

Stan frowned. "Is this true?" He looked at Mary.

"I'm afraid so."

"That makes no sense." Stan sounded a little defensive. "Christmas is about getting things. It's a materialistic holiday and nothing more."

"The commercialism of Christmas is materialistic," she said, gently, "but the true meaning of Christmas is all about love."

"Try telling that to the kid who wants an Xbox but gets a bike instead." Stan stomped away right as Catalina and Victor appeared on set.

"Seems we still have a lot more work to do on Mr. Larkin." Mary let out a long sigh.

"No doubt." Joe watched Elliot go over the scene with Victor. "Maybe Stan was told the couple had to be in their thirties. I heard age discrimination in Hollywood is alive and well."

"Either way, he can't proclaim to the world that Santa's mailbox is some cheap wishing well." She huffed. "We'll have flocks of people coming up here to wish for boatloads of cash."

"Look what's going on over there." Joe motioned to Catalina talking to Jay, who was crouched near the porch swing with his camera. Catalina said something that made Jay laugh.

"Interesting." Mary shifted in her chair when a camera assistant blocked her view. "Do you think he's the one?"

"Would make perfect sense if he was." Joe took another sip of coffee and winced. "They have a history as director and actor, so it's very possible."

"I hope they're meant to be together," she said, watching them. "Jay's such a stable, talented, and considerate young man. He'd be wonderful for her. We should talk to him when he takes a break."

Grayson came striding through the set with a skinny blonde. A PA immediately ran up to them and directed her to the sidelines.

"That must be his main squeeze." Joe motioned to the blonde.

"It's obvious Grayson has her around to make Catalina jealous." Mary glanced over at Catalina. "Luckily, Catalina seems too engrossed in her conversation with Jay to notice her ex's childish behavior."

Grayson walked up the porch steps and went inside their home with Isabella and Elliot.

"Settle," Mark called out.

"This is so exciting." Mary leaned forward in her chair as the chatter on set ceased.

"Action!" Victor yelled.

"I can do this," Catalina said as Blake, shaking out her hands and pushing out a deliberate breath.

The camera moved with her as she marched up the steps and rang the doorbell, activating loud chimes playing "Joy to the World," which could clearly be heard from outside.

"Cut!" Victor threw his hands in the air. "What the hell was that?"

"Language, Mr. Caviano," Mary called out, which got laughs from the crew. "That's our doorbell."

"Not anymore." Victor turned to the best boy electric. "Cut the wire."

"What?" Mary jumped to her feet.

"Hey!" Joe stopped the young man, who already had tools in hand, marching toward their front door. "You can't destroy our doorbell."

"Sorry," Catalina called out. "I didn't mean to ring the bell."

"See? Problem solved," Joe said.

"Thank you, Catalina!" Mary waved to her and blew her a kiss, which made her smile, and had more crew members chuckling.

"Back to one. We're going for a take," Mark called out as everyone took their places. "Roll sound."

"Speed," the production sound mixer called out.

"Roll camera," Mark said.

"Rolling," the camera operator said. The second camera assistant stepped in front of the camera, slated the scene and take, then cleared the frame.

"And...action!" Victor called.

Catalina said her first line, marched up the steps, and only pretended to ring the bell. A moment later, Isabella, playing Mary, answered the door.

"Hey, Blake. What's up?"

"I'm looking for Remington Savage."

"He's just finishing breakfast. Come on in."

"Mary? Who's at the door?" Elliot as Joe appeared. "Hey, Blake. I didn't expect to see you here. Isn't your yoga class today?"

Character Mary stared at her husband. "Since when are you interested in her yoga classes?"

"I can come back," Blake said.

"No need. Remington?" Character Mary called out, stepping inside.

A moment later, Remington appeared at the door, still chewing his breakfast. "Ms. Dickens."

"I'd like to speak with you, if you have a moment."

"Of course." Remington walked outside.

"And cut!"

The real Mary frowned. "What in the world was that?"

"Yoga?" Joe asked, seeming truly mystified.

"Holding!" Mark called out.

"See?" Stan came up to Mary and Joe. "We do know what we're doing. Did you love it, or what?"

"What...uh...catchy dialogue," Mary said with a plastered smile on her face.

"It works." Stan seemed very proud. "Too bad we have to shoot Mary and Joe's interior scenes in LA, otherwise you'd be able to watch those, too."

"Our loss," Mary said.

"Enjoy watching the magic of Hollywood. I've got to get back to work."

"Do you have any questions we can answer before you start writing?" Joe asked.

Mary really hoped he'd remove the couple's forever-young wish.

"No, though your doorbell is such a bizarre thing that it's given me an idea. Maybe one of our robbers gets electrocuted by it."

Mary scowled. "I thought you were taking out the robberies?"

"I did, but I missed them—" he shrugged "—so they're back in."

"A thief gets hurt by a doorbell?" Joe asked, confusion coloring his voice.

"Worse. Dead as a doornail by a doorbell." He laughed and hurried up the steps before they began shooting again.

"I've got to do something," Mary stood, but Joe pulled her back.

"No need to worry, my dear. He'll soon discover that one cannot be electrocuted by a doorbell."

"I'm sure he'll find a way." Mary sat back in her chair and wrapped her coat tighter around her body.

"We could use reinforcements, though." Joe pulled out his phone.

"Who are you texting?"

"Piper. She needs to know how her life is being portrayed."

"Stan doesn't seem to care, and Victor doesn't care, either. I don't know how to fix this one, Joe. The pre-Scrooges are getting in the way."

"Then we treat them like Scrooges," he said.

"I suppose it's the only way we're going to see any movement in a positive direction."

After they finished shooting the first part of the scene, Catalina took a break, giving Jay an opportunity to speak with the real Mary and Joe. "Hi, Mr. & Mrs. C."

"Jay." Mary gave him a hug. "The movie is lucky to have such a talented photographer, and I bet Catalina is very happy to see you again. She was so good as your leading lady."

"She was."

"Looks like you two are hitting it off." Joe nudged Jay.

"We're getting reacquainted."

"How wonderful." Mary clasped her hands in front of her. "You two would make a great couple."

Jay broke out into a laugh. "Nothing like getting straight to the point, Mrs. C. I'm not sure who loses the subtlety award—you or my mom."

"See." A smile widened on Mary's face. "Your mother and I agree, and we are very good at reading body language."

Jay shifted, feeling awkward.

"I'm sure Jay didn't come over to talk about that," Joe said.

He quickly changed the subject. "Can I ask you a Scrooge question?"

"Of course, dear."

He stepped closer to Mary, lowering his voice. "Is there anything I can do to speed up Victor's Scrooge journey?"

"I wish there was, but he's not an official Scrooge." She sounded displeased.

"He isn't?" Jay jerked back, stunned. "I would have bet money it was him." He frowned. "If he's not the Scrooge, then who is?"

"Why, Catalina, of course."

"What?" Another surprise he hadn't expected. "Are you sure? She's recently been dubbed the Ice Queen, but I think that's a mistake. Victor is so much more the Scrooge type."

"I'm with you there, son," Joe said, watching Victor yell at someone else.

"Why has she been deemed a Scrooge?" Jay asked, still not believing it.

"Like many of our Scrooges, she's given up on love.

And now she's cut herself off from the world so much that she can't even experience the joy of Christmas."

He couldn't deny Catalina's self-isolation. Actors who reached movie-star status often lived sheltered lives. In Catalina's case, the fortress she'd been building around herself was due to the fear of trusting the wrong people. "She's been burned, so she doesn't trust easily anymore."

"Understandable, but I have faith she'll be receiving help in that department," she said, her eyes twinkling.

"I hope so," he said. "I can confirm that the legend is definitely working on her. She swears she doesn't believe in magic or miracles, yet she's been defending the Scrooge Legend, insisting the screenwriter stay as close to Piper's real story as possible."

"That's a great step forward, and I have no doubt she'll continue in the right direction," Mary replied. "Unfortunately, Stan isn't listening to Catalina and is going in the wrong direction. He has thieves stealing Christmas presents and Piper stealing cars."

"He's back to that again?" Jay couldn't understand how the film had ever been green-lit.

She gave him an exhausted look. "We're working on him."

"You're obviously rubbing off on Stan, because he changed the names of the B&B hosts from the last rewrite."

"What were the names before?" Joe asked.

"Petunia and Kenzo."

Both Mary and Joe looked like they'd tasted a sour pickle.

Jay laughed. "I didn't care for the names, either."

Mary sighed. "I don't know if I'll ever understand the Hollywood crowd."

"Except we like Catalina," Joe said.

"Yes, very much so." Mary put a hand to her heart. "You know, Jay, Catalina spent a lot of time watching you before rehearsal, and you didn't even know it."

She did? He wanted to ask how she was watching him—with a smile, a longing, or was she simply distracting herself. "I'm sure she was just getting into character."

"If you say so." She gave him a big smile. "Well, we best get inside and start derailing some of the writer's bright ideas."

"Good catching up with you, Jay." Joe patted him on the back. "Say hi to your folks for us."

"I will."

Jay took a big breath and let it out. Catalina was a Scrooge? Any Scrooge who'd given up on love always found it within a week. Were Mary and Joe right about how she was acting around him? Could she be thinking about him as more than just a friend? Could he dare to hope she'd choose him?

Catalina was a real Scrooge. He smiled. This was a good thing after all.

Chapter Twenty-Two

Catalina finished looking over the latest revised dialogue, then stepped out of her trailer right as Brandi came around the corner.

"Ms. Jones?"

With a long sigh, she turned around, annoyed.

"I thought you should know that when Grayson asked if I wanted to hang out with him on his next movie, I had no idea you were in it," Brandi said in a shy manner. "I apologize if my presence has made you feel uncomfortable. That was not my intention. I told Grayson that I shouldn't be on set when you are, but he insisted and said not to worry about it."

Had she judged Brandi too harshly? Catalina scrutinized her, looking for any indication that the girl was lying, but she couldn't see any. What would be the point for her to offer up any of this information if it wasn't the truth?

"Grayson thinks of himself and his image first," Catalina said. "I appreciate what you've told me, but he's right. I'm not bothered by you being around, and you can let him know that." She was hoping that if Brandi mentioned their talk, he'd stop making a thing out of his

PDAs. Brandi was being used by Grayson, and the poor thing didn't even know it.

"I'll be sure to tell him." She started walking away.

"Brandi?"

She turned back. "Yes?"

"A word of advice? Make sure you really know what his true intentions are before you lose yourself in his world."

She thought about that, then smiled. "I will."

Jay stopped by the wardrobe trailer. "Hey, Valerie, did anyone by chance ask for elf shoes yesterday?"

Her eyes widened. "No. Is this a new scene I don't know about? Has the shooting schedule changed again?"

"No, sorry. I didn't mean to alarm you. I caught something in one of my shots yesterday that looked like elf shoes." He laughed it off because he didn't want to make a thing out of it.

"No one came by, but I do have elf shoes."

"Can I see them?"

"Sure." Valerie disappeared deep into the trailer then came back with a plastic box and took off the lid. There were shoes with red fuzzy balls and some with bells, but they were all red-and-green, not green only.

"You have a great selection, but none of these are what I saw. Thanks for letting me take a look."

"Anytime."

Jay had decided not to ask around, especially now that he knew they hadn't come from the wardrobe department, but he could at least ask Clayton. He hung out, waiting for him to finish giving instructions to his camera guys, then pulled him aside. "Got a minute?"

"Sure."

"Did you catch anything unusual in your dailies last night?" -

"Like what?"

Jay pulled up the photo and showed it to him.

Clayton inspected the elf shoes behind the mailbox. "That's a new one."

"So, you or your camera operator didn't see these before, during, or after filming?"

"Nothing before or during filming, and we went on break right after the take. Do you have another photo?"

"No. I moved on to taking stills of Catalina and Grayson."

Clayton looked at the photo again. "This would have been a good gag to pull on Stan, had he been present."

"Who are the jokesters on this crew?"

"My guys. Practically all of the teamsters, but yesterday was intense. No one would have risked their job pulling something like this." Clayton handed back his camera. "I'll keep an eye out."

"Thanks, Clayton."

"Lock it up!" Mark called out to get the crew to settle, ready to film the first take of the next setup.

Catalina and Grayson faced each other, outside on Mary and Joe's walkway. Catalina felt empowered and in full control of her emotions. She wasn't sure where her strength was coming from, unless it was from all of the self-reflection she'd been doing while getting to know Neil and reconnecting with Jay. Even Mary had gotten her to reflect on some of her recent choices. Now she felt so at ease standing toe-to-toe with Grayson.

"I heard you had a talk with Brandi," he said.

"More like the other way around. She's a smart

woman and knows you're using her to make me jealous. Only I can't figure out why. I didn't break up with you, and I wasn't the one who immediately took up with my next costar."

"So you are jealous."

"Of what?" She shrugged.

"My life. I now have more star power than you. I'm in a relationship. You're not. Should I go on?"

"Please do, since everyone is listening." She tapped her radio mic.

Grayson glanced over at Victor, who was waiting for them to finish.

"Whatever," he said.

Mark yelled for camera and sound to roll and Victor called, "Action!"

Blake squinted at Remington. "I can't get a real read on you, Mr. Savage. You barrel into town, salivating to snap up my mother's property, but then I see you helping one of my neighbors with a fallen tree. I also heard you donated a large sum of money to St. Nicholas's charity for a child in need."

"And you feel those are bad qualities?" Remington asked.

"Quite the opposite. It makes me want to believe that if I sell my mother's house to you instead of letting the bank take it, then you'll treat it with respect. Can you promise me that?"

"I said I would from day one."

"You also said you'd be making major changes."

"Change isn't always bad."

Blake looked away—conflicted, not knowing if she was making the right choice or making the biggest mistake of her life.

"I know you don't trust me, Ms. Dickens, but I keep my word. I will not do anything that will ruin your mother's house or taint her memory. Can you say that about the bank?"

She took a long breath and slowly let it out. "All right. The house is yours. Call me when you're ready to sign the papers."

Blake hurried away, leaving Remington looking after her.

"Cut!" Victor said. "Great."

"Back to one," Mark called out.

Catalina turned around and took her mark, locking her gaze on Grayson, realizing he had never been a man of his word like Remington. How had she missed that? She could have saved herself months of heartache.

Chapter Twenty-Three

Mary climbed the stairs to the second floor, carrying a tray of food. It didn't matter if Stan was a Scrooge, a pre-Scrooge, or just a writer because he was getting the Scrooge Legend all wrong, she needed to do something about it. At least he had no problem devouring whatever food she put in front of him. She shifted the tray to one hand and knocked on his door.

"I'm busy," he said, a little curt. "Leave whatever it is at the door."

"Thought you could use a midmorning snack," she said sweetly. "I know you're hard at work, so I brought you a grilled cheese sandwich and tomato soup."

The door whipped open. "How did you know?"

"Know what?"

"Grilled cheese and tomato soup is my writer's block meal. If a scene isn't working, I go to a diner by my house and order this."

"What a happy coincidence," she said, smiling. "Or maybe it isn't if this means you're having writing issues." She gave him a sympathetic look of concern.

"I am. Because of you." He pulled on his hair. "No offense."

"None taken. May I set this down?"

"Please." He stepped aside, then realized there wasn't a place to set the tray, so he hurried to the table and cleared off a space.

Mary stepped over several pieces of crumpled paper littering the floor, which seemed strange because there was a wastepaper basket right next to the table where he was working. "Sit, eat, and tell me all about it." She sat down, joining him.

"You'll make it worse."

"Did I make it worse when you came up with that incredibly sharp idea of not seeing the mail collector?"

He thought for a moment. "Okay. Here's—"

"Eat."

Stan took a big bite of the grilled cheese. "What is this?" he said with his mouth full, staring at the sandwich.

"Sorry?"

"This is insanely good. What have you put in this?" He took another bite, and she could see tension draining from his face.

She laughed. "Just cheese. Monterey Jack, a little sharp cheddar, and a pinch of oregano."

"Delicious." He took a spoonful of tomato soup. "You put my local diner to shame."

"You're too kind." She waved him away. "Now, tell me about your troubles."

"I don't know where to begin. Blake's shady past doesn't seem to be, I don't know, ringing true, now that I've tweaked other scenes. I don't understand it."

"Maybe you don't need it."

"We're already shooting!" He motioned out the window, stressed. "I've got to have something."

"Mr. Larkin, I'm glad you've taken the time to travel

here. Maybe now you can see for yourself that St. Nicholas isn't any town. The people living here carry a sense of responsibility to show outsiders like yourself how one's life is so very important. Every one of us affects so many others."

He looked at her, a little confused. "I haven't seen any of the town because I've been busy rewriting."

"Fair enough." She folded her hands in her lap. "What I'm trying to get at is this. If Blake were to arrive in a lifeless town, then I can see why your story would need to have all that heightened nefarious stuff going on. But…if Blake comes to an exceptionally special town, one that is so foreign to her, then maybe her exploration of that town would be more intriguing to watch than a bunch of common thieves."

He sipped his soup, mulling over what she was saying. "Okay. I can add more of the talking reindeer and Christmas fairies."

Mary pinched the bridge of her nose, took a deep breath, then focused again on Stan. "*Or* maybe she just needs someone special to listen to her."

"Talking reindeer don't listen?"

"I wouldn't know. I was thinking more on the lines of having deep conversations with her future husband."

He nodded. "The human connection."

"We all need it, but sometimes it's as scarce as gold."

He took another bite of his grilled cheese and stared out the window for a long moment. "It's hard to trust it—to know when it's real."

She saw a shadow of sadness cross his face. "You do understand."

He nodded. "A lot of disappointment during the holidays."

"I'm very sorry to hear that."

He brought his laptop back over and stared at the screen. "I see where this needs to go. Thank you, Mary."

"My pleasure." She got up and went to the door.

"Can I use your scarce-as-gold line?"

She suppressed a laugh. "It's all yours."

They finished shooting all angles on the first scene, and Catalina was told to take a break while they set up for the next one. She texted Neil that she was going for a walk should anyone need her. Even though she'd had total control in her scene with Grayson, it still drained her. What surprised her most was their interaction between takes. She was irritating Grayson, which meant he no longer knew how to manipulate her emotions so easily. The calmer she was, the angrier he got. It was liberating to feel her emotional ties to him slipping away. Coming from a place of strength, she started to see who he really was—a shallow actor who put himself above everyone else.

She bundled up and walked behind the B&B where a good portion of the Carrolls' property extended far into the woods. She stood on the edge of it, taking in the height of the massive trees—some bare branches, some not, but all were blanketed with snow. She closed her eyes and inhaled a deep breath of the clean mountain air, feeling newly energized. When she opened them again, she spied two bucks sparring in a small clearing. They were powerful and magnificent, and she couldn't believe she was so close to such gorgeous animals.

With every passing hour in St. Nicholas, she realized how very special a town it really was. It made perfect sense that Jay would be from here. She'd always felt he was different than the other men she met in LA. She just hadn't been able to pinpoint what it was. His roots were in a hometown with a close-knit community where everyone supported each other and took time to help complete strangers. It was a place that many dreamed of but never had a chance to experience. She could see why he had come back here after leaving LA.

Yesterday she'd wanted to quit, but now she was grateful she'd stayed. Victor's gotcha stunt had helped her to see the real Grayson Edwards through his fake façade. When she spoke her character's dialogue, it was as if she was becoming empowered with every take. She could feel herself starting to let go of her pain from her failed relationship with Grayson, and at the same time, she was finding herself more receptive to Jay.

She heard boots crunching on snow and turned to see Jay walking toward her.

"I thought that was you," he said, coming closer. "Everything okay?"

"Yeah, I just wanted to take a quick walk and get re-energized before I have to do the next scene."

"The scene where Blake and Remington are starting to fall in love."

"That's the one." She suddenly didn't want to talk about Grayson because it felt like she was allowing him to intrude on her time with Jay. "Hey, you know, I just saw two bucks sparring right over there."

He followed her gaze. "That's interesting. I usually see them sparring in October, at the beginning of their mating season, but maybe they've extended their season for love."

She laughed. "Smart animals. I saw a momma deer

and her fawn from my room—though I have no idea how old the little guy was."

"Probably around seven or eight months." He studied the woods, then took a few shots.

She watched him, so focused on his task. "What specifically are you taking photos of?"

"The snow-covered trees. I promised a friend of mine that I'd send him some for a website he's putting together."

"Can I see?" She leaned into him and was suddenly very aware of him—his face only inches from hers. They were the same height, yet he felt taller to her somehow, and she envisioned him putting his arm around her. "It's gorgeous. Reminds me of an Ansel Adams winter landscape, but in color. The snow is so pristine. Not one footprint, not one—wait. Where are the bucks' footprints?"

"We might not be able to see them from here."

They walked farther into the woods, to the clearing where she had seen them sparring, but they were no longer there.

"Listen to how quiet it is." She took a deep breath and looked up at the snowy pines all around her. "I'd forgotten how healing it was to be surrounded by nature."

"Whenever I need to clear my head, I take a long walk through the woods. I even wrote my screenplays out here."

"Really? Even in the winter?"

"No, but weather permitting, I drag out a table and chair and peck away on my laptop."

"Maybe I should suggest that to Stan. It might help to clear out some of his bad ideas."

He laughed, then gazed into her eyes. There was a

tenderness in the way he was looking at her, something she had hoped to experience years ago, before he had disappeared out of her life entirely.

A text dinged, and Catalina flinched. She ignored it, attempting to go "back to one" and reset the moment, as she did every day on set. But the connection was lost. Jay seemed flustered, and her phone dinged again, so she forced herself to look at it. "I'm wanted in hair and makeup."

He reluctantly nodded. "I should get back, too. I need to get some stills of Victor."

"I don't envy your job."

"Maybe he'll be in a good mood." His voice was full of optimism.

Catalina laughed, looking at him. "You're funny."

He smiled, staring into her eyes. "It's always good to dream."

She held his gaze, not letting go. "I couldn't agree more."

To his great surprise, Jay found Victor at the craft service table in a very good mood, though he suspected Piper had something to do with it. She had sent over Dina, her pastry chef, with some of their baked goods from her coffeehouse. Among them was a panettone.

"Are you really? I'm also first-generation Italian." Victor couldn't stop smiling at Dina as she unwrapped her panettone and began slicing it into pieces. "My grandmother always made a panettone for my brothers and me at Christmas," he said. "She spent days curing the dough and always made it in a coffee can. She served it with homemade mascarpone cream and orange marmalade, and it tasted like heaven."

"My mother did the same thing." Dina laughed. "I loved how good the house smelled while it was baking, and I was always right by her side to get the first slice. Over the years, I've tweaked my mom's recipe and have managed to get the prep time down to two days." She handed a slice to Victor. "I hope you like it."

He took a bite, closing his eyes. "Eccezionale," he said in Italian. "Brings me back home."

"I'm glad you like it." She gave him a sweet smile. "I work with Piper, and I'm rolling out a new bakery menu specific to Christmas. I'd love your opinion if you have time to stop by."

"I think I can make that happen," he said, taking another bite.

Jay took a few pictures of them together, and Victor was smiling in every one.

"You're welcome to stay and watch us film," Victor said to her.

"I'd love to, but we have a lot of orders to fill today, so I have to get back."

"I understand deadlines," Victor said. "Grazie, Dina, for helping me to remember home with your delicious panettone." He kissed her hand.

"Piacere," she replied.

Theo hurried over. "Sir, we're ready for you."

"Thank you, Theo." Victor smiled at Dina, then calmly walked away with his assistant.

"Amazing," Jay said to Dina after he left.

"What is?"

"Victor's dramatic personality change. I've never seen him smile or say thank you to anyone."

"I imagine there's a lot of pressure being a director,"

she said, then suddenly gave Jay an embarrassed look. "You, having directed yourself, would know."

"There is a lot of pressure, but some handle it better than others," he said. "Did you or Piper know he was Italian?"

"No, but I suspected he was from his last name. Turns out his family lived about twenty miles away from mine in Northern Italy."

"Are you serious?"

"Small world."

"You singlehandedly put him in a good mood for the rest of the day, and the crew and I thank you for that."

"I'm pretty sure it was the panettone," she said.

"He didn't kiss the panettone. He kissed the hand that made it."

After Dina left, Jay took a look at the photos he'd taken of the woods, wishing he and Catalina could still be out there. Was it his imagination, or had she been flirting with him a little? Jay clicked on the first photo he took for his friend and noticed something deep in the background. It looked to be a small herd of deer. Could they be the bucks Catalina had been talking about? He zoomed in on the background.

They weren't bucks but actually reindeer, which were not native to their area. One reindeer was in midair in an unusually high jump. If he didn't know better, he'd think it was lifting off the ground. Of course, he'd never know for sure. Half the photo was inexplicably whited out.

Chapter Twenty-Four

As Catalina walked by Grayson on the way to the set, he planted a kiss on Brandi, who appeared completely taken off guard. Catalina inwardly smiled, knowing his actions no longer held any power over her.

Once on set, Grayson stepped up to her. "This is a great little town," he said. "Not much nightlife, but then Brandi and I know how to entertain each other." He laughed. "What did you do last night?"

She peered at him, annoyed, growing weary of him. "What's the point of this conversation?"

"Just making small talk."

"It is small, so stop."

"Rehearsal's up," Mark called out as Victor came over, and he didn't look happy.

"Whatever is going on with you two, figure it out fast," he said. "You look no more in love with each other than my dog does with my neighbor's cat."

She didn't want to think about Grayson romantically at all. She glanced over at Jay and was flooded with good memories of their friendship on the set of *Sage Under Fire*. She thought about their dinner last night, and the short walk in the woods they'd just taken. She had really missed him, all these years.

"And action!"

"Don't tell me you're here to yell at me again," Remington said to Blake as he opened the door at the B&B.

"Just the opposite," she replied, smiling. "I wanted to thank you. The wall sconces you chose for my mother's house—they're beautiful, and they look like they've belonged there for years."

"You stopped by the house?"

"I did."

"To check up on me or on my work?"

"Maybe a little bit of both." Blake raised a brow.

Remington looked flattered but anxious. "What did you think of the kitchen?"

"Impressive. Your electrician said you've been working day and night."

"Guilty."

"How did you match the lights in the library?"

"A buddy of mine who also restores homes just so happened to have them."

"Incredible. Truly. Thank you."

Remington moved closer to her. "You're quite welcome." He gazed into her eyes and slowly reached to kiss her, but the B&B front door opened, startling them apart as it was written in the script. Grayson, however, pulled Catalina to him and kissed her anyway.

She jerked back, pushing him away. "What's wrong with you?"

"Cut!" Victor stormed over and glared at Grayson. "What are you doing?"

"Oh, I wasn't supposed to kiss her?" he asked innocently.

"We're behind," Victor said, staring down his rogue actor. "Stay on point."

"Back to one," Marked called out.

"Stick to the script," she warned Grayson.

"I thought I was." He shrugged with a gloating grin.

"Picture's up. Last looks," Mark announced.

Alyssa flew in and fixed Catalina's lipstick, while she got herself together and tried to calm down, but she was still so angry.

She glanced over at Jay, who was glaring at Grayson with an intensity she hadn't seen before. He was standing now and closer—just out of frame, as if he were a bouncer ready to pounce on her ex should he step out of line again. That alone made her smile—and feel secure.

When Victor called action, she thought about her dinner with Jay and how much fun they had talking and catching up. She kept visualizing him in front of her as she spoke her lines to Grayson, who barely managed to stay on script. This time the scene worked perfectly.

After they shot all angles on the scene, Jay came in to take several stills.

"Be sure to get my good side," Grayson said to Jay as he stood in front of Catalina, posing. "Oh, wait. I guess I don't have a bad side."

"Why are you being so obnoxious?" she asked Grayson as Jay moved around them.

"I'm just having a little fun. Where's your sense of humor?"

"I take my job seriously. Maybe you should think about doing the same."

"Great job, guys. We're now at lunch," Mark said, coming over. "We're moving back to the Andersons' for the mailbox pickup and Blake's scene with her mom. Take your time getting over there. The crew will still need to break down everything here, then set up over there."

"Looks like I'll get to kiss you today after all." Grayson chuckled as a sound assistant helped him and Catalina remove their radio mics. Grayson walked away, whistled to Brandi, who promptly ran over to him. He hooked her neck with his arm, and they walked off toward his trailer.

Catalina ignored his immature behavior and focused on Jay.

"I got some great ones of you just now." He searched through his photos, then found several good shots in a row and showed them to her.

She really did look good. And that was all Jay's doing. "When I think about the hundreds of stills from all of my movies, there are maybe twenty I've liked over the years. These are all great, Jay." She handed back his camera. "You're an amazing photographer."

"I've got a great subject." He took another one of her as she looked directly into his lens. "Stunning." He made her laugh, and she appeared embarrassed, so he kept clicking until she put her hand over the lens.

"Did you get any good ones of Victor earlier?"

"Actually, I did. Dina, Piper's pastry chef, brought over a bunch of baked goods. Her Italian sweet bread put a big smile on his face."

"Really? I wouldn't have expected Victor to like anything sweet."

"He not only devoured the panettone, but he seemed very taken with Dina."

Catalina let out a tiny gasp. Had suggesting Victor as a Scrooge actually worked?

Jay studied her. "What?"

She shook her head, smiling.

"You've got a twinkle in your eye."

"I do?"

"Yeah. You used to get it a lot, when you had a fun, little secret."

She felt heat in her cheeks. "I did?"

He nodded, grinning, stepping closer to her. "And you always told me what it was."

She remembered. She'd often search for things to tell him because Jay loved hearing secrets so much. He was very funny that way. It seemed so out of character for him—especially since he never gossiped about anyone.

"Okay, but you have to keep this quiet." She moved even closer to him. "Not that I totally believe in your Scrooge Legend, but I decided to suggest Victor as a Scrooge last night."

Jay's jaw dropped as his eyes shot wide. "What?"

She nodded, still keeping her voice down. "Neil found out that Victor had lost his parents at Christmas as a boy, so I thought maybe he'd be happier if he wasn't a Scrooge anymore."

Jay ran a hand over his mouth. "And in less than twenty-four hours, Victor's completely enamored by an Italian woman who brings over a panettone." He grinned. "I'd kiss you right now if we weren't surrounded by a production crew."

She laughed and found herself eyeing his lips. "Too bad we are." She could feel the charged electricity between them. She wanted to take his hand but couldn't without someone seeing it.

A few grips started working around them, so she reluctantly took a step back. "Do you believe Victor met Dina because of the Scrooge Legend?"

"Guaranteed. And I have the proof." He held up his camera. "Check out how different he is."

Catalina sat in her set chair and clicked through Jay's stills. "Wow. These are very rare photos. Victor actually seems happy." She studied the look in his eyes—a look of unexpected joy. "He's definitely smiling because of Dina—though he's seriously enjoying the panettone, too."

"Everyone has a weakness."

She handed Jay back his camera. "What's yours?"

He fixed his gaze on her. "You."

She shook her head, attempting to contain her smile. "I mean, what sugary sweet is your weakness?"

"You. With a chocolate silk pie."

She laughed. "So that's why you ordered it for us last night."

He scratched the back of his head. "I wish I hadn't. My mom made me an entire pie and surprised me with it when I got home."

"Oh, no. Did you have to stuff down another slice?"

"A tiny one." He enlarged his cheeks with a breath, commenting on how he felt afterwards.

"You poor thing." She playfully put her hand on his arm.

"What's your sweet-tooth weakness?" he asked.

"There are too many to count, but I'd say it's a tie between homemade banana ice cream and saltwater taffy."

"I would have pegged you for chocolate truffles."

"Those are good, too, but my dad used to make my brother and me homemade ice cream in the summer, and my mom taught us how to pull taffy in the winter."

"You pulled taffy?"

"Three Christmases in a row," she said. "It's really

hard to do. Come to think of it, the ice cream was hard labor as well since my family only had an old-fashioned hand crank ice cream maker."

"So you've pretty much had to work for your desserts."

"Burns the calories before you consume them."

Jay laughed. "You might be on to a new weight-loss fad."

Neil came over. "Sorry to interrupt, but here are the latest sides for your next scene. A few line revisions, and you'll be interested to see the revision that Victor personally asked for."

"Thanks, Neil." She took the sides, curious to see what he was talking about, skimmed through the new dialogue, and then gasped. "He took out the kiss."

"You're kidding." Jay glanced over her shoulder.

"It used to be after this exchange," she said, showing him. "I can't believe it. I love this scene now. Not only did Stan get rid of the ridiculous snowman, but Victor got rid of the kiss. I obviously didn't want to kiss Grayson to begin with. But as a scene, I thought the kiss was premature. Blake and Remington were only on their official first date."

"See? The Scrooge Legend is hard at work," Jay said. "It's opening Victor's eyes, heart, and mind. He saw how uncomfortable you were with Grayson's unexpected kiss, and it actually bothered him."

"I'd like to think that he was taking my feelings into account, but maybe he was just in a good mood because of Dina."

"Then I'd think he'd want to keep the kiss in. You helped him to see how his gotcha stunt is affecting you every day," Jay pointed out. "The Scrooge Legend often holds up a mirror to those needing to see their behavior and how it's affecting others."

"Something we all need to do," she said. "Though, if asked, I'll never admit to making him an official Scrooge Legend Scrooge."

"No shame in that," he said. "You know, I was so convinced that Victor was a Scrooge, I asked Mary how I could help him change faster. I was absolutely shocked to learn he wasn't an official Scrooge. Of course, now that you suggested him, he's going to change so fast. You'll see."

"Wait. Mary has some kind of Scrooge list?"

"No list, but a few of our B&B proprietors know who the Scrooges are since they host their complimentary stay."

"What?" Catalina shook her head quickly as if that would get rid of her confusion. "Are you telling me that the Scrooge invitation is a real thing?"

"I thought you already knew that." He gave her a surprised look. "Didn't you talk to Piper?"

"Yes, but she never told me she received an invitation, and it's certainly not in the script. Stan went back to his original idea. Talking reindeer and Christmas fairies lead her to St. Nicholas as she's fleeing from the cops in a stolen car."

Jay groaned, rubbing his forehead. "Here are the facts. Piper had been wanting to visit her mom, but they'd had a difficult relationship after her father died. She thought about coming for a visit several times, but she was low on cash. Then she received an invitation in the mail for a free week's stay at one of the B&Bs here in town. That invitation prompted her to finally come to St. Nicholas because she knew she could always stay somewhere for free if it didn't go well with her mom. I'm surprised she didn't tell you, since it's common knowledge in town."

Catalina sat back at this revelation. "It might have been because she was too stunned to hear that Stan had drastically changed her life on paper. I have to say, I'm a little stunned, too. I can't believe the invitation is real. I thought it was a clever marketing tool. Are they always for a free week at a bed-and-breakfast, and only for Scrooges?"

"Yes, why?"

"Because I got one."

Jay nodded. "I heard."

She jerked back and glared at him. "You knew and didn't say anything?"

"I just found out this morning. And the only reason I know is because of my inquiry about Victor."

"He was never considered a Scrooge, but I was?"

Jay didn't answer, but his very uncomfortable look did.

"You're trying to tell me that I'm considered to be a real Scrooge, not the pretend Scrooge in the movie, but a real Scrooge Legend Scrooge?"

"I was equally shocked to learn that from Mary," he said. "*I* don't think you are. I seriously don't see it."

"Well, somebody does!" She threw up her hands in exasperation. "Who suggested me?"

"I don't know. You'll have to ask Mary and Joe."

Catalina rose and stormed up the steps of the B&B. She whipped open the door, expecting to see some of the producers still in the living room, but everyone had already cleared out. She heard Christmas music coming from the kitchen and marched in to find Mary pulling out a tray of Christmas cookies from the oven while Joe was hovering next to a batch cooling on a rack.

"I'm a Scrooge?"

"Well, hello, Catalina." Mary smiled at her pleasantly. "Cookie?"

"No, I do not want a cookie. I want some answers!"

"Don't we all," she said with a sigh.

Joe took a sugar cookie off the cooling rack and shoved it in his mouth.

"Won't you have a seat?" Mary motioned to a barstool.

"I don't want to sit, either." Catalina remained firmly planted where she was.

"I'm afraid I'll have to insist," Mary said. "It's our one house rule, which all guests must abide by. We don't discuss anything of great importance until everyone has had a chance to calm down." She poured a cup of hot cider and set it by the closest barstool.

Catalina was cold, and now cranky, and though she didn't want to admit it, she could really go for a cup of hot cider. She inhaled a deep breath, let it out with an irritated sigh, then parked herself on the stool. "Who said I was a Scrooge?"

"We don't know. It's usually a family member or a best friend, but whoever it was did it out of love." Mary took a dozen cookies off a hot baking sheet and placed them on a cooling rack. She set an English toffee bar and a few decorated cookies on a plate, along with cheese and crackers, then set it in front of Catalina.

Catalina made the mistake of looking at the goodies. She wanted to eat all of it and called on her willpower not to do so as she dealt with the matter at hand.

"I thought my invitation was a clever way for you to get my attention for free advertising."

"We'd never do something so outlandish, and we have no control over who gets an invitation and when. We only host those who need our help." Mary rolled out the rest of the cookie dough.

Catalina glanced at the sugar cookie in front of her. It was a snowman decorated with a silver-starred blue scarf, exactly like the one the actor in the snowman costume wore yesterday. It was another weird coincidence. She took a bite of English toffee instead and immediately regretted it, knowing she'd be eating the rest.

She watched Mary cut the dough with Christmas cookie cutters, trying to make sense of everything. She sipped her cider, and she could swear it was relaxing her but energizing her at the same time. The cheese and crackers looked too good to ignore, so she helped herself, still trying to wrap her head around the fact that she was a Scrooge.

"I can't believe someone actually suggested me as a Scrooge to you."

"To Santa," Mary clarified. "We only host Scrooges."

"I don't believe in Santa, so who really gets the suggestions?"

"Just because you don't believe in him doesn't mean he doesn't exist." Mary raised a brow, looking at her intently.

She had to think about that for a moment. "Okay, I'll suspend reality and accept that Santa invited me here, even though I was already coming here because of the movie, but what I—"

"Were you?" Joe asked. "Or did you get the part in the movie because Santa wanted you to be here?"

She'd like to argue with Joe, but couldn't because the movie practically came out of nowhere, and her negotiations to star in it happened almost overnight. "I see what you're saying, but the big question is why? Why am *I* a Scrooge? If anybody is a Scrooge, it's Victor. And if *Santa* is so good at his job, why did I have to be the one to drop Victor's name in the mailbox before he was officially recognized as a Scrooge?"

Mary stared at her excitedly. "*You* were the one who suggested him?"

"Yes."

Mary gasped. "We just found out an hour ago. Now, it all makes sense—why our other guests went to Hawaii, and why Victor moved over here from the hotel. Your journeys are interconnected. You're helping each other. Because of you, his life is going to turn around. It's a wonderful thing that you've done, Catalina."

Could any of what Mary was saying be true? Was she connected to Victor? Would he become a better person because of her? If he changed, she'd not only have proof that the Scrooge Legend was real, but she'd have to change her whole way of thinking as to what was possible in this world.

"I don't see how I could be connected to Victor in any way," she said. "But I'm glad I could help." She sat back, having a hard time grasping the constant Scrooge Legend connections. Did she really need to understand it? No. The end result was what mattered. "So, what happens now? Do I get a certificate because I've graduated from Scrooge school?"

Mary looked to Joe, then back at her, then to Joe again.

"You can't be serious." She toggled her gaze between the two. "I can't possibly still be considered a Scrooge."

"Well…" Mary gave her a pained look.

"Why?"

"You don't believe in Santa, which means you don't believe in the magic of Christmas or have the Christmas spirit, and you swore off love," Joe said flatly.

"Joe!"

"Just cutting to the chase," he said to Mary.

"I don't see why any of that matters." Catalina scowled.

"Your beliefs and attitudes affect your behavior, which in turn affects all," Mary said, in a gentle, pleasant voice.

"No, my mood might affect a few at most."

"Isn't the entire crew affected by Victor's foul moods?"

"Okay, I see your point, but not everyone believes or gets excited about Christmas, and they do just fine. My skepticism isn't the reason for my unhappiness, and I didn't swear off love." She found herself getting angry and she didn't know why. She took a breath, and a sip of cider, suddenly feeling a little emotional. Maybe she had sworn off love. She took another breath, then began again. "I can't fall in love again because I can't trust it to be real, and I don't want to be hurt like I was with Grayson."

"Just because there's one bad apple in the bunch, it doesn't mean the whole jug of apple cider tastes terrible," Mary said.

"Grayson is more than a bad apple. Our entire relationship was a lie, which made me never want to get into another serious relationship again. Before coming here, I had resigned myself to the possibility that I might be single for the rest of my life, and you know what? I'm fine with that."

"How can you be fine with missing out on a deep,

honest connection?" Mary placed the cut-out cookie dough on a baking tray, then handed it off to Joe, so he could add colorful sprinkles and candied decorations. "You once gave Grayson your heart, but now you have it back to give to the one who deserves it."

"Or maybe I should just keep it safe and free from injury." Catalina sat back, crossing her arms.

"You can keep it to yourself, but then won't you be cutting yourself off from a wonderful part of life?"

"I make my living with emotions, and I can tell you for a fact that it's all fake. Present company excluded, of course. True love is a beautiful idea, but for the majority of us it remains just an idea. People only think they fall in love, and when they're hooked and have given part of themselves away, things change, layers of a person are peeled back, often revealing lies and deceit."

"I suppose that does happen more often than any of us wish, but true love is not just an idea. It's real," Mary said. "I can promise you that." She beamed at her husband.

"Thirty-five blissful years," Joe said, and the look on his face told Catalina that he meant it.

Even if she didn't want to believe them, her eyes didn't lie. The man was decorating Christmas cookies for his wife. "I can see the love between you two is real, but did you ever consider that you were just incredibly lucky to find one another?"

"Lucky, grateful, blessed. Yes, we are all those things," Mary said. "But it started with one simple belief. The belief in love, which is what Christmas is all about. You have to believe that love will find you, Catalina, just like love will find Victor."

Mary began icing a tray of cooled gingerbread cookies. "Do you know who is lucky?" she asked. "Those who get Scrooge invitations because, as a Scrooge, love envelopes you the moment you step foot in our town. Your true love is put in your path. You might not be aware of the incredible love surrounding you at first, but it begins to work on you." She winked with a nod of her head. "You've only been here for three days, and you are a much different woman than the one I met getting off of the helicopter."

She thought about her past three days. She was less anxious, more positive, trusted the people around her more. She was letting her guard down with Jay. "I do feel different."

"It shows. But there is one thing you haven't quite embraced." Mary looked at her.

Catalina already knew what it was. She didn't trust love to be real. She'd become unhappy when Grayson dumped her, and then everything started going wrong after that. She was miserable, and she was most miserable at Christmas. The holiday season was too joyful for her state of mind. Believing in the magic of Christmas, having faith that the right person was out there for her—they were two separate ideas connected by love.

She was just starting to feel more like her old light-hearted self whenever she was with Jay, but then she was about to sabotage it. For what reason? Because he hadn't told her she was a Scrooge? He'd only known for a few hours. She couldn't blame him for not saying anything. They were working. If the situation had been reversed, she wouldn't have told him until after they wrapped.

Jay, Neil, Victor, Grayson—it was as if they were all playing their parts perfectly in her journey as a Scrooge.

Before she arrived in St. Nicholas, she had dreaded the day she would run into Grayson again. She'd ruminated on it for months, wondering what she would say, worrying that she'd somehow reveal how much he had devastated her.

But then Victor had unleashed his nasty surprise, and she couldn't have planned it better herself. The first words she'd uttered to Grayson had not been her own. Hiding behind her character, speaking Blake's words, had given her cover. The shock of seeing him had infuriated her, which came across as being strong and in control, instead of bursting into tears as she'd assumed she would do. This had allowed her to finally have closure on a painful end to a relationship so that she could be more receptive to a potential future one.

Then there was Neil, who'd fast become a caring and considerate assistant. He'd allowed her to take down some of her protective walls and trust him. Could she finally be surrounding herself with good, solid, trustworthy relationships?

And what about Jay? She had never stopped thinking about him all these years. When their friendship dissolved after the film festival, his absence in her life had put a hole in her heart—one she'd never thought would heal. If she hadn't been cast specifically in a movie about his hometown legend, where the movie was not only shooting on location, but shooting a month early, she would have never reconnected with him.

The synchronicity of it all was like magic. *Christmas magic.* Her hosts would wholeheartedly agree—only she wasn't entirely sold. She had to give some credit to her Ice Queen persona. It had toughened her up—allowing her to handle Grayson and Victor. As for Neil, it wasn't Christmas magic that had given her such a great assistant. Erin had vetted him thoroughly. Jay might believe in Christmas magic, but she knew the reason they reconnected was nothing more than coincidence.

What about Neil meeting Iris? Was that also a coincidence? Victor had actually smiled today—a new world record. Could that be a coincidence, too? There were an awful lot of them that she couldn't explain away.

She wanted to believe, she truly did. She wanted to know what it felt like—to totally and completely entrust your heart to the person who was meant to be yours. But even if soul mates were real, being who she was, someone who lived in the celebrity spotlight, made it all the more impossible to experience that kind of deep connection. For people like her, real happiness and true love often remained just out of reach.

Chapter Twenty-Five

"Major news," Catalina said as she walked at a fast clip to the car with Neil. "And to be honest, I'm not sure what to think about it."

"What is it?" he asked, trying to keep up.

Catalina glanced around to make sure Victor wasn't within earshot. "Victor is officially a Scrooge."

Neil's eyes shot wide. "How do you know?"

"Mary told me. They host Scrooges. Neil, I'm also a Scrooge."

He stopped dead in his tracks. "What?"

"The invitation I got from Mary is an official Scrooge invitation."

"But you're not a Scrooge."

"It's okay. I am or was," she said as they kept walking. "I'm not exactly sure where I stand, but I don't want to be a Scrooge if I still am."

"You couldn't be." He looked at her, still confused. "Victor is way more of a Scrooge than anyone I've ever known."

"This is crazy. The more I try to dismiss this, the more it doesn't make sense if I do. I can understand how I got an invitation because of my growing Ice Queen reputation, but how did anyone know we suggested Victor as a Scrooge?"

"Surveillance."

She closed her eyes as her shoulders fell. "Yes, of course. Surveillance." She continued to walk with Neil, then slowed, feeling that wasn't quite right. "But how did Victor get injected with nicer-guy genes overnight? In less than twenty-four hours, he's different. He noticed Grayson's bad behavior toward me, actually cared about my feelings, and took out the kiss in the scene."

"Maybe it's a one-off."

"I thought the exact same thing, but he also met someone today." She eyed Neil. "Piper's pastry chef, Dina, is Italian—just like Victor."

Neil's jaw dropped. "Could the Scrooge Legend actually be real?" He held open the back car door for Catalina, but she didn't get in.

"How about I sit up front?"

A broad smile took over his face. "I'd love that."

Neil opened the passenger door and she got inside, desperately wanting to figure this out. She had to take herself out of the equation because it would only cloud her thinking. This left Victor and Neil.

Neil pulled out of the driveway and headed down a back road—a shortcut to the Andersons'.

"Mary said Victor would be a completely changed man in one week's time," she said, glancing at Neil. "It seems like fantasy, doesn't it?"

"A day ago, I would have said yes, but I watched him watch you and Grayson, and there was something behind his eyes. He looked uncomfortable, as if he was embarrassed by the gotcha stunt he created, and I think he's questioning Grayson as his choice for the leading man. The fire you had in your eyes when Grayson kissed you was also hard to miss. Victor suddenly got angry and was glaring at Grayson before he went over to talk to you two."

"And what about you and Iris? People meet all the time on movies. Do you think you might want to date her after we wrap?"

"Definitely," he said without hesitation. "I stopped by yesterday when you went to dinner with Jay. She's pretty cool. She loves sci-fi like I do, and hangs out at the beach in Santa Monica. Did I tell you that she lives in Encino? And here's something totally freaky. She lives in my apartment complex."

"What?" Catalina glanced at Neil, thinking he was kidding. "Are you being serious?"

He nodded. "I live on the first floor, and she lives on the third."

A Scrooge Legend orchestration? "And you had to travel to a small mountain town in Colorado in order to meet."

"How crazy is that?" He laughed. "And you had to travel here to run into your first film director, Jay. There seems to be an awful lot of coincidences happening up here."

"Yes, there are." Were there too many coincidences to be coincidence?

"I saw some of Jay's stills from yesterday." Neil gave her a quick glance. "They're incredible."

"He's very talented."

"Do you think he'll return to LA and continue directing?"

"Hard to say, but I hope he does." She wasn't sure if Neil was asking her if there was more to her friendship with Jay. "Like you, he's a good guy," she said, not able to hide the tenderness in her voice when she thought of him.

"Hollywood could definitely use more good guys." Neil turned on to the Andersons' street and started searching for Catalina's trailer.

"Have you reached a conclusion on your experiment? Do you think your wish is coming true with Iris?"

He parked right behind her trailer and turned off the car. "I'd like to think I was smart enough to recognize someone who had a lot in common with me. At the same time, with Victor being a Scrooge, and with what you just said—that it took Iris and me to travel here to meet—I do think my wish was granted." He looked at her intently. "And I truly hope that yours was granted, too."

After Jay grabbed a bite to eat, he talked with Mr. Anderson and showed him the picture of the elf shoes. Mr. Anderson was astounded to see how it looked so much like the one Jay's father had taken on the stakeout last year. He also confirmed that his grandkids hadn't been anywhere near the set.

Jay stood at the fake Santa's mailbox, ready to investigate the last plausible explanation for the photo. He checked out the shapes of the trees and any light reflections behind it. Nothing could be misconstrued as elf shoes behind a mailbox. He pulled up the photo in question for reference, in order to find the exact angle and distance from where he had taken the shot before. He looked through the viewfinder, snapped several shots, but wasn't seeing anything unusual.

"Already hard at work?" Catalina asked.

He whipped around, not expecting to see her so soon on set. "Oh, uh, just taking pictures of the mailbox." He threw his camera strap over his shoulder. "Look, about earlier, I wasn't trying to keep anything from you."

"I know. I shouldn't have reacted the way I did. I was just so surprised to learn that I was a Scrooge and that Erin, who's not only my manager but my dearest friend, is most likely the one who suggested me."

"She wouldn't have done it if she didn't care about you."

She nodded. "Erin's been worried about my reputation as the Ice Queen even though she knows it's just an act."

"I knew it! I knew you couldn't have changed that drastically."

"I have changed, but I'm finding my way back," she said, smiling at him, as if she were trying to say that he had helped in her transformation.

"That's what the Scrooge Legend does."

"Mary said as much, though apparently my being a Scrooge has nothing to do with the Ice Queen. It's more about my lack of the Christmas spirit, not believing in the magic of Christmas, and having lost my faith in love."

"All good things," he said, "which you're meant to have."

"I'm not disagreeing, though shouldn't I be a little wary of something that's promised to happen in less than a week? The time frame seems impractical. Even for a movie."

"You're in St. Nicholas, where the impractical and impossible happen all the time."

She smiled. "I'd really like to believe that."

"Have I ever been known to exaggerate?"

"Don't know." She met his gaze. "I haven't exactly been around you the past seven and a half years."

"Then I guess I'm going to have to prove it to you."

"You're going to show me real evidence of Christmas magic?"

He nodded, though he wasn't exactly sure what he was going to show her. He didn't have any hard evidence, and even if he did, it would only be explained away by a skeptic. But the people whose lives were changed knew without a doubt that it was real. He didn't need Catalina to believe in it wholeheartedly. He just hoped she would be open to the possibilities, and maybe allow herself to believe in something more tangible— like love, and him.

"So when am I going to see this evidence?"

"Tonight."

She laughed, then saw that he was being serious. "I'm going to hold you to it. Tonight, it is."

Chapter Twenty-Six

Grayson finally managed to come out of his trailer and join Catalina on set, and boy was he in a bad mood. "Did you see this?" he asked, waving the revised sides in her face. "They took out our kiss."

She tamped down her giddiness. "Well, Blake and Remington are only on their first date."

"A first date after they've fallen in love."

"It's an almost kiss." She shrugged. "Why are you so hung up on it?"

He shoved his hands in his pockets, and the expression on his face reminded her of a lost little boy she encountered one time at an airport. "I've missed kissing you."

She would have given anything to hear him speak those words months ago, even weeks ago, but now it just made her uncomfortable. "Guess you should have thought about the repercussions of your actions before you broke up with me, but you didn't." She narrowed her eyes on him. "Let me be clear. The feeling is not mutual."

His shoulders slumped as he cast his gaze to the ground.

"Wake up, Grayson. You have a new girlfriend."

"I really don't know if I do. She's an actress. I'm getting the feeling that she's only with me to further her own career."

Exactly what he had done to her. Karma had found him after all. "How does that make you feel?"

"How do you think it makes me feel?" Irritation ran through his voice.

"Then break up with her." Something she wished she had done with him. The only difference was that Catalina had been in love with Grayson, whereas Grayson clearly wasn't in love with Brandi.

Brandi was watching him from the sidelines. She waved at him and blew him a kiss. "I don't know," he said, pretending to catch the kiss. "She might not be able to live without me."

Catalina laughed at his sheer arrogance. "I did."

"Barely."

She stiffened. "Don't believe everything you read."

"All right." Victor clapped his hands together as he approached them. "Any questions on the scene revisions before we start shooting?"

"I don't like that Stan cut the kiss."

"I do. Any other questions?" Victor looked to Catalina, and she shook her head, smiling. "Good. Let's do this." Victor winked at her before he turned away.

"Last looks!" Mark called to the crew.

Catalina and Grayson took their places on the park bench by the mailbox. Alyssa flew in to put a little powder on Catalina's nose while her stylist fixed a stray hair.

Once everyone was settled, and camera and sound were rolling, Victor called, "Action!"

A featured extra made a deposit into Santa's mailbox, then walked away as Blake and Remington watched her.

"And just like that, someone's life is about to change for the better." Blake motioned toward the mailbox.

Remington laughed. "You want me to believe that the little piece of metal over there brought us together?"

"It's our town's history," Blake said. "The mailbox began with Christmas wishes. I've never believed in the magic of Christmas or the granting of wishes, but for my mother's sake, I wished for my soul mate, and then I turned around and ran right into you."

"Actually, you yelled at me and accused me of being a house thief."

She laughed. "I didn't know you then. If I'd been able to see what you were going to do to my mom's house, well, maybe I would have called you a house savior instead of a house stealer."

Remington held her hand. "I think I like that. Maybe I'll put it on my restoration website." He studied the mailbox. "Who picks up the wishes, and where do they go?"

"Like the Scrooge suggestions, they go to Santa," Blake said. "And they're picked up by one of his helpers."

He laughed.

"Right around this time of day."

"If you say so."

Bells jingled off-screen.

Remington squinted at the mailbox. "Is that...?"

Blake sat up straight. "What?"

"I thought I saw—No. Impossible." He shook his head. "I don't believe in stuff like that."

"What do you believe in?"

"Deep honest connections between two people. Real love." He brushed her face with his hand. "You." He stared intently into her eyes and moved to kiss her when a woman walked right by them to use the mailbox, interrupting the moment.

Remington stood and held his hand out for Blake. "Come on. I want to show you something."

"And cut!" Victor said.

"Great," Mark relayed. "Going again."

As Catalina went back to first position, she thought about the new dialogue, which was eerily familiar to the conversation she'd had with Mary and Joe. She was sure the words were lost on the very guy who spoke them, but they weren't lost on her. She just realized why love never felt real. Her past relationships, especially the one with Grayson, had been missing an honest connection. If she *could* finally have one, then maybe she'd be able to put her faith in love again.

She looked at Jay, who happened to be taking a picture of her that very moment. He lowered his camera, made eye contact with her and smiled. He, more than anyone else around her, understood what a deep honest connection really meant. And that was very real.

After their scene, Grayson wrapped out for the day, which meant Jay could take a moment to look through his photos while the crew set up for the next scene. He never wanted to step away from set when Grayson was around Catalina. Not that she would need his help. She had put her ex in his place more than once. Still, Jay told her he'd have her back on and off set, and he meant it.

Jay set down his gear at a table near craft service and started scanning the shots he took of the mailbox and the area around it. As he expected, nothing could be misconstrued as green elf shoes. He couldn't even blame a Christmas decoration being misplaced since Mr. Anderson hadn't started decorating.

He had a photo of elf shoes that appeared only in one frame, and another photo of reindeer that didn't inhabit the area. Nothing really earth-shattering there, but the position of the shoes really had him intrigued. If he were the mail collector sent to investigate, then saw someone else not only removing the mail but dropping it carelessly on the ground, he'd risk being seen to retrieve every piece. Though everyone on the film crew knew it was just a movie, Catalina's repeated heartfelt prayer as Blake could have easily drawn attention from someone who didn't know it was fake. It wasn't unheard of. There were reports of miracles happening on the set while filming *The Passion* and *The Bible*, so why couldn't it happen on their movie?

He headed over to Catalina's trailer to see if she was available for dinner when Grayson's door flung open with a loud bang.

"You're such a jerk! Forget I even asked," a tearful Brandi yelled at Grayson before she ran down his trailer steps.

Grayson, appearing somewhat confused, grabbed the door to close it when he saw Jay staring at him. Grayson looked as if he was about to say something, but declined, and shut his door right as Catalina opened hers.

"What was that all about?" she asked Jay as he came over.

"Trouble in Grayson's paradise. Brandi just left in tears."

"Uh-oh. I hope I didn't cause it." Catalina seemed genuinely concerned.

"How?"

"He was complaining to me earlier, and I literally said, 'Then break up with her.'"

"Good advice, but still not your fault," he said. "If they did break up, Brandi is better off."

Grayson came out of his trailer, saw her talking with Jay, turned back around, and left for the night.

"He creates more drama than any of my high school friends ever did," Catalina said.

"At least he's wrapped for the day."

"Yes." She seemed happy about that and let out a long, satisfied sigh.

That sigh made him suddenly think about their time on his film. They had just shot the last scene in the movie—Catalina's character was riding bareback on her horse along the beach. It had been an absolutely gorgeous day by the ocean. After they wrapped, she asked him to walk along the beach with her. As the waves splashed over their feet, she had let out a long vocal sigh of complete satisfaction. She'd then tucked her arm inside his and said, "I love my life."

He'd smiled, locking his gaze on her, and said, "I do, too."

Catalina cleared her throat. "What are you thinking about?"

"Oh." He snapped back to the present and looked away, a little embarrassed. "I'd forgotten how much you study people."

"Part of my job." Her stare was still intense, not letting him off the hook.

He placed his foot on one of her trailer steps. "I, uh…"

"Ms. Jones, we're ready for you on set," Mark said, stopping by.

"On my way," she replied, still keeping her focus on

Jay. "I remember that look. You were miles away." She lifted a brow. "See you on set."

"Yes. See you out there."

Chapter Twenty-Seven

On set Pauline, the actress playing Blake's mom, was standing by the mailbox. Catalina had hit it off with the older actress during the table read, but she hadn't personally connected to the scene—until now. The dialogue reminded Catalina of her conversation with Mary and Joe. *Another coincidence or the Scrooge Legend at work?*

Pauline greeted her with a big smile. "It's so good to see you again, Catalina."

"And you," she said. "When did you arrive?"

"Last night. This town is *gorgeous*. I've got to bring my husband here for a visit."

"It is beautiful. I felt like I'd walked onto one of our Christmas sets."

"Only this place feels magical, doesn't it?"

"Afternoon, Pauline," Victor said, coming over. "Pretty straightforward scene. Do a slow build with the emotional aspect of it. Any questions?"

"No, I'm good," Pauline said, and Catalina shook her head.

"Then let the magic begin," Victor said with a smile, and she couldn't help but notice how many times the word *magic* was being thrown around.

Victor stepped away, and his first AD took over.

"Rehearsal's up!" Mark called out. "Settle."

The women took their places in front of the mail-box. Catalina spied Jay crouching just out of frame. She loved having him near when she was working—and when she wasn't. She drew in a long breath, set-tled herself.

"And action!"

Blake had a confused look on her face as she studied the mailbox. "Why does everyone in town think throw-ing a name in this mailbox will change a person's life?"

"Because it does," Blake's mom said, matter-of-factly. "How do you think you got here?"

"I drove."

"I sent for you."

"By suggesting me as a Scrooge?" She laughed. "You could have just called."

"I did. Over and over," her mom said with sadness in her voice. "You've been emotionally unreachable these past few years."

Blake looked over the landscape, reflecting on that, and suddenly Catalina missed her own mom. Though her mother would never be so frank with her, she knew she'd been emotionally unreachable.

Catalina clicked back in to the scene. "I'm sorry. I've just had a tough time with work and relationships," she said, feeling the honest truth behind those words. "With Dad dying, I didn't want to burden you with my problems."

"Why would you ever think that? I'm your mother. I will always to be here for you no matter how old you are, no matter how difficult the problem."

"Thank you, Mom. It's just… I've felt so lost lately,

like I don't have a clear direction in my life. I don't know what comes next, and that terrifies me."

"None of us do, but the best advice I can give you is to focus on your dreams. Set goals for yourself. Don't worry about if and when you'll get there. See yourself already there."

"That's the problem. I don't see myself anywhere. I know I need a job in order to pay the bills, but nothing really speaks to me. I feel like I've let you down. You and Dad have always had such lofty aspirations for me, and well, I don't think I'm cut out for a high-profile or high-stress career. I think I'm one of those people who could be perfectly happy working in a coffeehouse."

"Not everyone has to aspire to be a doctor or lawyer, and you shouldn't apologize for that."

"I can't believe I'm about to say this, but ever since I moved here, I've thought a lot about wanting a family. You already know how out of character that is for me. But now I'd really like to meet someone who might feel the same way."

"That's wonderful, Blake. Family is so important. It's always been to me, and I'm so happy to hear that it is to you."

"So, what now? Take out a billboard which says, 'Seeking Mr. Right, who wants to start a family'?"

She chuckled. "I have a feeling it's not going to be that difficult. You're putting too much pressure on yourself. Stay with me as long as you like. Who knows, maybe you'll even meet someone here."

"I see that gleam in your eye. This conversation doesn't give you carte blanche to set me up with the single guy of your choosing."

"Now would I do that?"

"Without a doubt."

"I wouldn't mind a bunch of grandchildren running about my huge house."

"Good because I'm planning on four."

The women laughed, and Blake put her arm around her mom. "How about we go to the Sweet Shoppe and get a delicious cup of hot cocoa?"

"You read my mind."

"And cut," Victor said. "Beautiful, ladies. Let's get one in the can."

"Picture's up. Final touches," Mark announced to the crew.

Catalina caught Jay's eye. He was smiling, and she suddenly wondered if he wanted to have children. With his gentle disposition, he'd make a great father. She could just see him teaching little ones how to hold a camera, or talking to them about the difference between a cottontail rabbit and a snowshoe hare.

She hadn't thought about children until the other day, when she believed Jay already had children. Then last night, when she was working on the scene, she couldn't stop picturing what it would be like to get married and start a family. The scene had unexpectedly come alive for her. Catalina's parents had raised her to value family. Like her character Blake, she had pushed that away. After her breakup with Grayson, she had convinced herself that she couldn't have children if she wanted to continue to have a successful acting career. Why had she done that to herself? Having kids with a busy career would be challenging but not impossible, especially if the father was someone like Jay.

They continued to shoot the scene, covering all angles, and because it went so well, they wrapped a little early.

"A perfect scene in a perfect place," Pauline said after Victor called the final cut.

"It was a pleasure working with you," Catalina said.

"The pleasure was all mine." Pauline gave her a hug. "I'll see you back in LA for the interior scenes. Good luck with the rest of the shoot, and Merry Christmas."

"Merry Christmas."

As the crew began breaking down the set, Catalina made her way over to Jay.

"That scene rocked," he said.

"Thanks." She smiled, feeling confident that it worked well. "I've got to go over a few things with one of my producers, but I can be ready in about a half hour."

"Take your time. I need to grab more shots of the crew as they wrap out. Just text me when you're ready."

Neil caught up with Catalina as she made her way back to her trailer. "Got the revised sides for tomorrow. You'll be happy to know that Blake is no longer stealing cars or listening to talking reindeer and Christmas fairies. She does, however, get pulled over by a cop coming into town."

"Definitely more realistic," Catalina said. "Glad to see Stan is getting in the groove. I'll have to stop by Piper's to let her know."

"Excuse me, Ms. Jones?"

Catalina turned to see Brandi. Her eyes were puffy and red. "Yes?"

"Can I talk to you for a minute?"

Neil got between Brandi and Catalina.

"It's okay," she said to Neil. "In fact, why don't you take the night off. Check in on Iris?"

A big smile spread across his face. "Are you sure?"

"Positive."

"Thank you. Call me if you need anything at all."

She nodded, then returned her attention to Brandi. "Everything all right?"

"Grayson and I had a big fight over you."

Why did I allow myself to get pulled into Grayson's drama? "Sorry to hear that, but I'm not sure what it has to do—"

Brandi let out a sob. "All I said was that you were such an amazing actress, and that I felt you were outshining him in every scene."

Why would she say that? Catalina hid the shock from her face. "I imagine he didn't take that well."

"No, he didn't. I apologized, but he said a lot of hurtful things to me, so I stormed out." Brandi wiped tears off her face. "Now, I don't know if I should apologize again, or leave town?"

The girl was in a bad place, and Catalina couldn't help but feel sorry for her. "He's probably cooled off by now. Have you tried calling him?"

"I was afraid to."

"His call time for tomorrow isn't until the afternoon. Why don't you suggest something fun to do?"

"That's a great idea," she said, smiling at last. "Thank you." She started to walk away, then turned back. "Is this typical behavior from Grayson?"

"I don't think any man would appreciate his girlfriend telling him he's second best."

"I see that now," she said. "Can you tell me what

I should worry about with Grayson, like you did the other day?"

Alarm bells went off in Catalina's head. Too many questions, and the last one was an odd one. "Brandi, you are in a relationship with Grayson. I'm not. You'll need to navigate those waters on your own."

"Yes, of course. I'm so sorry. I don't know what I was thinking. Thank you for all the advice you've given me. Have a good evening."

Catalina watched her go. She was probably making too much of her sudden strange feeling about Brandi. She seemed very naive for someone in her mid-twenties.

Catalina opened her trailer door and went inside. Had she just given relationship advice to her ex's new girlfriend? *What's happening to me?*

Jay retrieved his equipment from the camera truck as the rest of the crew continued to pack up.

"I heard there's a great barbecue place in town," Clayton said. "The guys and I are going to go check it out, if you want to come along."

"Thanks, man. Ordinarily I'd say yes, but I need to go over today's stills."

"Did you figure out that photo?"

"No."

"Maybe Santa's mailman is hanging around our fake mailbox?" Clayton laughed.

Jay chuckled, but after exhausting all other explanations, he was ready to embrace that theory.

"See you tomorrow," Jay said, then went to his car, wondering if he could test the theory. He grabbed one of his night tracker video cameras, and attached it to a tree next to the mailbox. The tree was in the perfect location to get a side view of the mailbox. He'd be able to record any elf, or human, moving in front or behind the mailbox. Since he didn't know when the mail collector would show, he'd record the fake mailbox all night and retrieve the SD card in the morning for review.

Now, he just had one more problem to solve. Catalina hadn't used the mailbox today. Only an extra had dropped in a blank sheet of paper at the top of the scene. He had to get a real heartfelt wish or a Scrooge suggestion inside that mailbox.

Taking out a pen, he scribbled down the only wish he ever wanted. The chances that the Scrooge Legend's magic had extended to the fake mailbox were slim, but if it had, the mail collector would come and his long-awaited wish could finally be realized.

Chapter Twenty-Eight

Jay flung his camera strap over his shoulder and knocked on Catalina's door.

"Hey." Her eyes lit up upon seeing him. "One sec." She collected her things and shut the door. "I gave Neil the night off. Do you think we can hit the diner again and eat in a closed section?"

"I'll text Angel right now." He took out his phone as they walked to his Jeep.

"Have you had a chance to look through your photos from today?"

"About half." He set his stuff in the back. "I'll be going through the rest later tonight. Luisa mentioned they might want to have some funny photos of the production crew for the end credits."

"Don't you need funny ones of me and the rest of the actors?" she asked, getting in his car.

"Luisa just mentioned the crew, but I don't see why not."

"Amusing photos might help dispel my Ice Queen reputation," she said before she looked at him hesitantly. "Do you have any funny photos of me?"

"A couple—when you were laughing at the snowman, but since he's no longer in the film, I might not be able to use them. I'll make sure I get a lot more of you as your sweet, bubbly self."

Her laugh was sarcastic. "I haven't been bubbly in ages."

He gave her a sideways glance. "Why is that?"

She frowned. "You know why. The pressures of the job and everything that comes with it."

He suddenly realized that he'd just killed her light-hearted mood. "It's definitely a balancing act, but you seem to handle it better than I did." He parked near the diner's back door. "Maybe we can help each other so that the stress doesn't make us crazy."

"I'd like that," she said in a soft voice, and for a second she looked like the bright-eyed actress she'd been almost eight years ago. He'd known even back then that she was going to go far. He had loved her pure optimism about everything but worried she'd be blindsided by it one day, which she was. Her optimism had made her stand out from the other actresses. People had gravitated to her because of it, including him. She then buried that optimism, but he was starting to see glimpses of it in her eyes again.

He turned toward her. "I want to thank you."

She gave him a curious look. "For what?"

"Staying."

She held his gaze as her expression relaxed, and there seemed to be a sense of appreciation in her eyes. It got very quiet as they ever so slowly leaned into one another. He reached for her, ready to kiss her, when a loud metallic clank startled them. Angel had opened the back door and was waiting for them.

Catalina smiled at him, as if to say *thank you for the almost kiss*, then they got out and went inside.

"Good to see you two again." Angel ushered them to a booth in the corner. "I'll try to keep this section closed as long as possible, but it's already getting busy."

"Thank you," Catalina said, taking a menu from her. "What's the special tonight?"

"Did I hear right?" Angel smiled, catching Jay's eye. "Someone has her appetite back."

"Out of necessity. I'm freezing."

"We've got turkey casserole with homemade buttermilk biscuits, and our soup of the day is pumpkin."

"Sounds delicious, but way too filling," Catalina said. "Maybe I should just stick to the pumpkin soup."

"Or how about we both get a cup of the pumpkin soup, split the turkey biscuit casserole, and maybe split a dessert?" Jay suggested.

Catalina narrowed her eyes on him. "You are dangerous, Mr. Townsend."

His mouth raised in a half smile. "Only way to be."

"All right." She let out a light chuckle. "But you'll be taking home the leftovers."

"Done and done." Angel hurried away.

He studied the way Catalina's stunning sapphire-blue eyes turned up at the corners, making them appear doelike and vulnerable. He had wanted to know what she'd been thinking all day. He missed how she'd shared her feelings, opinions, and aspirations with him when they were friends. Even their one brief kiss had spoken volumes. It had literally taken his breath away, and he'd wanted to experience that again. He stared at her full-lipped mouth and inched closer to her—then two waters were hastily dropped off at the table, forcing them apart.

Catalina sat back with a light laugh. As tempting as it was, he knew a public kiss was out of the question.

"So." She looked away for a moment, a sweet smile lingering on her lips, then she refocused on him. "What's this Christmas magic evidence you have for me?"

"Right." He rummaged around in his bag, pulled out a blown-up photo of the elf shoes, and set it in front of her. "What do you see?"

"Elf shoes under our fake mailbox." Her brow creased. "When did you take this?"

"Right after Victor called cut. Here's a copy of the original before I blew it up." He set it before her. "You've seen this photo before. We were looking at this last night, but I think we were focused on the actor in the snowman costume and didn't notice the shoes."

She studied the photos. "Why would there be elf shoes under the mailbox?"

"That's what I'd like to know," he said. "It's more like the shoes are behind it. As you can see by the position of the feet, it appears like someone is either crouching down or in midstride."

"Who?"

"Good question. You were out there, and so was I. So was the entire crew," he said. "I didn't see anybody. Did you?"

"No, but to my eye, whoever is wearing the shoes is reaching forward."

"That aligns with what I discovered earlier today." He pulled out another photo. "This is the next photo I took. The shoes are gone, and so are the scraps of paper littering the ground. You can see the pieces of paper in this shot, with the shoes and the snowman walking out of frame. But in this next shot, the shoes and the paper scraps are gone."

"How far apart were these photos taken?"

"Under a minute, and then I came over to photograph you and Grayson."

She ran a hand through her hair and took a deep breath. "Okay, that's a little weird. I watched the actor dropping those pieces of paper everywhere, and I didn't see anyone picking them up before you came over."

"It gets weirder." He pulled out a copy of his dad's photo and set it next to his close-up photo of the shoes. "My dad took this last year at a stakeout."

"The one where the floodlights were used?"

"Yes. My dad got lucky as he happened to be snapping photos at the exact time the floodlights were triggered."

She compared the two. "The shoes look identical. Same size, same style. Wait. Is this the night where the residents said they saw an elf?"

"Yeah."

She laughed. "An elf? We're talking about a nonexistent being."

"A supposed nonexistent being—like Bigfoot or the Loch Ness Monster."

She smiled. "I don't have an explanation for the fast disappearance of all those scraps of paper," she admitted. "Or the fact that no one saw the elf-shoe owner out there, but an elf, Jay?" She looked at him skeptically. "Besides, this isn't even the real Santa's mailbox."

"Agreed, which is why I'm trying to get proof as we speak."

"How?"

"I set up a wildlife infrared video camera that will record any movement around our fake mailbox should anyone feel the need to stop by and collect whatever's inside."

Angel brought over their cups of soup and a basket of bread, then gasped. "Is that the mail collector?"

Catalina laughed. "Okay. I get it now. Is this another one of Victor's gotchas?" She looked around the restaurant. "Are we on camera?"

"No," Jay said.

"Absolutely not." Angel looked mortified. "There will be no Hollywood funny business in here." She wagged a finger between them. "I mean it." She walked away.

Catalina smiled at Angel's response, took a small taste of her soup, then glanced at his photo again, which meant she was still curious and not completely closed off to the idea of Christmas magic. "Those shoes are really small."

"Which rules out any of the teamsters and ninety-five percent of the crew. Did you see any kids sneaking around?"

"No. It had to be a crew member—though pretty daring on the first, very tense day of filming." She swallowed another spoonful of soup. "It's intriguing, I'll give you that, but I don't think you'll catch anything on your video camera tonight, other than deer."

"Speaking of which, take a look at these three photos." He picked up his camera and clicked through several images before he found what he was looking for. "Remember the bucks you saw sparring?"

"You got them on camera?" She leaned closer to the

viewfinder, and when she saw them, she got very excited. "I knew they were out there."

"They're actually reindeer, and male reindeer are called bulls, not bucks."

"How can you tell?" She stared at the animals.

"They're bigger and have a heavier coat than regular deer. Here's the thing though. There aren't any wild reindeer in this area."

"Maybe they're elk."

"You're talking to a wildlife photographer. These are without a doubt reindeer."

"Okay, so we've got reindeer in an area they don't usually inhabit. I overheard a crew member talking about a reindeer ranch he wanted to take his kids to. Maybe these are escapees."

"Possible, but the ranch is near Denver. Go to the next frame."

Catalina clicked on the next photo and saw one of the reindeers in a midair jump on the left side of the photo, but the other half of the photo was whited out. "That's weird."

"Very weird. This is a digital camera. Half frames aren't possible."

"Something has to be wrong with your camera." She gave it back to him. "Definitely unusual, but not hard evidence of Christmas magic."

He sighed, feeling defeated but not giving up. "You used to love this kind of mystery. You even said that if something existed but couldn't be proven, it didn't matter. It only meant that anything in this world was possible."

She huffed, looking away. "I was naive."

"No. You were right." He pushed the photos aside. "I remember that Catalina Jones, the fearless Catalina."

A shadow of sadness crossed her face. "She existed a lifetime ago."

"What happened?" he asked gently. "What changed?"

She released a long, slow breath. "If you really want to know, aside from my breakup with Grayson, I've had one disappointment after another. When they begin to stack up, it changes you."

"I can understand that," he said, feeling like they were finding their way back as good friends.

She studied him. "What happened to make you give up your dream?"

He sat back. "I thought I'd been given a big-budget movie to direct as I pleased, but then every one of my decisions was questioned at every turn. It was exhausting. I didn't feel like I was developing a good film anymore. The studio seemed to give me a beautiful canvas to create anything I wanted, and then I was suddenly told to paint by numbers. I began to compromise, and with every watered-down group-think decision, I felt like I was giving away a piece of my creativity. I became irritated, angry, and then depressed. I no longer recognized my own movie, so I quit. The whole experience was so stressful that I knew I needed to get out of that environment before I lost myself for good."

Concern flooded her eyes. "I had no idea you were going through all that, Jay. I'm so sorry."

"No need. It was short-lived. I should have handled it better. I know that now, and lately, I've been kicking myself for not sticking with it."

"Then come back," she said simply.

"I'd like to, but I burned a lot of bridges on the way out."

"Bridges can be rebuilt."

She was right. He was the only one holding himself back. Like Catalina, he'd lost faith in believing that anything was possible. He met her gaze. "You still give great advice."

"So do you." She touched him on the arm. "I'm beginning to wonder if St. Nicholas doesn't automatically make everyone examine their own lives and the people in them."

"See, you do believe in a little bit of the Scrooge Legend magic. Self-reflection is a big turning point in all Scrooge journeys."

"That I definitely believe. Ever since I got here, I've been reviewing my life—especially my first year in LA. I finally realized what my first devastating disappointment was."

"That's a huge breakthrough," he said. "May I ask what it was?"

"You're not going to like the answer."

"Try me."

"It happened at the last party we attended at the film festival. I kissed you, and you rejected me."

"What?" he said with a laugh because he thought she was joking. "I didn't reject you. Why would you ever think that?"

"Because it's true. I put myself out there, risking our solid friendship by kissing you, and what did you do? You ran away. You left the party, and we never talked about it again."

"No. I'd never do that. I kept getting bombarded by producers and studio execs. Every time I tried to break

away to go find you, I'd be pushed in a corner by someone else who had to talk to me. When I was finally able
to look for you, you had left."

She stared at him, bewildered, confused. "So we
both thought the other one left?"

He blinked a few times, realizing it himself. "It
sounds like it."

They shared a laugh as they let the mix-up sink in,
and then he leaned closer to her. "For the record, your
kiss was electrifying."

She smiled, then disappointment hit her eyes. "How
come you didn't tell me that the next day?"

"I wanted to, but not over the phone. I wanted to
see you in person," he said. "If you remember, we kept
missing each other. You were busy with career-changing
auditions, and I was taking meetings at studios. Our careers were going in different directions, and before we
had a chance to get together and figure it out, you were
off to England."

"It had happened all so fast," she said. "I remember
very clearly the day I called you and told you I'd booked
the miniseries. You didn't sound very happy for me, and
then you ghosted me."

"No, never," he said. "I was extremely happy for
you because I knew it was the type of role that would
take your career to the next level. I wanted to talk to
you about the lead role in *Lost in the Glades*, but when
you told me about the miniseries, I changed my mind."

"Why?"

"Because I wasn't going to be the sole decision maker
on who got the part. It was also going to start filming
before your miniseries wrapped. There were too many

unknowns with my project, and it wasn't the type of role that would advance your career."

"So, instead of discussing it with me, you decided to make that decision for me?" Her tone was terse. "It sounds like you didn't trust me to make a decision about my own career."

"No. I didn't trust myself. I was worried I'd convince you to turn down the miniseries for me. I wanted you right by my side, working together again. But what if the producers didn't agree with my casting choice, and if they did, what if I wasn't able to convince the writer to make your role more emotionally challenging?"

The tension in her face lessened. "I never understood why you hadn't even mentioned it to me. But when I saw the film and the role that I would have played, that's the first thing I thought. The role would have been physically challenging but lacked substance."

"It did," he said. "Something I had tried to change but couldn't." He took her hand and searched her eyes. "I'm deeply sorry that I never allowed you to be part of the decision process."

Her shoulders relaxed as she let out a long exhale. "We were young and had just come off of *Sage Under Fire* where we didn't have to answer to anyone. I understand now why you didn't tell me, and to be perfectly honest, I can't say what I would have decided. The miniseries was a supporting role and out of the country. Would I have turned it down? I honestly don't know."

"If you had turned it down, you would have done it for another role that I couldn't even guarantee," he said. "Your career could have crashed, landing you right next to me, freezing your ass off in the cold, trying to make a living as a wildlife photographer."

"Oh, no." She fought back a smile. "I would have dumped you long before it came to that."

He laughed. "You've done incredibly well for yourself, and you should be proud of your achievements. I've paid close attention to your career, cheering you on, even though you didn't know it."

"Thank you, Jay." She put a hand on top of his. "I've missed you so much."

"I've missed you—talking with you, sharing everything about my life with you." He caressed her hand. "If I could take back all the wasted years of missing out on our friendship, I would."

"Does this magical town of yours dabble in time-travel?"

"If it did, we'd already be back there—landing right at that incredible kiss."

She smiled. "All this time I thought I had crossed the line. I saw the shock on your face and read it wrong." She shook her head, seeming embarrassed. "If you had seen me before the party, you would have laughed. I was so nervous about kissing you. We were such good friends, and I didn't want to mess that up. You were the only one I could truly talk to because it seemed like you were the only one who not only knew the real me but understood me. I could always be myself around you. I could be vulnerable around you and not get hurt. You were my best friend. I couldn't imagine my life without you, and that's when I started to have feelings for you."

"I began falling for you almost immediately," he said. "I think it was the day you met our star horse. You were so timid and scared, but when you stroked her nose, she nuzzled you, and your face lit up like a child on Christmas day. In that moment, I saw how kind and gentle you were—so present and positive about life. I was so taken with you that I wanted to know everything about you. I wanted to be with you, spend all my time with you, experience things with you. I wanted a lifelong friendship with you, and of course, I had hoped for more. But as long as you were in my life, I knew I'd be happy—like I am right now."

They gazed into each other's eyes, and he so desperately wanted to kiss her, but couldn't.

"Do you think it was a coincidence that we ran into each other at the town square?" she asked.

"Not in the least."

"Do you think it was the Scrooge Legend?"

"Without a doubt."

She nodded, then set her gaze back on him. "Then if *you* believe, I can keep an open mind. Will you take me by our fake mailbox to view the videos after we eat?"

"I'd love to, but we need to wait until tomorrow morning before we can review the footage."

"Oh." She looked disappointed.

"I can take you to the real Santa's mailbox—though I can't guarantee you'll see the mail collector."

"Have you ever seen him?"

"Not yet."

"But some locals have seen him, correct?"

"That's what they tell everyone."

"Then, if we go there tonight, there's a possibility I might see him."

"A very slight one."

Her eyes twinkled. "I don't get what the big deal is. It seems fairly easy to be able to see who's picking up the mail."

"Oh, you think so? Super easy?"

"If we're standing right next to it, how can we not see him?"

Catalina zipped up her coat around her ears, standing with Jay, one foot from the mailbox. They'd only been out there for ten minutes, and she was already freezing.

Jay shoved his hands in his pockets. "He's not going to pick up the mail with us standing right here."

"Doesn't the mail have to be removed by midnight?"

"Yes, but let me save you a lot of trouble. Many Scrooges have stood right where we are, and do you know what happened? They were distracted by something that made them look away for a few seconds, which allowed the elf to retrieve the mail."

"You're trying to tell me that not one Scrooge could keep his or her eyes on this mailbox?"

"Not one, and believe me, there have been plenty who have tried. For those who refuse to look away, unexpected weather rolls in, forcing them to leave."

She laughed hard. "That's the most absurd thing I've ever heard. I will stand here until midnight, and I can guarantee that a severe snowstorm will not move me." She pulled out her phone, checked the weather app. "Look at this, Mr. Elf Expert. Clear skies all night long." She held it in front of his face.

He sighed and turned up his coat collar. "I guess we'll see, won't we?"

"Yes, we will." She stiffened as a blast of wind went through her, and she glanced up at the sky.

"Eyes on the mailbox."

She narrowed her gaze on him. "You're doing everything you can to distract me."

"I'm not doing a thing. If I wanted to distract you, believe me, you'd know it."

She suspected she would know because she'd have his warm lips on hers. She wouldn't mind that at all right about now. He moved closer to her, and she wanted to see what he was up to, but she refused to look away from the mailbox. "What are you doing?"

"Nothing."

She could hear the smile in his voice and knew he was up to something.

He deliberately nudged her. "Oh, sorry."

"You did that on purpose."

"Just trying to keep you warm." He tried to hide his smile but wasn't doing a very good job at it.

"Thanks." She stared at the mailbox, pretending he wasn't getting to her. She needed to have blinders on, to keep from looking at him, or from getting distracted by his charm.

A gust of cold winter air hit her cheeks, and she really wanted to check the sky but wouldn't take the bait.

He chuckled. "I know you want to look, so I'll let you in on a little secret. You will stand here all night, and he won't come. Then about ten minutes before midnight, the weather will drastically change."

"All right. I'll play. How exactly will the weather change? Is it going to suddenly start snowing? Big whoop."

"No," he said. "A few little snowflakes aren't going to scare away a woman from Maine. I'd say..." He glanced up at the sky, she could see him with her peripheral vision, and his long pause was killing her. "Hail. Big, fat, golf-ball-size hail."

She exploded with laughter and had to look at him for

a second. "I had no idea you were such a good actor—to deliver such a ridiculous line with a straight face—well done."

"I'll be taking a picture of your truly shocked face when it does." He raised his chin up a notch. "Eyes on the mailbox."

She chuckled to herself. He definitely had an advantage on her, having lived with the legend all of his life. Not that she believed something so ridiculous. She just wished it were almost midnight. She tightened her coat up. "What time is it?"

"Nine o'clock."

She groaned. Could she endure another three hours just to prove a point? When she and Neil had deposited Victor's name, the flag had lowered in seconds, and it happened right as she turned around. Was Jay telling the truth? Could she wait three more hours only to miss the mail collector if she was forced to look away for a split second? "Do you have any proof of these unusual storms?"

"News articles. Several past weather events have occurred in St. Nicholas ten minutes before midnight."

"Let's see them."

"I don't have them on me, though maybe I can find some online." He pulled out his phone.

"On second thought, bring them tomorrow. I'm not going to let you distract me."

He put his phone away, suppressing a smile as footsteps could be heard coming up behind them.

"Did you just text someone to become a distraction?" she asked.

He laughed at her paranoia. "Absolutely not. I don't need cheap tricks when I'm dealing with the real thing."

"I'm not looking away," she said, even though she desperately wanted to see who was approaching them.

"You can look," he said, waiting to see who showed. "Whoever it is, it's not the mail collector."

"How do you know that?"

"Because, when it's quiet out here like it is now, people always hear the bells jingle on his shoes."

She'd heard bells when she turned away from the mailbox just last night.

"Hey, Clayton," Jay said, casually.

Clayton glanced up with a surprised look on his face. "Oh, hey." He slipped whatever he was holding inside his pocket. "Hi, Catalina."

"Clayton."

"What are you guys doing out here?"

"Catalina wanted to—"

"Get some fresh air."

"Yes. It's a great night for a walk," Jay said.

"It is." Clayton nodded. "I'm doing the same thing." There was an awkward pause, and she realized it was not the night to elf-watch.

"See you on set," Catalina said, walking away from the mailbox.

Jay quickly followed. "I thought you wanted to stay," he whispered.

"He wants to use the mailbox."

"Oh. Right. That's what he was doing." Jay looked back. "We can keep an eye on the mailbox from my Jeep."

"Why didn't you suggest that in the first place?"

"I tried, but you were insistent."

She huffed. "I guess I was." She followed him, and the minute she got in his car, she felt relief. Jay turned on the heater to get her warm, and she was happy to see that the flag on the mailbox was still in the raised position.

"Have you ever put up a night vision camera on this mailbox?" She kept her eye on the mailbox.

"Yes, but I either got a snowy picture or the recording completely stopped every time the mail was picked up—as it happens to all the cameras around town. They all go out whenever the mail collector is around."

She eyed him, not sure if he was joking. "Is that true?"

"Yes," he said without hesitation.

"How many nights did you keep up the camera?"

"An entire year."

Her jaw dropped. "Seriously?"

He nodded.

"You ended up getting interference every single night?"

"Every night the mail was collected."

"Maybe it's your video camera."

"Nope. It works perfectly fine."

"So how are you expecting to get proof tonight with the camera monitoring the fake mailbox?"

"Easy. If nothing happens, if I don't get interference, then it was someone playing a prank."

"Ah, so the lack of evidence is evidence."

"Exactly."

She watched the mailbox for a few minutes, but she really wanted to give her attention to Jay. "I'm not going to see anyone tonight, am I?"

"Probably not."

She eyed the mailbox again and saw someone approaching. "Wait. Who's that?"

It was a guy about the same height as Jay. "Too tall for the mail collector."

The guy glanced around, then took something out of his pocket, threw it in the mailbox, and quickly walked toward them.

"That's Theo," Jay said and ducked.

She saw him and slid down in her seat. They waited for another minute, then popped back up.

"Poor guy," she said. "He probably suggested Victor as a Scrooge."

"I wouldn't be surprised if we see the whole crew showing up tonight."

She laughed, then settled back in her seat. "Why is Victor still yelling at everyone if he's supposed to be changing?"

"The Scroogiest can often take the longest," Jay said. "But he's already changing. He took out the kiss for you."

"He did."

"We'll see more changes shortly," he said, seeming confident.

She turned toward him, studying him. "You've lived here all of your life. Why haven't you asked for your heart's desire?"

"Santa's mailbox doesn't bring the perfect job or the cool car."

"I know, but it can bring you the love of your life."

"Yes, it can definitely do that."

"Then why are you alone? Why haven't you deposited a wish for love?"

"I almost did at one time." He stared at the mailbox. "But then I thought it wouldn't be fair to the woman I was wishing for."

She cocked her head, not understanding. "Why not?"

"Different career paths, different lives." He expelled a breath. "That was a long time ago."

She assumed Jay had dated like she had. He knew everyone she'd dated because it was always reported on, but she had no idea how many women he had dated over the years, or if he'd had a serious relationship like she'd had with Grayson. By the look on his face, the woman had really meant something to him, and he seemed sad just being reminded of her. "Maybe you should finally make that a wish."

He chuckled. "I kind of did tonight, at the fake mailbox, to see if it would bring anyone over to pick it up."

"An experiment?"

He nodded.

"I kind of made a wish for an experiment, too, but at the real magical mailbox."

"What?" He shot her a surprised look. "I thought you didn't believe in the magic of Christmas?"

"I don't," she said, halfheartedly. "Neil wanted to conduct a science experiment to prove the mailbox didn't work, so he wished for his soul mate, then he insisted I wish for mine."

"What happened?" He suddenly seemed very interested.

"Nothing." She shrugged.

"Impossible. If the wish is true and dear, the soul mate will appear.'"

She gawked at him. "Oh, come on. You're just making that up."

"No, I'm not. You were considered a Scrooge, which means that any wish you make gets immediate attention."

"How immediate?"

"Within the hour."

She stared at him intently as she held her breath.

"Who was the first person you met after you deposited your wish?"

"You." She couldn't move and he looked shocked, like when she had kissed him so many years ago, and then his features softened. She saw vulnerability in his expression.

"Me?" He searched her eyes as his became a little watery. "You wished for me?"

She nodded. "I didn't know it at the time, but yes. I wished for you," she said as she slowly realized it herself. "It's always been you."

She suddenly saw him the way she had wanted to for so long. He wasn't the guy who had rejected her all those years ago. He was not just a friend who was protecting her on and off set, or someone she could casually date. He was a man who shared her values, who cared for others more than himself, who had wanted her to be in his life as much as she wanted him in hers. He was the man she had wished for. Her heart began beating faster as time seemed to stand still.

"Want to know something funny?" He held her hand in his. "The wish I had wanted to deposit years ago and the wish deposited tonight were for you."

He took her breath away. He leaned over, cupped her face in the palm of his hand, and gently kissed her. The kiss was so tender. It was as if he were pouring his heart out to her as their eyes closed and their lips touched. She wrapped her arms around him, not wanting the feeling to end. When they at last ended the kiss, they shared a smile, and then a laugh.

"The most anticipated seven-and-a-half-year kiss in the making," she said.

"It was well worth the wait." His smile was that of absolute contentment. He was about to kiss her again when someone else walked by, going to the mailbox.

"Is that Valerie from our movie?" she asked.

Jay turned around. "Yes. Good for her—though I wonder if she has a Scrooge suggestion or a Christmas wish?"

"Can't she have both?"

"Not at the same time, and sometimes not in the same week. That's the one thing that doesn't seem to be a hard fast rule. Some people can suggest a lot of Scrooges or deposit more than one wish, while others only get one."

"Maybe my Victor Scrooge suggestion didn't take."

"If you got the door open, it did."

"I'm beginning to like your magic mailbox."

"I am, too." He got lost in her eyes, leaned closer, and found her lips.

It was a warm, sensuous kiss, and she pulled him to her, feeling the heat behind his kisses.

A woman laughed. Catalina remembered where she was, who she was, and immediately sat up straight.

A couple walked by, holding hands, going toward the mailbox. As soon as they moved past it, Catalina noticed that the flag was down. "Nooo! We just missed him."

"Yeah, we did." He couldn't help but laugh.

She playfully smacked him on his chest. "You distracted me."

"You tempted me, so we're even."

"I was so close to seeing him," she said, truly disappointed.

"We can always try tomorrow night," he suggested happily.

"And if we miss him again?"

"There's always the night after that, and the night after that."

"Oh." She smiled. "This could be fun."

Chapter Twenty-Nine

"But Santa doesn't pull from the naughty list," Mary said, making Joe yawn, as they sat with Stan by the fire.

Stan frowned. "Of course he gets them from the naughty list—that's why they're Scrooges."

"Perhaps in your version, Mr. Larkin, but I'm afraid you're missing the entire point of the Scrooge Legend," she said. "A Scrooge invitation is Santa reaching out to those who have lost their Christmas spirit and their sense of joy in life, which by definition makes them a Scrooge."

Stan was clearly having a difficult time wrapping his head around what Mary was telling him. "So there isn't a list of any kind?"

"No. Someone suggests a Scrooge by placing the person's name in Santa's mailbox. Santa goes through the suggestions, then invites those who are considered a real Scrooge."

"What about those people on Santa's naughty list?"

"The naughty and nice lists are for Christmas gifts only."

Stan stared at his script in his hand and let out a deflated sigh. "No Scrooge naughty list. Great. Something else I need to change."

"What are you changing?" Victor asked as he came into the living room with Theo following close behind.

"Mary has informed me that Scrooge invitations are not generated from Santa's naughty list."

"Does it matter? Our movie is fiction."

"Bite your tongue, Mr. Caviano." She waved a finger at him. "Your movie might be fiction, but the Scrooge Legend is very real. I would very much appreciate it, as would Dina and our other St. Nicholas residents, if Piper's story remained as close to the truth as possible."

Victor immediately softened. "Yes, of course. My apologies. I was just talking to Dina and Piper at the coffeehouse. Stan, Piper mentioned she had asked you for a few changes. Can we do those for her?"

Stan sighed. "I have so many changes that I no longer know what is what."

"Maybe Catalina could help you with that," Mary suggested sweetly.

"The mail collector is going to need a vacation after the film crew finally leaves town," Jay said as he pulled into the Carroll Inn driveway.

She laughed. "Too bad there isn't a magical mailbox in LA." She took off her seat belt and turned toward him. "I'd ask you to come in, but I've got to prep for tomorrow."

"I know. I'm just glad I was able to spend some time with you."

"This was one of the best nights I've had in years." She wanted to reach for him to give him a good-night kiss, but stopped short, not knowing where Victor was. "How am I going to concentrate on work now?"

He grinned, leaning toward her. "Do you need my help?"

"No." She gave him a stern look. "I think you've done enough."

He laughed. "One kiss for the road?" She glanced at the front door, then gave him a quick kiss, and he looked disappointed. "How about another?"

"And then another. I know what you're up to." She hopped out before she could change her mind. "Sweet dreams."

He clutched his heart. "You are cruel."

She opened the front door, waved, then headed inside.

"There she is," Victor called out from the living room, all smiles.

"What's going on?" Catalina asked, walking into the living room as Neil came down the stairs and joined her.

"We desperately need your input on the script," Victor said, sitting with Stan and Theo.

Catalina whispered to Neil, "This is a first."

Mary picked up a few dirty dishes off the coffee table. "I'll be back out with drinks and snacks." She hurried into the kitchen.

"How can I help?" Catalina asked, as she and Neil sat with them.

"Let me start with the good news," Stan said. "I've dropped the robbery scenes and added more Blake and Remington scenes. The first one I'll be working on will have the couple shopping in an antique store for vintage kitchen cabinet pulls."

"That's fantastic, Stan." She sat back, relaxing. "I can't wait to read it."

He sat up a little taller. "Now on to the issue I'm

dealing with. I got an email from George. He said the studio isn't clear on when Blake believes in Christmas magic and wants a specific Christmas magic event that converts her to a believer. I'm thinking an elf and flying reindeer can take her on a magical sleigh ride to the North Pole."

"Oh, dear." Mary dropped the food tray on the coffee table with a loud bang. "Apologies," she said, composing herself. "Stan, I have a grilled cheese and tomato soup for you to help you think clearer."

"Mary, you read my mind. Thank you."

"Italian Christmas cookies for you, Victor. My first batch." She handed him a plate filled with them.

"That's very kind of you, Mary." He took a bite and his eyes lit up. "Delicious."

"And for you, Catalina, apple cider with a hint of caramel."

"Caramel?" She was truly shocked. "How did you know?"

"It's my job to know."

As a kid, caramel apples were one of Catalina's favorites. She loved Halloween because of them. Whenever she craved something sweet, she'd dip a few slices of apple in caramel. She took a sip and almost died. It was incredible.

"For you, Neil—" Mary handed over a mug "—hot cocoa with extra marshmallows."

"My favorite. Thank you."

"And, Theo, here is your gingerbread eggnog."

"Awesome." He immediately tasted it and moaned with pleasure.

A silence fell over the group as they all stared at Theo, then at Mary.

"It's a new recipe," she said. "How about I bring out a small taster for everyone?"

There was a collective agreement to that suggestion as they got back to enjoying the treats in front of them.

Catalina sipped her cider. How could she politely tell Stan that he was going in the wrong direction again?

"Have we mentioned a sleigh ride before?" Victor stuffed his mouth with another cookie.

"No, but I thought it would be a good example of Christmas magic," Stan said with his mouth full.

Victor shook his head. "Something seems off."

"Though the North Pole definitely screams Christmas magic, it might overshadow Blake," Catalina said.

Stan nodded. "When do you think Blake becomes a Christmas magic believer?"

Catalina thought back on her evening with Jay, which had been truly magical. "She believes in Christmas magic when she finally regains her faith in love."

"Yes!" Mary cheered, bringing in the gingerbread eggnog samplers, which were snapped up immediately.

Stan tasted it, and suddenly his fingers were flying across his computer keyboard. "Keep talking to me, Catalina."

"Through the magic of Christmas, Blake's enveloped in love, and because of that love, she finally feels safe enough to trust the man who's been put in her path. The man who has so much love to give. The man who is her soul mate. The magic of Christmas allows her to experience joy again and finally realize that true love is real—something that will stay with her forever and not just at Christmas."

Mary was nodding enthusiastically, but no one said a word, afraid to break Stan's concentration.

A few minutes later, Stan looked up. "Victor, do you think we could get permission to have a scene by the tree in the town square? I can have Blake and Remington enjoy the tree-lighting ceremony surrounded by all of the beautiful decorations. There can be plenty of Christmas spirit with laughter and singing and sampling great Christmas treats. Then as they are enveloped in the magic of the Christmas season, they turn to each other, both knowing they are very much in love and meant for one another. Blake finally trusts that love has found her and they kiss—a kiss like no other. A kiss that will…" Stan paused. "Oh! A kiss that will curl her toes." He grinned, looking at everyone. "Get it? Because elf shoes have curled toes."

Victor laughed and Catalina couldn't stop smiling. Jay's kisses had curled her toes, and with all of the elf talk, she knew her own personal experience was somehow being injected into the script, yet again. She loved where Blake's life was headed, and she wanted to go there with her.

"I love it!" Victor ate another Italian Christmas cookie. "Theo, do you think we could get our permit back?"

"I'll try my best, sir. I'll work on it first thing in the morning."

"Scratch that," Victor said, suddenly standing. "Picture this! Instead of filming in the town square, we use our mockup set so that we can go big, really big. We'll make it a winter wonderland. We'll have ice-skating and ice sculpting, snowman building, and hot cocoa all around. We'll have every branch of every tree decorated, and an enormous Christmas tree right in the center. We'll have coordinated music, and all the trees will light up, one by one, with the last one—the center tree—exploding with lights. We'll have fireworks and invite the townspeople to be in the movie. There'll be carolers, and roasting chestnuts, and eggnog. Mary's gingerbread eggnog! We'll have ten times more decorations than there are in the real town square. We'll go big, Hollywood big, so big that the astronauts at the International Space Station will be able to see it from space!"

Catalina gawked at Victor, wondering who had taken over his body. Then Mary giggled, ecstatically happy, and everyone else broke out laughing.

"Yes, sir," Theo said. "I'll talk to our production designer and see if she can have something ready by next week."

Catalina leaned over to Neil and quietly whispered, "I think we just got confirmation on our science experiment."

Neil nodded, still in shock. "The Scrooge Legend is real."

As Jay headed back home, he replayed the night over in his head. It had taken all of his willpower to stop kissing Catalina. He'd said their initial kiss had been electrifying, which was the truth, but their kissing tonight went beyond words. She had turned his insides to jelly, including his brain, and now he could think of nothing but her.

How was he going to stay focused on work tomorrow, unless he could only take pictures of her? How was he going to handle Grayson cozying up to her? They were actors and would only be pretending to care for one another, but it was still going to be difficult to stand by and watch him put his arm around her. And make her laugh. And kiss her.

He wasn't going to go there. His relationship with Catalina had started with a solid friendship years ago, and after everything they discovered tonight, he was fairly confident their bond would grow stronger with every passing day.

He was so grateful that the Scrooge Legend had sought them out, as every resident in town knew the legend righted lives that had been knocked off-kilter. Had he been the one to change their future trajectory by that one fateful decision, or had it been a series of circumstances? He'd never know for sure. At least the truth came out about why their friendship had ended, and she had taken it remarkably well. He was relieved she had understood how he'd only been trying to do the right thing by her and for her career.

Now he wanted his career back more than ever. He had so much to say through filmmaking, and he wanted to be given the chance to do that. He also wanted to develop projects with Catalina. Their work together on his first film was magic, and they could again create something that was meaningful to them both.

He pulled into his parents' driveway and went inside. He'd had an amazing time, and he could see that Catalina had, too. The night had started out by promising to show her hard evidence of Christmas magic, and she finally saw it—not in the photo of the elf shoes, but by believing in him. She had put her faith back in love again, and he couldn't wait to see where they were headed.

Chapter Thirty

Catalina sat in the driver's seat of an old beat-up car. It was idling on the side of a deserted road at the far end of St. Nicholas. While she waited for Victor to call action, she looked over at Jay who was taking photos of Victor, Clayton, and the camera crew. Victor was changing before her eyes. After an incredibly fun writing session last night, she had worried he would wake up grumpy and slide back into his usual unhappy self. But that wasn't the case at all. He was actually sharing a laugh with the guys.

Stan was even changing. His rewrites were getting better with every pass. Piper had been very happy to learn that the character based on her no longer stole cars for a living.

"Ready to roll!" Mark announced. "Roll sound."

"Speed," called out the sound mixer.

"Roll camera," Mark said.

"Rolling," replied the camera operator.

Catalina focused and put her hands on the steering well, as if Blake had just pulled over her car.

The second assistant camera operator stepped in front of the camera to slate the scene and take, then cleared the frame.

Victor called, "Action!"

Blake looked in her rearview mirror at the flashing police cruiser lights and frowned. "Just what I need." She gathered her license and registration to hand the officer.

The actor, dressed as a highway patrol officer, knocked on her window.

Blake lowered it with a smile. "Hello, officer."

"May I see your license and registration, please?"

"Of course." She handed them over. "Did I do something wrong?"

He examined her license. "You seem to be in quite a hurry, Ms. Dickens. What's so important that you couldn't maintain the speed limit?"

"Oh, I'm visiting my mom. I haven't seen her in a while. I didn't realize I was speeding."

The officer bent down and studied her face. "Is your mother Ann Dickens?"

"Why, yes. Do you know her?"

A smile took over his face. "Your mother made the best Christmas cookies at last year's festival. I must have eaten a half a dozen."

Blake laughed. "She's quite the baker. I'll let her know that you're a fan. Maybe we can whip up a batch or two and bring them over to the station."

"We sure would sure like that," he said. "All right, Ms. Dickens. Be on your way." He handed back her license and registration. "But please slow down. We have a lot of deer crossing our roads."

Or flying over them, Catalina suddenly thought. "Yes, sir."

"Oh, and Ms. Dickens, do try to enjoy your time

here. Life moves a lot slower in St. Nicholas. Don't be in such a hurry all the time."

"Great advice," she said. "Thank you."

The officer walked back to his car, and Blake breathed a sigh of relief.

"Maybe my luck is changing after all," she said to herself.

"And cut!" Victor looked up at the sky. "What's with all these clouds?"

"It's crazy how fast the weather changes here." Clayton checked his light meter, made a few adjustments, and they continued to shoot until they had full coverage of the scene. Just as Victor appeared ready to move on to the next scene, producers George and Luisa went over to talk to him. Catalina was too far away to hear what they were saying, but when Stan was called over to join the discussion, she knew a rewrite was in the works.

She sighed and hoped for the best. She liked the scene and couldn't help but notice how the rewrite, once again, seemed to be mirroring what she was feeling. She really could use at least a month off, where her life could move at a slower pace.

While they were waiting, Jay took an establishing shot of her behind the wheel, then took a few close-ups. "New wheels?" Jay joked, looking over the rust on the lower side of the car.

Catalina laughed. "This actually reminds me of my first car in LA. It was a real clunker."

"At least you had one. I got around town on a used motorcycle."

"Take five," Mark called out.

"This can't be good," Catalina said as she got out.

They leaned against the car, watching the impromptu meeting that was going on behind the camera.

"Victor's been in such a good mood today," Jay said. "But now he doesn't look so happy."

"Neither does Stan." She groaned. "I better go see what's going on."

Catalina made her way over to the meeting.

"But I liked the drama," George said. "And that's what the studio's expecting. Not this sugary scene."

"No one had a problem with it earlier this morning," Luisa replied. "We don't have time to be shooting two versions of the movie."

"Then we stick with the original script," George insisted. "Having Blake steal cars gives her a bigger character arc. Don't you agree, Catalina?"

"No." She crossed her arms, irritated how George had completely derailed their great day. Scrooginess was like a virus; it jumped from one person to another. Victor was on his way to recovery, and now George was trying to take his place. "Look, George, we've been over this before. Piper, the real woman behind this story, never stole cars a day in her life. She was very upset by that negative characterization of her. I can't do that to her, and Stan's new rewrite is good. It shows just how magical this town is. The second she's within city limits, her luck changes. It's a precursor to what's about to happen if she allows it."

"The studio doesn't care about Piper, and I don't, either."

"Which studio exec is complaining?" Victor asked. "Because I'm not seeing it. In the original shooting script, Blake's chase ended as she entered the town because Stan made her car invisible by magical elves. If anyone is to believe that our movie is based on a true story, then Stan had to take out the magical elves, talking reindeer, and Christmas fairies. I agree with Catalina. Stan has written a very good realistic scene."

"This movie is about Christmas magic," George reminded everyone. "How about we combine both ideas? She steals the car, the cop pulls her over, but the magical elves hypnotize the cop so he has no idea she's stolen the car."

"You can't be serious." Catalina glared at George.

"It won't change the current scene much," he said. "Instead of saying, 'Just what I need,' Blake will say something like, 'Oh, no! I'm about to get busted for stealing this car.'"

Catalina groaned. "That's the worst dialogue I've ever heard."

"That's why we have a writer on payroll." George motioned to Stan. "Stan can fix it."

"Stan doesn't want to fix it," Stan said as snowflakes hit his glasses.

Catalina cast her eyes upward. "Where did this come from?"

"It's snowing?" George asked, checking his weather app.

Good observation, Catalina wanted to say.

"It can't be snowing. I've got two more scenes to shoot today." Victor's mouth turned down into a scowl. "Theo!"

Theo ran over to his side. "Yes, sir?"

"It's snowing."

"Yes, it is."

"Why is it snowing? I didn't call for snow. Make it stop!"

"I…uh…can't."

"Whoever didn't read the weather forecast correctly is fired. You got that?" Victor stormed off.

Great. And now Victor is back to being a Scrooge.

"The weather app says it will be snowing until four thirty." George scowled at his phone as he refreshed his weather app and checked it again. "Can this really be right?" He looked at Stan.

"I'm not a weatherman, just the writer." Stan walked off.

"George, calm down," Luisa said. "Let me go look at our options and see what we can do." She hurried away.

"You." George snapped his fingers at Jay, who was taking pictures.

"His name is Jay," Catalina said as Jay stopped what he was doing and came over.

"You're a local hire. Mind telling me what's going on here?"

Jay shrugged. "What exactly are you referring to?"

"The dramatic change in weather. Is this an anomaly, or are your weathermen completely inept?"

"We often get hit with storms out of nowhere. That's mountain weather for you."

"Well, this is just terrific." George huffed. "Is this going to last all day?"

Jay glanced at the sky. "Hard to say, but we're pretty socked in."

He groaned. "But it's only eleven thirty. This is going to blow the rest of the day." The snow began falling at a faster rate as he looked up at the sky. "I don't know which studio genius decided to begin filming right before Christmas, but I'm going to find out and tear him a new one!" George stomped off, ranting, punching numbers into his phone.

"They're all so ridiculous," Catalina said to Jay. "Why can't the money people let the creative people create?"

"Because money people would rather be creative people."

She sighed, shaking her head.

"Just breathe."

"Best advice I ever received." She took a deep breath and immediately felt better. She held out her hand, catching flakes, as the snow started to clump together. "I'd forgotten how beautiful snowfalls are."

"We're shutting it down, folks," Mark called out. "See you tomorrow."

"A snow day?" Catalina looked at Jay, excitedly. "We actually got a snow day?"

"Let's not waste it," Jay said. "How about I show you the real St. Nicholas?"

She broke into a huge smile. "Yes!"

It didn't take long for Catalina to change out of her wardrobe, or for Jay to wrap up what he was doing.

"I need to drop off my equipment at my parents' house first," he said as they got in his Jeep. "If that's all right."

"Sure." She watched the snowflakes collect rapidly on his windshield. "Colorado is so much warmer in the winter than Maine." She unzipped her coat, feeling a little too warm.

"I'm glad to see you're starting to acclimate to the cold."

"Hard not to when you, Angel, and Mary are fattening me up."

Jay turned the windshield wipers up a notch. "What exactly was George so upset about?"

Catalina groaned. "He said the studio wants to return to the original version of the script with Blake stealing cars."

"Typical." Jay shook his head. "Please tell me that's not going to happen."

"It was heading in that direction," she said. "And then George decided to throw in a few suggestions of his own. He pitched the idea that when the cop pulls Blake over in a stolen vehicle, he gets hypnotized by elves and lets her go."

"Ah. Now this day makes sense." Jay glanced at her. "There's your reason for the weather change."

"What?" Catalina gave him a skeptical look. "Are you trying to tell me the snow shut us down because Santa didn't like the idea of another rewrite?"

"Strange things happen when someone tries to mess with the Scrooge Legend."

She laughed. "The weather change is a coincidence and nothing more."

"Coincidence is the most overused word by Scrooges. No offense."

"First, there are weather changes so an elf can pick up the mail, and now a snowstorm brought on by a possible revised scene in a movie? I don't see the connection."

"They're connected because of the Scrooge Legend. The scene change is a bad one. It not only paints Piper in a bad light, but it's also claiming that elves have the ability to hypnotize law enforcement. The whole thing is so absurd that it should never be filmed. It can't be filmed in a snowstorm."

She shrugged. "They'll just film it tomorrow."

"Then I predict it will be snowing tomorrow."

"Then they'll film the day after tomorrow. It can't snow forever." She checked her weather app. "Says clear skies for the rest of the week."

"Just like it did today," Jay reminded her.

The weather app had said clear skies. She'd checked it herself when she was getting dressed this morning.

"I know what it sounds like, but I grew up here," he said. "I've seen weather interference over and over again when a Scrooge is involved."

The snow was really coming down now. "It definitely came out of nowhere, I'll give you that," she said, finding herself a little curious. "Exactly how often does the weather step in to change the future?"

"A lot. Last summer St. Nicholas hosted a miserable, loveless, thickheaded Scrooge, like Victor. He refused to believe in anything, so he packed his bags and headed out of town after just one day. But he didn't get far because a massive thunderstorm came out of nowhere and flooded the streets."

"What happened to the Scrooge?"

"He met his soul mate in a coffee shop, waiting for the storm to pass." Jay stopped at a red light, and took a moment to look at her. "Our town has come to learn that when a person is unhappy, it's usually because they've had some form of loss in their life, which often leads them to giving up on love."

"So love fixes everything."

"Doesn't it?" The light turned green, and he continued driving to his parents' house.

"Not everything. I had an assistant who recorded a private conversation between me and a producer, and when I caught her, she edited my reaction, making me look like a horrible prima donna. Was she an unhappy person? Who knows, but I don't know how love could have fixed that incident."

"I'd be willing to bet that assistant had removed love from her life. She then became jealous of you, thinking you had it all, and saw nothing wrong with trying to destroy your career. Did you know anything about her personal life?"

She shook her head. "She was my assistant for a whopping two days."

"It's a good thing she wasn't with you any longer. Who knows what kind of damage she could have inflicted? But trust me. Her attack on you wasn't about you."

"That's an interesting way of looking at people," she said. "I suppose we all make too many snap judgments of others. We rarely think about the pleasant people we encounter, but we remember those who ruined our day. The short-tempered saleswoman might have been up all night with a sick child."

"Exactly."

"Now I really am curious about my ex-assistant. I never thought to consider she was lashing out in pain."

"You could always suggest her as a Scrooge, if the mailbox will open for you."

"That's a good idea, though maybe I'm not the best person to suggest someone. I'm a little worried that Victor slipped back into his Scroogy ways. He was yelling at Theo about the snow."

"He's still a work in progress, as Mary would say, but come day seven, he will be a happier man."

She was on day four, and she had definitely changed.

She had finally cut her emotional ties to Grayson. She was stronger around him, less wounded, surer of herself. Before coming to St. Nicholas, she'd convinced herself she never wanted to fall in love again. Now she understood that had been a knee-jerk reaction—a short-term fix for her fear of getting hurt again. She wanted love in her life. She wanted to be in a long-term relationship again, and she wanted it with Jay.

She studied him as he pulled into the driveway. Not only did Jay have the character traits she wanted in a man—honesty, integrity, empathy for others—he was really very handsome. He had a strong chin in perfect alignment with his thin, straight nose and alluring lips. He was clean-shaven, which she found very attractive. She had grown tired of the five-o'clock shadow seen everywhere in her industry. Perhaps Jay's best attribute was his deep, mesmerizing eyes—eyes that reached her soul whenever he held her gaze—which he was doing right at that moment.

He leaned toward her, touched her face with his hand, and brushed his lips over hers. She responded and moved closer to him. He pressed his mouth onto hers, and she could think of nothing else.

The garage door suddenly clanked loudly as it began to open in front of them. They jerked apart like two teenagers caught kissing on the living room couch.

Jay glanced in his rearview mirror. "It's my mom," he said, regaining his composure. "And she's a big fan." He closed his eyes with a grimace.

She let out a breathy laugh. "That's okay. I'm used to it."

"We won't stay long."

"I'm in no rush." She got out of his Jeep and walked

to the back to help him carry in his equipment as his mom drove by them and into the garage.

"I had a feeling you'd be home early with this snow," his mom said, getting out of the car. When she saw who was with Jay, she screamed with excitement. "Oh, my goodness. It's you!"

"Yes, it's me," Catalina said with a smile.

"Mom, Catalina, Catalina, my mom, Denise." Jay handed Catalina his camera case, then grabbed the rest himself.

"Come on in, Catalina. Please excuse our messy garage." His mom opened the door to the house as Jay closed the garage door behind them.

"This storm came out of nowhere." His mom took off her coat and set her things down. "Must have something to do with the Scrooge Legend."

Catalina caught his eye, and he gave her an I-told-you-so look.

"It sure surprised all of us." Catalina removed her hat and shoved it in her pocket. "We'd only been shooting for a few hours when it shut us down."

"I bet you were perfect in every frame," his mom said, gushing. "I've seen every one of your movies, but my favorite is *Sage Under Fire*, of course."

"That film is one of my favorites as well." Catalina noticed how cozy their home was with all the Christmas decorations. Their Christmas tree was nicely decorated with shiny multicolored glass balls mixed with the right amount of personalized and homemade ornaments. Four stockings were hung on the fireplace mantel, and garland with fairy lights wrapped the banister to the second floor.

"Take off your coat and make yourself comfortable."

His mom motioned to the coatrack. "Who's up for some hot cocoa or tea?"

Jay parked his equipment on the bench by the door. "Don't trouble yourself. We can't stay."

"What?" His mom was aghast. "You can't go out in that."

"We're only going into town."

"Why? If it's an early lunch you're looking for, you've come to the right place. I've got homemade chicken noodle soup and corn bread."

"Thanks, Mom, but—"

"Sounds delicious, Mrs. Townsend." Catalina looked to Jay. "We can stay for lunch, can't we?"

"Uh…sure. If that's what you want to do." He went into the kitchen to help.

"Wonderful!" His mom's face lit up as she heated up the soup.

"Tea, coffee, cocoa, water?" he asked, glancing at her.

"Water, please. Can I help?" she asked.

"No need." His mom warmed up the corn bread. "How's the movie going?"

"Lots of changes and we're behind schedule." Catalina sat down at the kitchen table.

"As all movies are." Jay brought over a glass of water.

"I'm sure your producers weren't happy about today's weather." His mom gave the soup one last stir.

"No, they weren't, especially since we're only shooting exteriors here."

"It's too bad you can't shoot the entire movie in town," his mom said as she brought the soup and corn bread to the table and sat down with Catalina and Jay.

Catalina tasted the soup. "This is excellent, Mrs.

Townsend. My mom used to make chicken noodle soup for me when I was little."

"It's the best on a snowy day." His mom passed around the corn bread. "I bet you're not used to this cold weather, being from LA."

"Actually, I grew up in Maine, and my parents still live there."

"A beautiful state," his mom said. "Do you get back there often?"

"Unfortunately, no. I'd promised my mom I'd be home for the holidays, from Thanksgiving through New Year's Day, but then the movie's schedule was pushed up."

"We're still supposed to get the week off at Christmas," Jay reminded her.

"Oh, I hope so." His mom looked a little alarmed, no doubt realizing that her own Christmas plans could be easily canceled. "I'm sure your parents are looking forward to seeing you."

The door to the garage slammed shut. "You won't believe it! I just saw Grayson Edwards!" Hailey came around the corner and stopped dead in her tracks when she saw who was sitting at the kitchen table.

"Catalina, this is my sister, Hailey."

"Oh my gosh. I can't believe this! Two movie stars in one day." Hailey retrieved her phone from her handbag. "Can I get a selfie with you? My friends aren't going to believe it."

"That's a big no." Jay raised a warning brow to her.

"Hailey, put your phone away and come have some lunch." His mom went back into the kitchen to get her a bowl of soup.

Hailey looked truly crushed.

"It's all right," Catalina said. "I haven't had to take any pictures with fans since I've been here, and I kind of miss it."

Jay caught Catalina's eye and knew she was stretching the truth, but she seemed happy to pose with his little sister anyway.

"You are so awesome, Catalina. Big brother, can you do the honors?"

She handed him her phone while she bent down next to Catalina.

He took several, then handed back her phone. "No posting on social media."

"I won't." Hailey examined the photos and smiled, looking pleased, before she set it aside. "Are you going to film around Grayson, now that he has a broken leg?"

"What?" Catalina, Jay, and his mom all said at once.

"You didn't know?" She ping-ponged her gaze between all three. "I saw him getting into an SUV with crutches."

"Are you sure it was him?" Jay asked.

"Positive. I was with one of my friends, and she yelled out to him to feel better."

Catalina immediately texted Neil. "My assistant is finding out."

Jay's mom set a bowl of soup in front of Hailey. "Anyone else need anything?"

"We're fine," Jay said. "Come eat before it gets cold."

"How do you like St. Nicholas?" his mom asked Catalina.

"I haven't seen much of it, but the people seem very friendly, and of course it's beautiful with so many Christmas decorations."

"Do you like filming on location?" Hailey asked.

"Absolutely. I love going to new places, and I've been fortunate that my movies have filmed in beautiful settings." Catalina got a text and opened it. The production office was in chaos, which she wasn't willing to share with her captive audience, but the rest she could. "Hailey's correct. Grayson broke his leg skiing. They're figuring out a workaround for tomorrow."

"Guess filming the ice-skating scene is off the schedule." Jay spooned in his soup.

She set aside her phone. "You know, I don't remember working on a movie that had so many setbacks."

"Why did they decide to shoot now?" his mom asked.

"Our director had a scheduling conflict, so we needed to start early if they wanted to keep him."

"They should have asked Jay."

"It doesn't work that way, Mom."

"Well, it should."

"Yes." Catalina smiled at Jay. "He would have been a much better choice."

Seeming uncomfortable with the spotlight now on him, he glanced out the French doors. "Looks like the snow is tapering off." He ate the last bite of corn bread. "Might be a good time to get going before it starts again."

Catalina nodded and finished off her soup. "Thank you so much for the delicious lunch," she said to Jay's mom as she took her dishes into the kitchen.

"You're very welcome. Stop by anytime."

Jay grabbed his camera, and they headed out to his Jeep.

"So where are we going?" Catalina asked as they got in.

"It's a surprise."

Chapter Thirty-One

When Jay found a parking spot at the town's one and only hotel, Catalina gave him a confused look. "You know most of the crew is staying here, right?"

He glanced at the sky. "The snow has stopped. At least temporarily. I'll take it as a good sign." He grinned. "We're not going inside."

"We're not?" she asked as they headed right toward the front entrance, but then he walked past it and over to a bench on the side of the hotel's pickup and drop-off area.

"You might want to bundle up," he said, keeping an eye on the street leading into the hotel grounds.

Catalina pulled her hat from her pocket and put it on, along with her scarf and gloves.

He chuckled to himself. "I guess George lost the argument."

She gave him a funny look. "George?"

"Our producer who wants Blake stealing cars. The snow stopped."

"Oh, right." She laughed. "Yes, I'm sure that's the reason." She got a text, then narrowed her eyes on Jay. "You knew."

"How would I have known?"

"By a text, just like me."

"I don't think production cares if I know what is being reshot and what isn't."

"Hmm. This still doesn't mean I believe you."

He smiled again and continued to watch the entrance to the hotel grounds.

"Just what are we waiting for?"

"This."

A horse-drawn carriage appeared from around the corner, came up the drive, and stopped right in front of them.

Catalina's eyes sparkled. "Is this for us?"

"Yes." Jay put his camera strap around his neck.

"Afternoon, Jay." An older man with white hair and rosy cheeks tipped his hat, then looked at Catalina. "Afternoon, Ms. Jones. You bring sunshine wherever you go," he said, bowing to her.

She laughed at his over-the-top performance. Right on cue, the sun briefly made an appearance, which had her raising a brow. "I really can't command the weather, but I'm not entirely sure about Jay."

"You are quite right, Ms. Jones. Jay is more in tune with nature than anyone I know." He held out his hand and helped her into the carriage.

Jay hopped up and sat beside her as the man set a blanket over their legs.

"I hear Ms. Jones enjoys hot apple cider." He handed Jay a thermos with two mugs.

"Thank you, Samuel."

Samuel climbed aboard and commanded his horse to begin walking on a private road near the back of the hotel.

Jay opened the thermos and poured out hot cider into the two mugs before handing one to Catalina.

She took a sip and hummed with pleasure. "On my first day here, I saw a horse-drawn carriage in town and wanted to climb aboard right then."

"I remember how much you fell in love with horses when we were filming *Sage Under Fire*. Samuel takes great care of his carriage horses. Duke is the one who's pulling us. He goes crazy for carrots, which we can feed him later."

"Sounds like you've taken quite a few rides."

"The first job I ever had was helping Samuel at his stables. I also helped him with his carriage rides on the weekends when he had back-to-back bookings."

"Your first job was much better than mine. I worked fast food." She grimaced. "I stood over hot grease cooking French fries all day. The only good thing about it was that I lost my craving for French fries forever."

Jay chuckled.

"This is so incredibly beautiful." Catalina inhaled the clean, mountain air. "I love how everything is blanketed in fresh white snow."

"Isn't this similar to your parents' place in Maine?"

"They live in a brownstone townhome in Portland. It's still beautiful, but in a colonial sense with brick sidewalks, cobblestone roads, and gas streetlamps. There are lots of tourists in the summer, but in the winter, it gets bone-chilling cold—being so close to the water."

"I've never been."

"I'll take you."

"I'd love that," he said as the carriage slowed in order to go over a snow-covered bridge. A couple of snowshoe hares hopped out of the way, and Jay quickly snapped a few photos of them before they fled.

Catalina looked over the side of the carriage at the

stream below them. Jay took pictures of a fox along the water. He then made a clicking noise with his tongue, and the fox glanced in his direction.

"Gotcha." Jay shot several photos.

"Do you remember the two baby bears we saw hiking that one weekend after we wrapped *Sage Under Fire?*" she asked.

"Yeah, they were adorable," Jay replied. "But from a distance."

"I was determined to get closer, even though you had warned me not to, and you pulled me back right as mama bear appeared on scene. I'd hate to think what might have happened if you hadn't been with me."

"I imagine you would have figured it out fast."

She laughed a little, then looked into his eyes. "Seems you're always protecting me one way or another."

"It's a job I'm more than happy to do." He put his arm around her and she snuggled into him as the carriage took them into the woods.

"It's so peaceful here. I can see why you love it."

"When I was a kid, I didn't appreciate it like I do now," he said. "I've come back here more than once to regroup, to figure things out."

"Have you decided if you'll be staying with the film when it moves back to LA?"

"I hadn't planned on it, but that was before things started going so well with you."

"Really?" Her heart felt like it was going to leap out of her chest. "You'll stay?"

He nodded. "I talked to Luisa this morning, and I'll definitely be staying with the film."

"Good." A feeling of serenity washed over her. "I love being on set with you again. I would have preferred that you were directing me, but even as a still photographer my work is better with you around."

He seemed to sit a little taller. "I'm glad I can make a difference."

"More than you know," she said, looking deep into his eyes. "Will you stay in LA after we wrap?"

He searched her face, as if he wanted to know how serious she was being. "If things keep moving in a good direction, I'll make the move out there again."

"I'm so happy to hear that." A sense of relief encompassed her as she cuddled into him. "I was thinking about what you said—that we need balance. I've realized, being here, that I need a place like St. Nicholas to retreat to. But I'd want someone special to share that retreat with." She fixed her gaze on him. "Someone who'd want that, too."

"I'd like to be that someone." He brushed her hair out of her eyes. "If you'll have me."

She blinked away her misty eyes. "I want that—more than anything." She tugged on his jacket to pull him closer. He lowered his head and kissed her—a long, heartfelt kiss before he wrapped her in his arms and held her tight. She let out a vocal sigh of true contentment. She couldn't believe how happy she was in that moment, being in Jay's arms, feeling love all around her as they rode together through the magical winter wonderland of St. Nicholas.

An hour later, Catalina fed Duke the last bit of carrot as Jay paid Samuel. "Thank you, Samuel, for a wonderful afternoon."

"My pleasure." He tipped his hat, then rode away as it began to snow again.

"That was such a beautiful tour," Catalina said, walking back to the car.

"It isn't over yet, unless you need to work."

"Nope. I thought I'd save myself some time and wait until tonight to get the latest rewrites."

"Good plan," he said with a chuckle. "I pulled the SD card from my night camera early this morning but haven't had a chance to view the recordings. Do you want to check it out with me while we wait for the snow to stop again?"

Her eyes lit up. "Absolutely."

As he drove to the diner where they wouldn't be disturbed, he couldn't be happier that he was getting a second chance with Catalina. There was no doubt in his mind where she stood, especially since she said her performance was better when he was around. That had touched him deeply.

Angel brought over two hot tea setups with an assortment of teas. "I might have to name this section of our diner after you two."

"Works for me," Jay said. "Thanks, Angel." He turned on his laptop, loaded the SD card, and positioned it so Catalina could also see the footage. "The video camera is motion activated, and begins recording in zero point two seconds."

"Wow. That's fast."

"That's what I love about it. I won't miss anything if I can't physically be there." He started combing through the footage. The first triggered recording was of two curious raccoons, followed by deer. More wildlife passed by in the next five recordings. Then at a timestamp of eleven forty-five, the video showed interference. The recording went black for a good twenty seconds and when it resumed, a herd of reindeer were surrounding the mailbox.

Jay sat up straight, staring at the recording.

"Reindeer?" Catalina leaned into the screen. "What are they doing?"

"I've never seen this before," he said. "It's like they're protecting the mailbox."

The reindeers' heads jerked up, paying attention to something off-screen, then the video went black again.

"I think your camera is damaged," she said.

He couldn't believe it. Hailey was right. The Christmas magic had extended to the fake mailbox. "Nope. It's definitely not damaged."

The video came back on for a few more seconds, then as the reindeer began moving away from the mailbox, it went black again.

"Is this the interference you were talking about?"

"Yes."

"Have you ever seen the reindeer before yesterday?"

"First time, and now this." He rewound the recording and viewed it again.

"What do you think happened?"

"I think the mail collector stopped by."

He expected her to break out in laughter, tell him he was being ridiculous, that Christmas magic didn't exist, but she didn't do any of that. Instead, she asked him to play it for her again. And then again.

"Wait, stop," she said.

He stopped the video and slowly backed up frame by frame. Barely visible, hidden behind one of the reindeers looked to be striped material—like a shirt sleeve. The infrared camera had automatically switched to black and white, so the color of the stripes could not be confirmed. Even if they could, only a small portion of the striped sleeve was visible for half a second.

"You have a good eye," he said. "What does it look like to you?"

"A striped sleeve."

"Agreed." He viewed the frames in slow motion. "It's definitely a striped shirt."

She studied the slo-mo images. "I really don't think it could be someone on the crew."

"It couldn't be. The reindeer definitely know whoever is with them."

"Another mystery in St. Nicholas," she said, viewing the recording one more time. "How come you never wrote a screenplay about your own hometown?"

"It's kind of sacred, you know, and I didn't want to make money off something that shouldn't be for sale."

"But we're making a movie about it right now."

"Are we, really?"

She laughed. "I guess not."

"Piper's story will be told properly," he said. "Or the Scrooge Legend will find a way to have the movie shelved. But I'm fairly certain the secret of the real Christmas magic is not in danger of being exposed." He paused the video on a reindeer looking directly into the camera, with a sliver of the striped sleeve exposed in the background.

"Let me ask you something. If the Scrooge Legend is everything you say it is, how is a movie being made at all?"

"It's not about the movie." He shrugged. "It's about who's making it. Look who's here in town being helped. Victor would have never come here. Stan wouldn't have either. You definitely wouldn't be here right now, and we would never be."

"That's depressing to even think about," she said, leaning closer to him. "I'm beginning to understand how powerful this legend is. That mailbox really did bring us together."

"And for that I'm forever grateful." He tipped her chin up and gave her a gentle kiss right there in the diner.

If he had any control over the Scrooge Legend, he would end Catalina's journey right now—with him, and in his arms. But he knew it didn't work that way. She now had the Christmas spirit, which meant she'd need to pay it forward to a future Scrooge, and when that happened, there was always a possibility of losing it all.

Chapter Thirty-Two

It was early evening by the time Jay got Catalina back to the B&B. As much as neither one wanted to say good-night, Catalina had too many texts from Neil she could no longer ignore, and Jay still needed to download his photos from the morning. Then he got a text from Clayton telling him to come immediately to the diner, as his career depended on it.

Curious, Jay headed back into town, and as he walked through the diner doors, he understood. Clayton was talking to Peter Wells.

"Hey, Jay," Clayton called him to come over. "I was just telling Peter that you and I had worked together on *Sage Under Fire*."

"Hi, Peter." Jay shook his hand. "Good to see you again."

"I wondered what happened to you. I saw your name on the contact list and couldn't believe it." Peter furrowed his brow in confusion. "You're a still photographer now?"

"No, just filling in for the guy who couldn't make it. My parents live in town, and I was already here for the holidays."

"Lucky us—to have a real director as our still photographer," Peter said. "Whatever happened to that psychological thriller you had planned to shop around?"

"I decided to make a few changes after speaking with you. I had planned on taking it out, but then I got busy with another project."

"I'd like to read the latest version if you think it's ready to be seen."

"It's good to go. I'll bring you a copy tomorrow."

"Great. See you on set." Peter walked out with one of his assistants.

"Man, I owe you one," Jay said.

"Don't mention it. Right place, right time. Peter will be with us for the rest of the shoot, so hopefully you'll have more time to talk with him."

"Yeah, that would be great." Jay unzipped his coat. "Have you eaten?"

"I was just about to get something."

"Let me buy you dinner."

Jay felt a little bad about missing another dinner with his family, but he knew they'd understand. After his day with Catalina, he was more than ready to get back to work in Hollywood.

"Your script must really be good for Peter to still be interested in it," Clayton said, wiping grease off his fingers from the fried chicken. "Have you talked to Catalina about it?"

"It hasn't come up." Jay took a bite of his ham sandwich.

"It would be great to get her on board. Her name attached would make your film a done deal."

Jay nodded, swallowing. "I plan on talking to her about it soon. I'd like to get the whole gang back together. You as my DP and Catalina as my leading lady, but I want to see what Peter has to say after he reads the rewrite. Catalina has a lot on her plate right now, and the last thing I want is for her to misinterpret my attentions toward her."

"So things are moving in a good direction between you two?"

"Yeah." Jay could barely believe how fast it happened. Even though he knew the Scrooge Legend had thrown them together, it was always up to the Scrooge to embrace it.

"That's awesome. I'm seriously happy for you. And she obviously cares a lot about you. Her entire demeanor has changed."

"I don't know if I've had anything to do with that, but she's definitely more confident around her ex. She's more settled, more relaxed."

"Settled and relaxed is definitely all you," Clayton said. "Will you be staying on with the movie now?"

He nodded. "I was able to work it out this morning."

"That's great, man. You're welcome to crash at my place, if you need somewhere to stay."

"Thanks, Clayton. I might take you up on that."

When they finished and were getting up to leave, Jay noticed Brandi sitting alone at a table right by them. "Hi, Brandi. I heard about Grayson's ski accident. How's he doing?"

"Oh, um, I don't know." She ran a hand through her hair. "We're no longer together."

"I'm sorry to hear that."

"Yeah. Thanks." Brandi's hat suddenly dropped in front of Jay.

He reached down and picked it up. "Well, enjoy the rest of your stay in St. Nicholas. I think this is yours."

"Oh, right." Brandi gave him a quick smile. "Thanks."

"No problem."

Jay walked away with Clayton. "That was a weird conversation."

"She probably didn't know what to say."

He glanced back at Brandi sitting all alone and staring at her phone. He hoped Clayton was right, but he had a feeling there was more to the story.

As Catalina walked into the B&B after a great day with Jay, she almost forgot that she was in St. Nicholas for work. She'd never prepared as little for a movie role as she had for *The Scrooge Legend*, yet her performance didn't seem to be suffering. In fact, it was just the opposite. Victor and the producers seemed quite happy with her work. She couldn't exactly take all the credit. She meant what she told Jay. Her work was better when he was near because he made her feel safe. In order to reach the emotional level she needed for each scene, she had to remain open and vulnerable. This had become increasingly difficult over the past year because of her own emotional wounds and not trusting those around her. But with Jay close by, she felt safe to be vulnerable.

Neil was sitting by the fire in the living room with his computer open and piles of paperwork on the coffee table. "I just received your sides for tomorrow." He handed them over.

She sat, skimmed them, and groaned.

"What's wrong?"

"They've nixed the ice-skating and replaced it with a carriage ride."

"I saw that. Don't you think that's a great idea? They can hide Grayson's broken leg with a blanket."

"It is. It's just—" She shook her head, realizing the script was once again mirroring her life. "Jay and I took a carriage ride this afternoon."

"That's awesome." Neil's smile disappeared. "Oh. That's a weird coincidence."

"An unfortunate coincidence." It was going to be weird. Weird for her and for Jay.

"At least he took you first, and for real."

"You're right."

Neil had a point. She'd experienced a wonderful afternoon with Jay—good memories that Grayson couldn't touch.

"Did you have a good time?" he asked.

"The best." She smiled, thinking about it. "The ride was very romantic. I highly recommend it for you and Iris."

"She hates snow."

"How? It's so beautiful."

"I don't understand it myself." Neil seemed disappointed.

"Surprise her, then. If you go during the day, she'll be warm enough. I bet she'll love it."

"Good evening, Catalina." Mary handed Neil a cup of hot cocoa. "I didn't hear you come in. Let me get you a cup of hot cider."

"You know what, Mary? I think I'll try your famous hot cocoa."

"Really?" Her face lit up.

"Neil raves about it. It's time I taste it for myself."

"Oh, you won't be disappointed. Be right back." Mary did a little hop-skip as she turned and went back into the kitchen.

"You finally made that woman happy," Neil said. "I

think you must have been the first guest who turned down her cocoa."

"If I'm in a sugar coma within the hour, you can tell the hospital what did it."

He laughed.

"Have you seen Victor?" Catalina asked.

"He's still at the production office. There was an emergency meeting with the producers over Grayson's broken leg. Victor wanted to replace him with Landon Barnes, but Luisa said it was too late. Landon just signed on to a Melissa McCarthy movie."

"That's fantastic," she said. "I was so upset about how Landon had been treated."

"I think Victor's finally regretting his little stunt."

"Hopefully it will cure him of ever wanting to pull another on his unsuspecting actors." She remembered what Jay said about the legend—that it righted lives that had gone off-kilter. If the legend needed Victor to pull his gotcha stunt in order for her to heal and move on from Grayson, did it mean the legend had helped Landon since he lost out on work?

"Here you are, dear." Mary appeared next to Catalina. "Hot cocoa topped with whipped cream and toasted caramel."

"Toasted caramel? What are you doing to me?" Catalina took the cup of cocoa and inspected it. "This looks too good to drink." She set it to her lips, took a small sip, and tasted the rich, deep chocolate, the light, sweet whipped cream, the buttery toasted caramel and almost died. "Oh, wow." She took another sip and let it linger on her tongue before she swallowed. "This ought to be illegal."

Mary giggled, elated. "I'm so glad you like it."

"I have a feeling that I'll be craving this on a cold night in LA. What will I do then?"

"Come for a visit."

"Ah. So this is how you lure everyone back to St. Nicholas."

Mary smiled proudly. "There's plenty more for as long as you're here."

Catalina took another sip, realizing she'd be back much sooner than she had planned.

Chapter Thirty-Three

"Morning." Catalina's beautiful voice filled the air.

Crouched on the ground with his camera, Jay turned to see her shining face above him. "Morning," he said, rising.

She took a deep breath and scanned her surroundings. "I can't believe we're shooting here on the same road we were on yesterday."

"Out of all places." He was just as surprised as she was when he got the updated call sheet. He'd wanted to remember their carriage ride as something he had only shared with her. But now she'd be taking one with Grayson.

"The snow has already covered our tracks from yesterday." She sounded a little sad.

"At least everything is glistening in the sun."

She nodded. "Gorgeous."

"You sure are." He snapped a photo, and he couldn't believe he made her blush.

"Hand it over."

"Why?"

"Because the movie needs a photo of their still photographer."

"I doubt that." He shied away.

"Then I want one of us." She pulled out her phone and took a selfie of them together. "Now, that's one good-looking couple," she said, seeming pleased.

Jay leaned over her shoulder to check it out. "Especially the woman, but the guy looks pretty darn happy."

"I have a feeling the woman is just as happy."

"Morning, Ms. Jones. Here's your tea." A PA handed her a cup.

"Thank you." Catalina tucked her phone away, then looked at Jay as she took a sip. "I almost died when I saw the ice-skating had been changed to a carriage ride." She moved closer to him. "I want you to know that this new scene doesn't hold a candle to yesterday's real one."

It was as if she knew what he'd been thinking last night when he read the new scene. He had worried that the movie version would lessen the magic of his carriage ride with her. He smiled, happy to hear her say that. "I happen to agree." He had to stop himself from kissing her. He glanced around to make sure they didn't have an audience. "I really want to kiss you right now."

"So do I, but I have to keep reminding myself where I am."

The crew started clapping as a golf cart drove up with Grayson inside. He got out with a cast on his leg. He leaned on his crutches and addressed the crew. "Thank you for all of your well wishes. I appreciate it, and I apologize for any delays I might have caused. As you can see, I am not a skier."

The crew laughed.

"I can't believe I just heard Grayson apologize," Catalina muttered.

"There's hope for him yet."

"Morning, everyone." Victor approached Catalina and Grayson, full of energy. "How are you feeling?" Victor inspected the cast on Grayson's leg.

"I'm ready to knock it out of the park," he said.

"That's what I want to hear." Victor raised his hand in a cheer, then eyed Catalina. "And how is my beautiful star today?"

"The sun is shining. I get another carriage ride. What more could I want?" She risked a glance at Jay, who had retreated to the sidelines.

"Excellent," Victor said. "Let me introduce you to Samuel, who has agreed to be in our movie today."

"It's so good to see you again." Catalina took Samuel's gloved hand in hers. "Yesterday's ride was wonderful."

"And your second will not disappoint." Samuel helped her up into the carriage. He then helped Grayson, who wasn't so graceful with a cast on his leg. Samuel set a wool blanket over their legs, hiding Grayson's cast entirely.

Jay took establishing shots of the scene, and then moved in closer to get shots of Catalina and Grayson only. He found it difficult to look through the viewfinder and see her with Grayson, who was sitting in the exact spot he'd been in only yesterday. Grayson whispered something to her and she smiled. It didn't look forced, which meant they were getting along. Not that he wanted them to be fighting. It just irritated him that Grayson was using his injury for sympathy.

"When I heard the snap," Grayson said to Catalina, "I knew it wasn't good."

"Oh, how horrible." She put a hand to her chest. "I probably would have fainted."

"It was incredibly painful—I'm not going to lie. But I couldn't allow myself to think about how much pain I was in because I knew I had to get down from that mountain."

Jay rolled his eyes at his dramatic storytelling, and couldn't tell if Catalina was getting totally sucked in to his story, or if she was just faking it.

"You were skiing alone?" she asked.

"I didn't start out that way. Brandi was with me, but then we broke up on our first run."

"I'm sorry," she said, and by Jay's keen eye, it seemed as if Catalina didn't feel one way or the other about Grayson's breakup.

"Thank you, but it's probably for the best. We were too different," Grayson said, not looking at all broken up about it. "Of course, now I don't have anyone to take care of me." He laid it on thick as he put his head on her shoulder.

"I'm sure you'll survive," she said, stiffening.

Jay jumped in. "Grayson, can I get you to look off in the distance—a look that says Remington has finally found where he's meant to be?"

Grayson sat up. "How's this?" He gazed over the horizon with a small but satisfied smile on his face.

Jay caught Catalina's eye and she mouthed a thank-you.

"Picture's up," Mark called out. "Last looks!"

The hair and makeup artists stepped in for final touches as Jay moved out of frame. Once the crew settled, and they were rolling, Victor called action.

Blake and Remington were smiling and laughing as Samuel set out on their journey.

"Cut! Excellent," Victor said.

"Going again," Mark announced.

Samuel's horse handler led Duke around in a circle until they were back to their first position.

Victor requested a few more takes before they moved on to closer shots of the actors.

Catalina finally looked to be having fun. Jay never thought he was the jealous type, but it seemed like Grayson was trying to flirt with her again.

He took a breath and cleared his head. He was being ridiculous, and he was not going to allow his sudden insecurity to cloud his judgment or lessen his professionalism. He'd remain a cool, levelheaded still photographer, but he couldn't wait for the scene to be over.

After a short break, the sound department miked the actors while the camera operator climbed aboard, situating himself next to Samuel but sitting backwards. Mark called for the crew to settle.

Catalina was in such high spirits. The weather was perfect, Grayson wasn't being smug or throwing Brandi in her face, the new scene worked better than the ice-skating scene it replaced, and Jay had even rescued her from an uncomfortable moment with her ex. She was truly enjoying herself.

"And action!" Victor called out.

Blake held up her champagne flute to Remington. "Here's to the completion of the most stunning home in all of St. Nicholas."

"Thank you," Remington said.

She clinked her glass to his before taking a sip. "Does this mean I'll finally be able to see the inside of my mother's house?"

"Hmm. I suppose I can make that happen."

"You better. I've waited long enough."

"Yes, you have." He gazed into her eyes, and she blushed, looking away. He put his arm around her, and they both set their eyes on the horizon, taking in the gorgeous landscape. "This is incredible," Remington said. "I can't believe you booked this carriage ride for us."

"I wanted to show you what makes St. Nicholas so beautiful."

"*You* make St. Nicholas so beautiful." As he stared into her eyes, Blake got lost in his.

"And cut!"

They broke apart.

"I like this scene," he said. "How do you feel about it?"

This was a first. Even when they were dating, he'd rarely asked her opinion. "It's good."

Grayson's cell dinged. He quickly retrieved it from his pocket, looking embarrassed. "I forgot to take this out of my jacket." He flipped the switch to silent. "Good thing I didn't ruin that take."

"Holding for sound!" Mark called.

"Guess I can check my phone while we wait."

Catalina sneaked a peek at his cell screen. It was a text with a video attached, from Brandi. Grayson groaned.

"If it's from Brandi, feel free to open it," she said. "She doesn't bother me."

He eyed Catalina. "She never did bother you, did she?"

Brandi had definitely bothered her at first, but she'd never admit it. "Why would she? You're allowed to move on, like I have."

Grayson studied her, and she thought she saw admiration in his eyes. "I was a jerk, parading her around in front of you. I'm sorry."

Another mature step taken by Grayson. I could get used to this. "Apology accepted."

A second text came in. "Please call me as soon as you watch what I sent," he read aloud, and sighed. "I should have never gone out with her."

"She seems…uh…very young."

"You can say it. She's immature. But she wasn't the only one. I didn't realize how immature *I'd* been acting until I recognized it in her." He sat, staring at the screen.

Catalina could tell he was dying to open the video. "You two broke up. Seriously, Grayson, nothing she says in that video is going to bother me, so if you want to open it, go ahead."

"Thanks." He opened it and turned the sound back on.

"Hello to all my fans out there," Brandi said into the camera. "When last we spoke, I told you I was going to St. Nicholas to get the real scoop behind the Ice Queen, and let me tell you, I've got the goods."

Grayson fumbled with his phone, closing the video as fast as possible.

Catalina steeled her spine as a wave of dread washed over her. "Keep playing the video."

"Why? She's nothing." Grayson turned pale. "I should have known she was going to do something like this."

"Give it to me." She held out her hand.

"Tech issue," Mark called out. "Take five!"

"Grayson, now."

He took a big breath and let it out. "I want you to know something first," he said, looking directly into her eyes. "The reason I broke up with Brandi was because I found out she was using me to get to you. I'm kicking myself for not figuring it out sooner. She kept mentioning you, asking how I felt about working with you. When I didn't say what she wanted to hear, she stepped it up a notch—comparing my acting to yours. She told me I was a terrible actor compared to you, and she said you had agreed."

Why had she been nice to Brandi? She knew something had been off during their last conversation. "That's a lie, Grayson. I never said that."

"I know." He nodded. "I knew it then, too. I told her that *she* was the failed actor, and she needed to stop being jealous of you. I told her the only thing going for her was that she was clinging on to me. I was out of line, and I regretted it the second it came out of my mouth." Grayson looked away, his jaw tightening. "Yesterday, I took her skiing and apologized. I thought we had moved on, but she brought you up again, right as we got off the chairlift. I couldn't understand why she was talking about you instead of us, and then I finally got it. It was never about me. It had always been about you. I broke up with her right then. I took off down the mountain, and she followed me. She overtook me and skied in front of me, cutting me off to stop me, which made me run into a tree and fracture my tibia."

She never thought Grayson would end up being a victim of jealousy like she had. She could tell how shaken up he was, and she felt bad for him—especially since he'd been physically hurt. "Grayson, I'm truly sorry this happened to you; that *she* happened to you."

"I am such an idiot. Something didn't ring true when I met her, but I ignored it because I wanted to make you jealous." He shook his head, angry with himself, and seeming to feel ashamed of his behavior. "I deserve getting injured, but you don't deserve getting wrapped up in her vengeance."

"You do not deserve getting physically hurt. No one does. Look, I've dealt with people like her before. As much as I'd like to never have to think about her again, we need to see the rest of her video."

"Why? It's not going to be flattering. Besides, who's really going to see it? She doesn't have that many followers."

"Doesn't matter. These types of things go viral. You know that. Play the rest of the video."

With a loud sigh, he tapped on it, and handed it over.

Brandi looked to be in a hotel room, filming herself, and she seemed quite pleased. "Let me tell you, I've got the goods. No one on the crew likes Catalina Jones. She's playing a female Scrooge in her new movie, and she is the biggest Scrooge I've ever met. She actually ruined my relationship with her ex-boyfriend Grayson, and he can't stand her. None of the crew likes her, either. Here's a small sampling."

Brandi turned the camera to a video on her computer screen, which was cued up. She hit play and Grayson said, "She's a failed actor. The only thing she has going for her is that I make her look good."

"I didn't say that." Grayson's eyes widened in shock.

The video cut to two grips being secretly recorded on the first day of filming. "I heard she lives up to her name as the Ice Queen."

"She'll freeze you out," the other guy groused. "I can't believe I turned down a trip to Puerto Vallarta for this."

It then cut to a PA, also on the first day. "Guys, chill. The Ice Queen is on her way."

Brandi popped back on. "I've been so upset about my breakup, but karma is swift. Turns out she's fallen for some low-level photographer, but he's just using her and she doesn't know it. Take a look."

The next cut showed Jay and Clayton having dinner together. Catalina recognized the shirt he had on yesterday.

"Have you talked to Catalina about it?" Clayton said in profile.

"It hasn't come up," Jay replied.

"It would be great to get her on board. Her name attached would make your film a done deal."

"That's the plan. I'll get Catalina as my leading lady. No problem."

"So things are moving in a good direction for your film?"

Jay laughed. "Yeah."

Brandi hopped back on. "Stay tuned for more Ice Queen drama."

The video ended. Catalina's hands were shaking as tears streamed down her face.

"Catalina, I am so sorry. I know you saw me saying those things, but I swear to you I didn't." He gave her a bewildered look. "I don't understand it." His phone dinged with another text. "Brandi says she hasn't posted this yet. She's waiting for me to call her. She's using the video as a bargaining tool."

"She's using it as blackmail, and she's a horrible person." Catalina got up and jumped out of the carriage.

Jay started toward her, smiling, but she quickly turned away from him.

"I'll make this right," Grayson called after her. "I promise."

Head down, Catalina marched toward her trailer, afraid she was going to lose it in front of everyone. She'd been a fool to trust again.

"Catalina?" Jay called after her, prompting Neil to look up and see she was on the move. The second AD radioed in that Catalina was walking off set. Mark asked if everything was all right, but she ignored him.

She made it to her trailer, hurried inside, and closed the door on all who pretended to be concerned but really weren't. She only wished she could shut out the world forever.

Chapter Thirty-Four

Mark and Neil were pacing outside Catalina's trailer as Jay stood on the steps and knocked on her door. "Catalina, it's Jay. Would you open the door, please?"

Neil kept calling her on her cell.

Mark listened to someone talking in his headset. "Unknown," he replied into his mic. "I'm trying to find out why she walked off... Copy that."

"I need to know what happened," Neil said to Mark.

"I don't know."

"She had a live mic on. What did you hear?" Jay asked.

"Unfortunately, nothing," Mark said. "Sound went down. We'd been troubleshooting for five minutes before she walked off set."

Jay saw Grayson being dropped off at his trailer and marched over. "What the hell happened out there?"

Grayson turned around and glared at him. "Who are you to be talking to me like—" He did a double take. "Wait. You were in the video." Grayson's brow furrowed in confusion. "You're the still photographer. You're using Catalina to get a movie made?"

"What?" Jay craned his neck forward. "No, of course not. Where did you hear that?"

Grayson cued up the video and handed it to him.

Jay's pulse began to race as his gut twisted into a knot. "That's not what I said. This thing has been edited. Did Brandi post this?"

"Not yet. She wants to talk to me in person about something."

"She's blackmailing you." He handed Grayson his phone.

"That's exactly what Catalina said."

Jay dragged a hand over his face, his mind racing. He and Catalina had gotten together at last. She was finally in a good place. She trusted him, and this woman they barely knew was trying to ruin what they had together. "Unbelievable!" Jay banged the palm of his hands against the side of Grayson's trailer, walked it off, then finally came back after he contained his rage.

"This is what you're going to do." Jay's fury flashed in his eyes. "You're going to agree to meet her, and I'll be there with you to record everything she says."

Grayson shifted on his crutches. "You'd do that for me?"

"For you, for me, for Catalina, and for everyone else she is lying about in that video."

"So you think all the videos are edited, including mine?"

"Without a doubt. Let me show you." Jay took back Grayson's phone, pulled up the video, and scrubbed through the images. "Here. You said this first line, but your second line has been pieced together." He slowly rocked over the edited frames for Grayson to see.

Grayson watched it again, and only then did he see the jump cut in the picture, giving away that it had been edited. "You're right. I see it now. I couldn't understand why I didn't remember saying that."

"Because you didn't. Your mouth is not on camera for the words you didn't say. She was obviously recording the entire fight. She then selected your words and edited them together."

"How did you catch that so fast?"

"I'm a director. I've spent many hours in the cutting room."

"I'm so confused. I thought you were a photographer."

"I am, but I first met Catalina on *Sage Under Fire*. It's the first film I directed."

Grayson's jaw dropped. "You're Jay Townsend?"

He nodded.

Grayson expelled a breath, appearing blown away. "I...uh... I'm so embarrassed that I didn't recognize you. I love your work. In fact, you're the reason Catalina and I initially hit it off. We were talking about your flawless shot composition on set one day. I can't believe she didn't tell me who you were." He leaned against his trailer. "Then again, she was talking about you so much at the beginning of our relationship that I started to get jealous. I told her to stop bringing you up."

"She did?"

"Nonstop. I assumed you two had dated."

"We were very good friends."

"I've never had that. A great friendship with a woman. Maybe that's why my relationships never last." Grayson had a bittersweet expression on his face. He then hobbled up the steps of his trailer. "Not sure what the rest of the day looks like, but I'll see if I can meet with Brandi later tonight."

"Great," Jay said. "Keep me posted."

He walked back to Catalina's trailer. Mark had left, but Neil was still there, trying to talk to her through the door.

Jay jammed his hands in his pockets and stood in front of Neil. "A video has surfaced."

The color drained from Neil's face. "What? When? Who?"

Knowing Neil was a solid guy, Jay told him everything, and what he had planned on doing about it.

"I didn't like Brandi from the moment I met her." Neil was fired up, clenching his fists. "She stopped Catalina one night, crying about Grayson, and Catalina was gracious enough to speak with her. I told her to go away, but Catalina insisted."

"That's the Catalina I know," Jay said. "She cares about everyone around her."

"She needs to know the truth now," Neil said, working his phone. "I'm letting her know that the video has been edited and is all lies."

"I did the same thing, but she wouldn't reply. Maybe she will now that she's heard it from both of us."

Neil glanced at her door, hoping it would open, but it didn't. "I'm going to get a copy of the video from Grayson, in case this goes south."

"Good idea," Jay said. "I'll be here."

Jay stepped up to her trailer and knocked on her door. "Catalina, I don't know if you're looking at your phone, but the video is fake. It's been badly edited. Grayson's sentences were pieced together, and my conversation with Clayton was edited as well. Please let me in so we can talk about this."

He was met with silence, so he texted her saying he

would never do anything to hurt her, but she wouldn't reply.

"I'm getting a little worried about your silence," he said through the door, "so I'll tell you what I'm going to do. I'm going to give you another minute to open this door, and if you don't, I'm going to assume you're unconscious, and I will get production to open it for me."

Silence for another few seconds, and then he heard movement in her trailer. She finally unlocked the door and hastily opened it, but didn't make eye contact.

He stepped inside, and she turned her back to him. "I've seen the video," he said calmly. "It hasn't been posted."

She still wouldn't look at him or say anything. She just stood by one of the windows, staring out, watching the crew through the tiny slits in the blinds.

"Brandi will be dealt with," he said through gritted teeth. "Grayson is handing a copy of it over to Neil should there be a need for legal action." He took a step toward her, wishing she would at least say something. "Catalina, Grayson never said those things, and—"

"Do you think I care about what Grayson said?" She whipped around, facing him. "I care about what you said." Her eyes brimmed with tears. "And right now, I can't see any difference between you and Brandi."

He felt like she'd just stabbed him in the heart. "Don't say that. My conversation with Clayton was completely taken out of context."

"Taken out of context." She glared it him. "But not totally made up, which means that a lot of what you said was true. You've been hanging out with me in hopes that I will say yes to one of your scripts so that you can get your career back?"

"No. Let me explain."

"So you weren't talking to Clayton about wanting me to star in your next movie—a movie that hasn't even been sold. You're saying I can walk over to Clayton right now, and he can confirm that for me."

Jay sighed. This looked much worse than he'd realized. "I do have a script that is in the hands of Peter Wells as of this morning. I didn't tell you about it because I didn't want you to think, even for a second, that my intentions toward you were anything other than what they are."

"Which is what, exactly?"

"I care so much about you, Catalina," he said, softly. "I want you in my life. I always have. Do you honestly think I'd jeopardize that?"

She brushed away tears that kept rolling down her cheeks. "I really don't know what to believe anymore."

She sounded so defeated that it shattered him inside. He moved toward her, to take her in his arms, to show her how she never needed to doubt his feelings for her. But when he reached for her, she jerked away.

"Please leave," she said barely above a whisper.

He couldn't. Not like this. "I can prove it to you. Let me show you the edits in the video."

"And then what? It's your word against hers. I'm tired of trying to figure out who's fake and who's not. Out of all people, I shouldn't ever have to figure that out with you."

"You don't."

"But I do. I can't unsee that video, Jay. Please. Get out of my trailer."

"Catalina, if you would just—"

"Now."

Her words crushed him. He loved her, and he wished he had said those exact words, because the look in her eyes told him she wouldn't be giving him another chance.

Jay couldn't believe Catalina managed to get herself together in order to finish out the day. to his amazement, her pain hadn't colored her performance at all. He couldn't say the same for himself. He took stills on autopilot, barely keeping his emotions in check. The only thing that saved him was keeping his mind busy, trying to figure out exactly how he was going to get hard evidence of the truth for Catalina. By the time they wrapped, he had it figured out.

"I think today was the most painful day I ever had filming, and I'm not talking about my leg," Grayson said as he leaned on his crutches, entering the hotel with Jay. "In between takes, I tried several times to show Catalina the jump cuts in the video, but she wouldn't even look at me."

Imagine how I feel, he wanted to say, but he didn't want to get too chummy with Grayson. "I hope we can fix this." Jay pushed the call button on the elevator. "Catalina has had enough of this gotcha crap to last an entire career."

"Neil was filling me in. I had no idea what she's been dealing with," Grayson said as they got into the elevator. "This is my fault. One way or another, I will make this right."

Jay hit the button for the third floor. "Keep your cool. Do whatever you have to in order to get Brandi to admit to editing the video, and get whatever footage you can. I want to show Catalina the unedited versions."

"Got it." The elevator doors opened, and they got out

on the third floor. Grayson stood in front of Jay. "Is my mic still hidden?"

"Yeah. Turn around." Jay checked to make sure his battery pack was also well hidden. "You're good to go. Just try not to move too much on your crutches when she's talking so we can get clean audio from her."

"Okay."

"Good luck." Jay put on his headphones and looked out the window while Grayson made his way around the corner to room 308.

Jay could hear everything clearly as Grayson knocked on the door. When he heard it open, he hit Record on his digital recorder.

"Hi," Brandi said sweetly. There was a pause and Jay imagined her taking in Grayson's injury. "Oh, Grayson, I feel so awful about your leg, and I want to make it up to you."

Grayson hobbled into the room on his crutches. He waited for the door to shut and Brandi to settle before he spoke. "Have you posted that video?" Irritation ran through his voice.

"I told you I wouldn't." She sounded a little miffed. "I only sent it to you so you'd talk to me again."

"You created the video just for me?" Grayson sounded truly mystified. "You didn't come to St. Nicholas to spy on Catalina like you said in the video?"

"No, I did," she admitted, like it was no big deal. "I have ten thousand followers waiting to hear from me."

"I thought you were a struggling actress, not a gossipy reporter secretly filming people without their knowledge."

"My quick vids to my fans is a side gig. You know I'm not a reporter, Grayson. I'm an actor who cares about her industry, and I've taken it upon myself to shed light on the truth behind rumors."

Grayson laughed. "Talk about false advertisement. *You* are the one fueling rumors. You put words in my mouth to make me look bad."

"I organized your thoughts better to help you express what you were really feeling."

"You have no right to speak for me, so hand over the unedited versions."

"Not a chance." She laughed and could be heard putting something away.

"What do you want?" Grayson asked, and Jay could tell the man was seething.

"For starters, I'd love a career like yours and Catalina's."

"Then do the work," Grayson said sharply. "Take acting classes. Get representation and start auditioning like we did."

"Wow. Did you listen to anything I said while we were together? I was a child actor on a sitcom for five years. I've taken acting classes, I have representation, I am auditioning, quite regularly I might add. You said you were going to get me a sizable part in *The Scrooge Legend*."

"I never said that."

"You promised you'd introduce me to Victor and talk to him about me."

"I did introduce you, but I never said I'd get you a part. How could I? It was already cast before I came on."

There was a long silent pause which had Jay checking his equipment to make sure their conversation was still recording.

A moment later, Grayson said, "If you post that video, you'll be hearing from my attorney."

He walked out and luckily Brandi didn't follow. Jay stopped the recording and took off his headphones as Grayson came around the corner.

"We got her," he said. "You okay?"

Grayson expelled a big breath. "Yeah. I'd feel sorry for her if I weren't so angry."

"You kept it together, man. Good job." Jay held the elevator doors open for him to hobble inside.

"I still don't understand why she did this." Grayson leaned against the back of the elevator. "She's a beautiful girl. She's young. She can obviously act. She could have a full-time acting career if she put some time into it."

"Jealousy destroys more careers than anything else. Hopefully she'll wake up before it's too late."

"I'm sorry I couldn't get the originals," Grayson said as they made their way through the lobby.

"We have more than enough audio to play for Catalina."

"Hi, Grayson. Can I have your autograph?" a preteen girl asked, holding out a journal and a pen.

"Sure." He steadied himself with his crutches, then took pen and paper in hand. "What's your name?"

"Ava."

Grayson scribbled a note to her and handed it back. "There you go, Ava."

"Thank you so much!" She squealed and ran back to her parents.

"Is the Scrooge Legend real?" Grayson asked him as they walked out of the hotel.

"Yes," Jay said without hesitation.

Grayson nodded as if he knew it was but wanted someone to confirm it for him. "Can I ask a favor?"

"Sure."

"Would you mind stopping by the real Santa's mailbox? I'd like to suggest Brandi for a Scrooge invitation, in hopes it will help her find her way."

Jay looked at Grayson, surprised by his request. "It would be my pleasure."

Chapter Thirty-Five

Catalina hadn't left her trailer even though she had wrapped two hours earlier. She sat with a tissue box talking to Erin. "I don't know what to believe."

"What does your heart say?"

"That he's telling the truth."

"Then why can't you accept that?"

"I don't know. I think it's because I let my guard down with him so quickly. I felt so safe with him. I honestly don't think he would hurt me intentionally. I just wish he had told me about the script, even though I understand why he didn't."

"So what exactly is the problem?" Erin asked. "You know he's been thinking about coming back to LA. You've encouraged him to return to directing. Why wouldn't he have a script or ten scripts that he'd want you to star in? I'd think you'd be more upset if he didn't want you in his movie."

"It was his laugh in the video at the end of his conversation with Clayton. I keep hearing it in my head. It seemed so self-serving and out of character for Jay."

"Then maybe it was. Jay told you the video had been edited. Your own ex-assistant edited your conversation with her. It's not a big leap."

"I know." Catalina rubbed her forehead, exhausted. "It's a horrible video, but I can't stop thinking about it. To have Grayson say what he did, followed by crew members I don't even know, and then to see Jay talking about me behind my back—it was shocking. I'm sure she fabricated most of it, but not knowing which part is real has me totally stressed out. I'm so tired of this happening."

"As long as you are famous, I'm afraid there will always be another Brandi. Shake it off, Catalina. If she ends up posting it, we'll deal with it. Okay?"

She let out a big breath. "Okay. Thanks, Erin. I'll call you later." Catalina disconnected the call, then pulled up the selfie she'd taken earlier of her and Jay. They truly looked happy together, and staring into his eyes, she knew he hadn't lied to her. He wasn't self-serving. He had integrity. He cared as deeply for her as she did him. When he'd come into her trailer, he wasn't worrying about what Peter would think if he saw the video. He was worried about her. He had to be telling the truth, and she should have never doubted him.

Erin was right. This would continue to happen, and she didn't want to feel like a victim anymore. This time she was going to do something about it. She texted Neil to come to her trailer. While she waited, she washed her face, put eye drops in her bloodshot eyes, and fixed her makeup.

Neil showed up with a white rose. "To cheer you up," he said.

"You're so thoughtful. Thank you, Neil." Catalina took the rose and inhaled its light scent. "My mom got the cookies you bought for her, and she loved them." She filled up an empty water bottle and set the rose inside.

"I'm glad she enjoyed them. I also wanted to let you know that everyone is still in the dark about why you had walked off set. I wanted to take this situation to the producers, but Jay and Grayson thought it would be better to talk to Brandi first."

"She's still in town?"

Neil nodded. "They went over to her hotel together to talk to her."

Catalina's jaw dropped, not able to picture the two of them doing anything together. "What happened?"

"I'm waiting to hear."

"They're over there right now?"

"I don't know. They left right after we wrapped."

She grabbed her coat. "Let's go."

"I don't think that's a good idea."

"She's after me. Not them. She said so in her video."

Neil hesitated. "Why don't we go to dinner and talk about this first?"

She recoiled at the thought. "I'm not going to be smeared without a fight. Now, are you driving me or am I going by myself?"

Neil sighed. "I'll drive."

Ten minutes later, Neil pulled up to the hotel. She thought about calling Jay but didn't want him talking her out of it like Neil had been trying to do.

"Do you know her room number?" she asked, getting out of the car.

"Three-oh-eight," he said. "But let me park and go up with you."

"I'll be fine."

"Please wait for me in the lobby." Neil pulled away.

Catalina headed into the hotel and straight into the elevator. She wasn't exactly sure what she was going to say to Brandi, but she decided to record the conversation in case it went poorly. She hit the record button on her phone as soon as she located her room, and then she knocked on the door.

"You changed your mind?" Brandi asked, whipping open the door. Her smile instantly vanished when she saw Catalina standing there.

"Hello, Brandi."

"How did you find me?"

"It's a small town."

"Grayson's not here. Or Jay." Brandi started to close the door, but Catalina stopped it with her foot.

"I saw the video," she said, staring her down.

Shock widened Brandi's eyes. "Grayson showed you?"

"Why wouldn't he? It's fake."

Brandi made no effort in trying to deny it. "Doesn't matter." Her mouth tightened. "It's what you deserve."

Catalina's first thought was that Brandi was a hateful woman who wasn't worth another minute of her time. She needed to walk away and let her attorney take care of her in court. But then she remembered what Jay had said about how many people were miserable because they were in pain. She clearly saw pain in Brandi's eyes.

"If it will make you feel better by posting that video to try and ruin my career, I won't stop you," Catalina said calmly. "But can you at least tell me why? I've been nothing but nice to you."

"You know why." Brandi scowled. "There aren't any cameras here so you can drop the act."

It was all Catalina could do to remain calm. "I honestly don't know what I did to offend you, so please enlighten me."

With an exaggerated sigh, Brandi let her in and closed the door before she walked over to the window and looked out. "Remember the TV series you did in England?"

"Of course."

"You took my part," Brandi snapped. "I had the role of Elizabeth—the role I absolutely loved, the role I was born to play—and then all of a sudden you were going to England and not me."

Catalina's mouth fell open. "You were the one I was up against?"

"What are you talking about?" She glared at her. "You were handed the part after one of the producers saw you in some little film at a stupid film festival."

"No. My agent called the casting office and asked for me to be seen for the role, but she was told I didn't have enough experience. My agent then sent over a copy of *Sage Under Fire*, which had just won awards at the film festival. Aaron, one of the miniseries producers, had been at the film festival and had seen the film. I finally got an initial audition, then a callback, then another. After that, I was told it was between me and another actress. I waited five more days on pins and needles, certain I'd lost out on the role, but then at eight o'clock on a Friday night, I got the call."

Brandi eyed her. "If that's the case, how is it that everything I heard or read about the miniseries said you'd been handed the part?"

"Because that's what happens with publicity on a long-awaited miniseries. I corrected the record a few times on talk shows, but people love the idea of an overnight success rather than one that was years in the making."

"Is this true?" Brandi's brow creased as she collapsed onto the nearest chair. "My agent told me I all but had it. And then I didn't." She looked at Catalina with fresh eyes. "All this time I thought you had just waltzed in and agreed to take the role, kind of like what Grayson did on this film."

"Victor pursued Grayson and persuaded him to take the part. It was a lousy thing to do to Landon, but that is on Victor, not Grayson."

She slowly nodded, taking it in.

"I know this doesn't help much now, but if it took the producers days to decide between you and me, then you have to know you did a great job," Catalina said. "I have no idea what made them finally choose me, but I'm willing to bet it was something that you or I didn't have any control over."

Brandi let out a little laugh. "Probably something ridiculous like hair color."

"I was once turned down for a job because my voice sounded just like the director's ex-girlfriend," Catalina said. "One of my other friends got a job over someone else because he was an inch taller and fit into an extremely expensive costume already made for an actor who had dropped out."

Brandi nodded, as if a similar thing had happened to her. "I have to ask, why do you seem so unhappy with such a charmed life? You mope around as the Ice Queen living a life that I would give anything to have. Why don't you appreciate it?"

"I do, Brandi. I appreciate everything I have. The Ice Queen evolved to combat fabricated stories about me. I tried to dispel them at first, but when that didn't work, I embraced her and used her as a defense mechanism."

"A defense mechanism against what?"

"People like you who only see one side and who choose to judge me and sentence me without knowing the whole truth."

"What truth? All I see is an entitled actress who walks off set whenever she feels like it. You did that on day one."

"I walked off the set because I was so shocked to see Grayson in Landon's role."

She gave her a bewildered look. "They didn't tell you?"

"No. Victor kept it from me just so he could film my real reaction. That's the truth you didn't see."

Brandi's jaw dropped. "Your own director did that to you?"

Catalina nodded.

"I would have been furious."

"I was. Things aren't always as they seem. You should know that by now."

Brandi stared off in the distance, looking a little lost.

"Want some advice? Focus on you. Love what you do, and it will show in your work. Honest hard work gets noticed."

"I feel horrible and embarrassed." Brandi lowered her eyes. "I'm truly sorry for all the trouble I've caused. Is there is anything I can do to make things right?"

"Well, don't post that video, for one."

Brandi laughed. "Done."

"Take a breath and take a break. Give yourself time to figure it out."

"Thank you, Catalina."

She nodded and showed herself out.

"I owe you." Brandi held the door open.

"No, you don't." Catalina walked down the hallway.

"I'm going to make it up to you," Brandi called out.

Please don't. "No need." She looked back and forced a smile. "Just concentrate on yourself. Good night."

"Good night, Ms. Jones."

Catalina took a big breath and let it out as Brandi closed her door. She hoped that was the end of the Brandi saga.

Neil hurried out of the elevator right as Catalina rounded the corner. "I thought you were going to wait for me in the lobby?"

"Oh, sorry." She stopped the recording on her phone.

Neil grabbed the elevator door before it closed. "What happened?" he asked as they stepped in.

"She thought I had stolen a part away from her, and all these years she's been carrying a grudge." Catalina couldn't help but think about her own feelings of rejection by Jay years ago.

Neil looked a little stunned. "How did she get such poor intel?"

"Probably a miscommunication from the casting director to her agent or her agent to her. Who knows? At least I got it straightened out. Have you heard from Jay or Grayson?"

"Yes, they're now at the B&B where Grayson's staying. They said it did not go well with Brandi. Grayson threatened legal action."

"No."

"Not to worry," Neil said as they walked through the hotel lobby. "They have recorded audio."

"That's not what I'm worried about. We need to get over there before this blows up any further." Catalina pulled out her phone. "Do you have the address?"

"No, but I can find out."

"I'm already on it." She texted Jay, saying she believed him but needed to speak to him and Grayson immediately. "I've got it. Let's go."

Chapter Thirty-Six

"Something big is going down," Felicity said quietly into the phone, sitting at her desk in the office of her bed-and-breakfast.

"What?" Mary sounded excited but a little terrified at the same time.

"Grayson is with Jay as we speak."

Mary gasped. "What? Why? What are they doing?"

"They're listening to something on a digital recorder, and they keep talking about Catalina."

"She's not with them?"

"No."

Mary paused. "That's curious."

"It is. I hope nothing's wrong between them." Felicity chewed on her lower lip. "You know Grayson and Brandi broke up, right?"

"Oh, yes. Angel reported it to me, but Brandi's apparently still in town."

It was Felicity's turn to gasp. "Do you know why?"

"Not yet, but I'm sure it will circulate around soon."

Felicity glanced toward the hallway to make sure no one was around. "Whatever it was must have been really bad because I heard Jay tell Grayson that visiting

Santa's mailbox on behalf of Brandi was a very cool thing to do, considering what she had done to him."

"She's a Scrooge? Oh my gosh, Felicity. This is huge. Brandi could be Catalina's Scrooge."

"Of course! I can't believe I didn't put that together. So Catalina has obviously regained her Christmas spirit."

"Absolutely," Mary said. "Do you know she suggested Victor as a Scrooge?"

"After he shoved her ex in her face? That's incredible. Catalina has turned around so quickly. I'm sure she'll pay forward the Christmas spirit to Brandi, if she hasn't done so already."

"I've no doubt," Mary said. "You know, for what looked like an impossible task with so many difficult Hollywood egos getting in Catalina's way, she's done a remarkable job."

"I knew she would, and now she's dating one of our own. Can't you just see how perfect she and Jay will be together?"

"I'm already planning the wedding in my head."

Felicity's doorbell rang. "Gotta go. Someone's at my door. I'll call when I know more."

"This place is almost as beautiful as the Carroll Inn," Catalina said as she and Neil waited on the porch of Felicity and Nolan's B&B.

Neil nodded. "Iris wants to come back for a week and stay here."

"You should take her up on it, especially since you said she didn't like snow."

"I think she's coming around."

Felicity opened the door and gasped. "Ms. Jones."

"Good evening. You must be Felicity. I'm here to see one of your guests, Grayson Edwards."

"Oh, uh—" She looked nervous all of a sudden. "He's, uh, in a meeting."

"With Jay?"

"Yes." Relief spread over her face. "I was afraid… Never mind what I thought." She stepped aside so they could come in. "Right this way."

Catalina was immediately drawn to the beautiful seven-foot Christmas tree in their living room adorned with silver bells, blue lights, and gold glass balls. She suddenly had a desire to decorate one herself. Would she be trimming her own Christmas tree with Jay?

Felicity took them down a short hallway into a cozy sunken family room with rich leather furniture, large picture windows, and a grand stone fireplace. Grayson was sitting lengthways on the couch in order to keep his leg elevated while Jay wore headphones, working opposite him.

"Catalina." Grayson smiled, then threw a wadded-up piece of paper at Jay to get his attention.

Jay looked up and immediately took off his headphones. "Hi." He locked his gaze on her as he quickly stood.

"Let me know if you need anything," Felicity said before she disappeared down the hallway.

Grayson swung his casted leg to the ground so Neil could have a seat. "Jay saved the day by putting a wire on me."

"It was a team effort," Jay said. "But now we have proof that Brandi doctored those videos."

Catalina couldn't stop smiling at the camaraderie between the two. "I appreciate your valiant efforts on my behalf, but I just spoke with Brandi myself."

"What?" Jay looked very concerned, then glared at Neil. "You let her go over there without me?"

"I tried to stop her."

"You didn't try hard enough." Grayson frowned.

Catalina wasn't sure how she went from no one other than Erin having her back, to three men fighting with each other over not protecting her enough. "Gentlemen, please." She suppressed a smile. "I can hold my own against women like Brandi."

"And she did," Neil said.

"You got Brandi to listen to reason?" Grayson asked, seeming skeptical.

"Yes. She thought I had stolen a role away from her, but now she knows the truth."

"So she's not posting the video?" Jay asked.

"She said she wouldn't, and she genuinely seemed remorseful about everything."

Grayson heard a text come in. "It's from Brandi." He opened it. "I hope you can forgive me," he read the text out loud. "Please show these original, unedited versions to Catalina." A moment later, several videos came in.

She sat down next to Grayson, and he hit Play. She saw an angry Grayson as he was before, but this time she heard the real dialogue. "Brandi, you're the failed actor. The only thing going for you is that you're clinging on to me."

"Not my finest moment," Grayson admitted before he played the video of the two grips being secretly recorded on the first day of filming. "I heard she's much nicer than any Ice Queen."

"Good because it's freezing," the other guy groused.

"I can't believe I turned down a trip to Puerto Vallarta for this."

The next video was of a PA, also on the first day, and the two electricians she was talking to. The first electrician said, "Catalina Jones is such a babe."

"Totally," replied the second one.

The PA then said, "Guys, chill. Ms. Jones is on her way."

After that, Catalina watched the only video that mattered.

Jay and Clayton were having dinner together.

"Have you talked to Catalina about it?" Clayton asked.

"It hasn't come up," Jay said.

"It would be great to get her on board. Her name attached would make your film a done deal."

Jay nodded, swallowing. "I plan on talking to her about it soon. I'd like to get the whole gang back together. You as my DP and Catalina as my leading lady, but I want to see what Peter has to say after he reads the rewrite. Catalina has a lot on her plate right now, and the last thing I want is for her to misinterpret my attentions toward her."

"So things are moving in a good direction between you two?"

"Yeah." Jay didn't laugh as he had in the edited version. Instead, he had a sweet smile on his face, lost in thought.

The video ended and Grayson set down his phone. "The truth at last."

Catalina shifted her gaze between Grayson and Jay. "I'm sorry I doubted you two, even for a second."

"Doctored videos, deepfakes. They're becoming more common these days," Grayson said. "Not good."

"No, it isn't," she said.

Felicity appeared in the doorway. "I just set out warm cookies and milk in the common area if anyone is interested."

"Oh?" Neil's eyes lit up.

"Help yourself," Felicity said with a chuckle before walking away.

Neil eyed Grayson, who looked equally excited about warm cookies. "Do you want to check it out?"

"Do you have to ask?" He reached for his crutches, then followed Neil out.

Jay came over to Catalina and took her hands in his. "As you heard, I wanted to make sure I had a solid, tight script before I showed it to you."

"Why? You know I'd work on any of your projects."

"Exactly why I want to hear Peter's opinion first. I want to make sure my screenplay is up to par with the other Catalina Jones projects."

She put her hands on his chest as Jay encircled her with his arms. "You don't give yourself enough credit. You're a fantastic writer and a brilliant director. I've always said that."

"And you're an equally brilliant actress."

"Some would say we're a perfect match, but we both know that high-powered Hollywood couples rarely ever last."

"Then I'll remain a wildlife photographer forever." He brushed her hair away from her eyes and held her gaze. "I'll be anything you want me to be, as long as I can be with you."

"That's all I've ever wanted. But I want whatever *you* want to be."

He studied her face as if he were committing this moment to his memory forever. "I choose to be the man who truly loves you and who always will."

She smiled, blinking back her misty eyes. "Then I choose to be the woman who fiercely loves you right back." She wrapped her arms around his neck and kissed him. "Thank you," she said, looking deeply into his eyes.

"For what?"

"For helping me to remember who I used to be."

"It was easy because I never forgot." He reached for her and gave her the most passionate kiss she'd ever experienced on or off-screen. She knew without a doubt that she had experienced a true Christmas miracle. Her wish had been granted. She had finally found her one true love.

Epilogue

One year later

Catalina reached for Jay's hand as she stepped out of the limousine at the premiere of *The Scrooge Legend*. A barrage of flashbulbs went off in her face, but this time she didn't need to fake her smile. She was with the man she loved, walking the red carpet, for a film she was finally proud of.

Stan had done wonders with the script and had at last told Piper's true story. Victor had finished the film with a much better directing style. He'd given his actors a safe space to work in and welcomed their input, while giving his crew the respect they deserved.

Catalina glanced around the red carpet and saw him giving an interview with Dina at his side. They'd been married over the summer and looked incredibly happy. Neil and Iris were there as well, along with Stan and his longstanding girlfriend. Grayson was with another new girlfriend, one who was not in the industry, and that appeared to be working well.

"Catalina, it seems like a big congratulations is in order." Lindsay from *Entertainment Spotlight* spoke into her microphone. "Your critics who got a sneak peek of your performance are talking Oscar."

"That's very kind," she said, "but I'm just honored to be part of such a wonderful film."

"And may I take a look at that gorgeous ring on your hand?"

Catalina held up her two-carat diamond ring and smiled at Jay.

"Absolutely stunning." Lindsay shifted her focus between her and Jay. "Have you two set a date?"

"We're working on it," she said, "but it depends on the shooting schedule of *Silencing Sarah*."

"Jay, you must be thrilled to be back in the director's chair with one of your own projects and working with Catalina again."

"I am, and I couldn't have asked for a better leading lady." He intertwined his hand with hers as the cameras went off with lightning speed.

"Now that you've been to the town with the famous Scrooge Legend, is Christmas magic real?" Lindsay asked Catalina.

"I believe it's real, but sometimes you only need to look no further than the one you love to find it."

"So, you're saying love is the answer to everything."

Catalina shared a knowing smile with Jay. "Isn't it?"

* * * * *

Acknowledgments

I'm very blessed to be working with such an incredibly gifted and talented editor, Deborah Nemeth. Thank you, Deb, for your fantastic suggestions and your incredible insight. I'm so grateful to Lynn Ferrin, my wonderful sister and best friend, who reads every version of every story I write. Lynn, I couldn't write without you.

A big thank-you to Stephanie Doig for believing in another one of my books. I'm thrilled to be counted among your talented authors.

Many thanks to my good friend, Dina Morrone, for helping me with the Italian in my story. Thank you to my wonderful support team: Steve Apostolina, Faa Brimmo, Joan Crossman, Wendy Cutler, Lori Gordon, Luisa Leschin, Lucy Lin, Carole Rycki, Suzi Sadd, Maura Swanson, DeEtte Tikotzinski, and Lynnanne Zager. Your love and support mean so much to me.

Thank you to my amazing husband who always puts me and my writing first. I'd be lost without you.

Last but not least, thank you to all of my readers. I so appreciate you. Have a blessed holiday season full of love, laughter, and cookies!

About the Author

Ever since she can remember, Caitlin McKenna has always loved a good story. Whether it was in the form of a long-winded joke told by her dad around the dinner table, or an outlandish story of alien abduction and missing homework imagined by one of her classmates, she loved to hear every one of them. Naturally, her love of a good story landed her in Hollywood where she embarked on an acting and screenwriting career.

While in the theatre, she had the opportunity to play complex characters like Anne Boleyn in *Anne of the Thousand Days*, and Eliza Doolittle in *Pygmalion*, which has helped her tremendously as a writer when fleshing out her own characters. Even though Caitlin saw her stories as movies in her head, she felt the need to have more control over them, so she switched her focus from screenplays to novels.

Now she enjoys writing any story where love drives the narrative. Her previously published novels include *Colorado Christmas Magic*, *No Such Luck*, *My Big Fake Irish Life*, *Super Natalie*, *Manifesting Mr. Right*, and her dystopian thriller, *Logging Off*. When not writing, she can be found at one of the major studios working as a voice-over actress and voice-casting director for an upcoming movie or television show.

Caitlin lives with her husband and two spoiled dachshunds in Southern California, and is working on her next novel.

Website: www.CaitlinMcKenna.com
Twitter: www.Twitter.com/CaitMcKenna
Instagram: www.Instagram.com/AuthorCaitlinMcKenna/
Facebook: www.Facebook.com/AuthorCaitlinMckenna/
Email: AuthorCaitlinMcKenna@gmail.com

Bah, humbug. Charley Dawson's sent on assignment to St. Nicholas, Colorado, to debunk their claim that even the Grinchiest visitor will end up loving Christmas. Baffled by unexplainable events, she pairs up with her high school sweetheart to investigate.

Keep reading for an excerpt from
Colorado Christmas Magic *by Caitlin McKenna.*

Chapter One

Hearing insistent meowing, Charley Dawson glanced up from her laptop to find her three-year-old cat perched on top of his treehouse, staring out the window of her one-bedroom apartment.

"What is it, Clarence?" She rose from the kitchen table to see what held his interest—the house directly across the street was lit up like a Christmas tree with big bright bulbs of red, blue, green, orange, and yellow. She ran her fingers through his short white fur and had him purring instantly. "I know you like the lights, bud, but we're not decorating this year. We're through with Christmas."

Clarence gave a short meow of disappointment before jumping down and running off, leaving Charley mesmerized by the lights. She used to love Christmas—how it ushered in that warm, comforting feeling of home where nothing seemed impossible. The Christmas season sprinkled happiness in the air, ordained love to reign supreme over everything, and made the world feel like it was a better place.

But for her, the magic of Christmas was gone. Over the past several years, the season only managed to bring her heartache. Last year's sorrow came from her then-fiancé, Hunter, who coldheartedly dumped her on Christmas Eve. After he left her, she'd cried on the couch with Clarence, staring at her Christmas tree, believing no Christmas would ever be joyful again.

With a sigh, she turned away from the window, gathering her long blond hair into a ponytail, then slid into the chair in front of her computer. She took one last bite of the sweet and sour pork before pushing it aside. The cold Chinese takeout reminded her of her love life—every relationship started sweet but ended sour.

She couldn't believe she was twenty-nine and still single—not that being single was a bad thing—but she had envisioned herself as a happily married career woman by twenty-five and a new mom by thirty. She was nowhere near meeting her goals, and she couldn't understand how true love kept eluding her—especially at Christmas.

She frowned at the blank page on her computer screen. For an hour's worth of work, she'd only come up with the title of her next blog post: "The Truth About Christmas." Did her readers sincerely want to know? Her popular blog, *The Cold Hard Facts*, was a real hit with *Authentic Lifestyles* readers. She debunked myths, urban legends, and uncovered the accurate but sometimes unpleasant truths behind long-held beliefs and traditions. She also exposed too-good-to-be-true business opportunities, shameful vacation getaways, and other consumer scams. Because of this, her boss suggested she break tradition and write something nice about the happiest time of year.

Bah, humbug. For Charley, Christmas was the most miserable time of year. Without having anyone to share things with, what was the point? Holiday parties became obligations; cooking ended up being a chore. She'd have to spend too much time baking for people who didn't appreciate it, and endure too much shopping chaos to buy gifts no one really wanted. "The truth about Christmas? Skip it!"

Abandoning her blog, she got up to pour herself a glass of wine and moved her pity party to the couch. Turning on the TV, she searched for anything that didn't involve love or hopeless romantics or jovial couples enjoying Christmas together. Even the commercials needled her with actors appearing so darn cheerful. No, she was definitely done with Christmas *and* love, once and for all.

But when channel surfing brought her to *It's A Wonderful Life*, her favorite Christmas movie of all time, she was immediately sucked in. "Clarence!" she called, putting her feet up on the coffee table. "Your show's on."

Clarence appeared from behind the couch and jumped into Charley's lap, as if he sensed she needed some affection. She snuggled in with her beautiful white angel and found herself weeping not twenty minutes into the movie. Then when George Bailey bitterly wished he'd never been born, puffy-eyed Charley found herself making a different kind of wish—a last attempt before she gave up for good. She wished—and out loud, mind you—for her soulmate to come find her since she wasn't getting the job done herself. The second this heartfelt wish passed her lips, the electricity in her apartment cut out.

"Just perfect. Exactly what I need. Oh, I get it. Are you trying to tell me that another one of my wishes will never see the light of day?" She cast her eyes upward into the darkness, assuming the power would snap on at any moment. But it didn't. "I figured as much."

With a loud meow, Clarence jumped off her lap. The tiny bell on his collar jingled as he ran down the hallway toward her bedroom.

Wiping off her tear-streaked face with the bottom of her sleeve, she rose and fumbled around in the dark, attempting to locate a flashlight. She finally managed to find one in the junk drawer right as the power popped back on and her favorite Christmas movie was playing once again.

As she started to close the drawer, she caught sight of an old photo strip buried under takeout menus. She and her high school sweetheart, Jack, had spent the day at the Santa Monica Pier, eating cotton candy, riding the Ferris wheel, and taking silly pictures of themselves in a photo booth.

With a bittersweet sigh, she caressed the strip of photos. How happy her sixteen-year-old self looked. Why hadn't she been able to find that kind of deep connection with anyone since Jack? *Because Love lost my address.* She shoved the photo strip back in the drawer and slammed it shut.

"Chocolate. I seriously need some chocolate." *Anything to get my mind off Jack.*

On the hunt, she scrounged around in the pantry, surprised she couldn't find one little morsel. She moved on to her handbag, her workbag, yes, even her gym bag. When she came up empty-handed, she checked the freezer for bits of chocolate in the form of ice cream, but to her dismay, she was cleaned out. She had no choice but to settle for the two complimentary fortune cookies she'd received with her takeout. She never cared for fortune cookies. The fortunes never applied to her and the cookies tasted dull and boring—much like her love life.

Charley snagged them off the kitchen table anyway, slumped on the couch, and popped opened the plastic wrapping on the first one. She snapped the cookie in half, crumbling it everywhere, then yanked out the fortune. **YOU WILL REUNITE WITH THE ONE THAT GOT AWAY**.

"Yeah, right." She crumpled it up, tossed it on the coffee table, then opened up the second cookie for a redo. **YOU WILL REUNITE WITH THE ONE THAT GOT AWAY**.

She sat up straight. It was a little weird to get the exact same fortune in two different cookies, and even more strange to get them right after she found pictures of Jack. "Ridiculous."

Jack had stolen her heart from the moment he'd spoken to her only to trample it to dust a little over a year later. She had tried to forget about him, she really had, but couldn't. She often wondered what had happened to him. She'd attempted to find him on Facebook but eventually gave up. Jack hadn't cared much for social media when it became popular, so she suspected he'd never changed his viewpoint on the subject. That made her even more curious as to where he lived and how he was doing. Did he ever think of her, or was he happily married? Maybe he had a gorgeous girlfriend and they were one of those couples she had recently passed by on the street, so happy and jolly that Christmastime had finally arrived.

Stupid fortune cookies.

Irritated at herself for thinking about him, she took to her blog and told the world *exactly* what she thought of Christmas. She was so certain her writing on the subject was sheer perfection that she posted it without waiting to reread it when she was in a better frame of mind.

The following morning, while shoving down smashed avocado on toast before darting out the door for work, she wondered if her life would ever change. It felt like every time she moved forward, she ended up right back in the same place.

As she drove to work, she couldn't stop thinking about Jack. Even though they'd met in high school, their relationship ended up being more than just infatuation or young love. The spark between them had been incredibly honest and deep. They had shared so much with each other that she truly felt she'd found her soulmate. She hadn't been able to see herself with anyone other than Jack. *Why did his parents have to move him so far away?*

Charley pulled into an underground parking lot off Sunset Boulevard and discovered she'd forgotten to turn on her phone. As she headed into the lobby and straight into an elevator, her cell began blowing up. She smiled, feeling downright confident her readers were, at that very moment, agreeing wholeheartedly with her sentiments about Christmas.

Yet when she stepped off the elevator and opened the onslaught of messages, that wasn't the case at all. She remained glued to her cell screen, reading negative comment after negative comment. Heart pounding, she weaved her way through the hallways of *Authentic Lifestyles Magazine* without ever looking up.

"Miss Scrooge?" she uttered in shock, abruptly halting in place. She bristled as she kept reading, frozen to her phone.

Bright, peppy Olivia Lancaster came bounding up

from behind Charley and glanced over her shoulder. "You bashed Christmas?" her best friend asked incredulously before she snatched the phone and scrolled through the barrage of insults left on the blog.

"I didn't bash Christmas, Liv. I merely suggested skipping it."

"You did more than that." Liv's eyes widened with every comment she devoured. "'Despicable,' says Devoted Fan, 'Unforgivable' comes from Fact Junky, and 'You've lost me forever,' cries Quirky Girl."

"That seems a little extreme." Charley plucked her phone out of Liv's tight grip. "I'm *not* going to apologize for telling it like it is."

"No, of course not," Liv said with a big snort of a laugh. "No one would ever accuse you of holding back."

"It's my job." Charley raised her chin. In truth, she actually *enjoyed* squashing people's over-joyous perceptions of long-held beliefs. (Wrong-held beliefs, according to her.)

"I'm just glad I get to write about fashion. Lunch later?" Liv asked, walking back down the corridor.

"Sure." Charley headed to her desk where she fired up her computer, anxious to defend her position to her readers. She took a determined breath, let it out, then pulled up her blog. The comments continued to pour in, an additional fifty-four in a matter of minutes. She skimmed through the newest ones, trying to find anyone who would agree with her. Finally, her eyes fell on:

I despised Christmas—

At last, a like-minded reader.

Until I fell in love.

"Bah, humbug." She slammed back in her chair.

"Here ya go!" An overly enthusiastic guy held out her morning mail, and she could only assume he was a new intern.

"Thanks." She rifled through a half dozen letters and stopped on a silver envelope embossed with gold script. She took note of the return address. *1 Kringle Lane, St. Nicholas, Colorado.*

Intrigued, she opened it.

Dear Charlotte Dawson,
You're invited to spend a complimentary week at
The Carroll Inn, a five-star bed-and-breakfast
in St. Nicholas, Colorado: Home of the famous
Scrooge Legend.

Scrunching up her face, she flipped over the letter, expecting to see additional information, but the back of it was blank. *Pretty expensive solicitation for a gimmick.* Without another thought, she crumpled up the paper and pitched it in the trash.

Now, where was I? She returned to her keyboard and began typing:

Dear Devoted Fan,
While I understand—

"Charley?" the familiar voice of her boss rang out. Paul was standing in the doorway of his office, twirling his glasses in his hand. "Can I see you for a moment?"

She rose and followed him. Paul was a cool boss. Being called into his office was usually a good thing. He advanced his employees faster than any editor in chief around. She'd already reaped the benefits from working for him. When she'd come to him as an intern, he noticed her hard work and promoted her to fact-checker only one month later. Then, when he learned how successful she was as a blogger, he allowed her to become a permanent guest blogger with the magazine. Hopefully, Paul's request to see her meant another promotion.

He waved her in. "Great initiative, Charley. Yes, you can go and investigate the legend. I'm sure you'll want to debunk it."

She gave him a puzzled look. "What exactly are we talking about?"

"The invitation you received to St. Nicholas, Colorado." Paul held up the crumpled letter she'd thrown away minutes earlier.

She widened her eyes in astonishment. "How did you get that?"

"Didn't you leave it on my desk?"

"No. I *just* threw it away. As in minutes ago."

"Doesn't matter." He rocked back in his chair. "The important thing is you're going."

"To Colorado?" Charley asked with more disdain in her voice than she'd intended. "In the dead of winter? People can actually die in the dead of winter. That's a cold hard fact."

"Here's another cold hard fact—you leave first thing tomorrow."

She refused to budge. Her level-headed boss obviously wasn't thinking clearly. "But, Paul, it's freezing there."

She had lived in Los Angeles her entire life, and

rarely had she ever ventured into the land of snow and freezing temperatures.

He pushed out a loud sigh, crossing his arms on top of his desk. "Charley, your blog is a great money-maker for our magazine. Separating fact from fiction has driven your readership and our subscriptions to an all-time high. But you might have crossed the line this time."

"My blog is titled *The Cold Hard Facts* for a reason."

Paul reached over piles of paper on his desk and snagged a printed version of her latest post. He cleared his throat before reading it aloud. "'Face it. The holidays are a chore—the decorating, the shopping, the never-ending line at the post office, not to mention the hours of cooking, baking, and cleaning. Why torture your-self? No time to make Christmas cookies? That's what store-bought is for. Tired of spending hours wrapping presents? Send an eGift card instead. No time to trim a tree? Do yourself a favor and just skip Christmas alto-gether. It's not worth the hassle.'" He tossed the print-out back on his desk and eyed Charley over the rims of his reading glasses. "You keep writing like this and you can rename your blog *The Cold Heartless Facts.*"

She ran her hands over the arms of the chair, trying to feel justified for her comments even though, deep down, she knew she'd been off the mark. "I'm doing everyone a favor. I'm only voicing what everyone's thinking."

"Is that so? Then why does this *one* post of yours have more negative comments than all of your previ-ous posts combined? Care to explain, *Miss Scrooge?*"

Shoot. He had seen the comment, the very comment that still gnawed at her. "Fine." She let out a defeated sigh. "I'll go." If she could debunk a legend *and* put the screws to Christmas, then subjecting herself to miserably cold temperatures would be well worth it.

"That's the *spirit*." Paul had a playful smirk on his face, so she knew the pun was intended.

"You know, the legend has to be a hoax because I've never heard of it."

He took off his reading glasses and leveled his gaze on her. "I thought that's why you put the letter on my desk."

"I didn't put—" She stopped herself. How the letter got to his desk was truly a mystery, but one she'd have to tackle later. "Have *you* ever heard anything about this famous Scrooge Legend?"

Paul put his glasses back on and pulled up the town's website. "It's right here. 'Welcome to St. Nicholas, Colorado, home of the famous Scrooge Legend, where any Scrooge who enters the town will end up loving Christmas as much as Santa.'"

Charley exploded with a laugh. "Ridiculous."

Paul arched a brow. "Prove it."

Don't miss Colorado Christmas Magic
*by Caitlin McKenna, available now
from Carina Press.*
www.CarinaPress.com